PRAISE FOR IMMORTAL

"I knew the Cincinnati Reds drafted wisely in selecting Ken. He skillfully uses America's pastime to provide us with a hero that is grounded in traditional American values. *Immortal* is an aspirational tale of a transcendent athlete's historical season and his desire to use his platform to do good."

—**Kevin Jarvis**, MLB Pitcher 1994–2006

"One may think that playing baseball is all glamour, women, and money. Some play for that notoriety, some play for the love of the game. *Immortal* gives us this expected insight, but it also projects another side of baseball, especially for Theodore Hunter! It shows us his love for the game but also the turmoil that Theodore also struggles with; it shows us reality under the cover of fame. Great read!"

—**Tod Gohl**, USAF Desert Storm Veteran, Author of *Saving America's Citizens*

"Our country needs a hero like T. C. Hunter. Kudos to Cav for introducing us to an intriguing character who brings baseball, tradition, and patriotism to the forefront. When the past beckons, we should all listen and not be afraid to act!"

—**Keith Glauber**, Former MLB Pitcher for the Cincinnati Reds

Immortal
by Ken Cavazzoni
© Copyright 2023 Ken Cavazzoni

ISBN 979-8-88824-104-2

All rights reserved. No part of this publication may be reproduced, stored in a retrieval system, or transmitted in any form or by any means—electronic, mechanical, photocopy, recording, or any other—except for brief quotations in printed reviews, without the prior written permission of the author.

This is a work of fiction. All the characters in this book are fictitious, and any resemblance to actual persons, living or dead, is purely coincidental. The names, incidents, dialogue, and opinions expressed are products of the author's imagination and are not to be construed as real.

Published by

3705 Shore Drive
Virginia Beach, VA 23455
800-435-4811
www.koehlerbooks.com

IMMORTAL

IMMORTAL

A NOVEL

KEN CAVAZZONI

VIRGINIA BEACH
CAPE CHARLES

*Tina, I thank you for your patience.
Isabella, Giulianna and Gabriel, you are my inspiration
and the reason for my being.
Immortal is dedicated to you.*

"If we take eternity to mean not infinite temporal duration but timelessness, then eternal life belongs to those who live in the present."

—Ludwig Wittgenstein

"Baseball is the greatest game in the world and deserves the best you can give it."

—Babe Ruth

CHAPTER 1

THE AIRPLANE IS on the small side, akin to some of the private jets I have chartered for weekend getaways from Tampa to Las Vegas. It's too big to be a Learjet 60 like I've flown to the Caribbean, and much older than a Gulfstream IV or V. The loud, deliberate maneuvering creates a jarring bounciness unlike other aircraft.

Behind in the cabin I see a dozen or so passengers, all looking toward the floor. Their body types indicate they are athletes, although I can't make out any of the faces. Each has unrecognizable characteristics, yet they somehow show an expression of subtle fear, sadness, and indifference.

"Tyson, Cory, Jim, Irv, Ken, you okay back there?" one of the pilots asks over the intercom. "Marv, Elmer, Tom, Charlie, Roy, Nestor? Is everyone good?" Nobody answers. They're not asleep, just incapable of speaking as their lifeless faces continued looking downward.

The gentleman beside me grips the arms of his seat. His dark, muscular forearms are tense, and his veins ready to burst through his skin. Unlike the others I recognize him.

"We are having some engine difficulty, everyone please try to stay calm," says one of the pilots. This time he did not use the intercom and turned his body toward us sticking his face into the cabin.

I recognize him too. I'm close enough to the cockpit to get a good visual of the two men flying the plane. The copilot on the right who just made the announcement is a spitting image of Thurman Munson, the late, great catcher from New York who died in a private plane accident decades ago. I do a double-take and consider how he matches the picture jacket of the biography I have on my bookshelf. The face shape, the sideburns, the mustache, all match precisely, except this man wore a pilot jacket instead of a pinstripe jersey.

The plane veers sharply before starting a hard descent. The nose plunges then levels off before dipping yet again. The pilot on the left vigorously fights the controls while the lights in the cabin flicker.

"Everyone, please brace yourselves. We need to make an emergency landing," announced the copilot.

The pilot remains stoic and intensely focused. Danger looming, yet he calmly turns to his partner and says, "Buckle in Yankee, this could get rough."

I search for movement or reaction from anyone in the plane, but each passenger remains still. Their faces are unremittingly blank as if fine with whatever might happen. Needing some sort of human emotion or reaction I grab the wrist of the gentleman sitting next to me. He turns and the fear in his eyes and ghastly expression make me panic.

"*Salvame,*" he says.

I'm fixated on this man's face, but not understanding his words. The more I stare at his features the more I recognize him as Roberto Clemente, the legendary outfielder from Pittsburgh who also lost his life in an airplane crash.

"*Salvame,*" he repeats, "*Salvame!*"

"What? *Salvame?*" Though utterly engrossed, I can't process the word. I'm sitting beside a baseball legend about to tragically perish just as he did decades ago.

"*Si. Salvame! Salvame!*"

The plane takes another dive and I hold on tightly. I glance again at the legendary figure sitting beside me, his expressionless face looking downward, his hands no longer gripping the armrests, his body flopping lifelessly in the seat.

I search his face for humanity, hoping for calming salvation to push me through the tormenting seconds. Like the others, he's unresponsive, and the gripping disappointment of losing all human interaction is just as frightening as the pending crash.

Scanning the cabin, I seek out anything that might remedy the situation. Deficient in logic, my brain urges me to stay strong and not display weakness despite the stillness of the other passengers. Helpless and nauseous, I battle the urge to vomit and focus on the cockpit.

The pilot is still battling the plane while his copilot slumps in his seat. With his right hand the pilot flips a couple of switches above his head and uses his left hand on the plane's yoke to try and steady the aircraft.

Salvame, salvame, I repeat in my head. *He was saying save me.*

"That's right, damn it," barks the pilot, his terse smirk not matching the seriousness of the occasion. We lock eyes, and I immediately recognize his face and booming voice.

"What'd you forget Spanish?" he asks. The plane veers hard to the left and feels like it might make a corkscrew rotation. Instead, we level off and regain control.

His steely demeanor and unbridled confidence prevent a crash. Like he had once done in the Korean War, the pilot averts disaster and makes an unconventional landing.

The plane skids across the water before finally coming to rest. Water fills the cabin, but at least for now we were safe. The boyish looking pilot stands and stares out from the cockpit. "No, not just save me," he says, "save them, save you, save us all."

His sturdy, echoing voice twists my reality until I confidently recognized the man as my namesake. I try to respond but can't even manage a squeak. Who am I to save? The men on the plane were already taken from this earth. *Save myself? Save the pilot? Save my friends and teammates?* None of it makes sense.

I shake my head violently to unscramble my thoughts. Soaked with cold sweat I'm no longer in the cabin of the plane. Alone, I sit up in my bed to survey the room, the shock of the graphic ordeal slowly subsidizes.

Unconvinced I might ever find peace, I consider the declaration, *"Save us all."* Even if I knew the meaning, where would I start?

CHAPTER 2

PULLING UP TO the pump, I glance at the reflection in the tinted glass window of the gas station's mini mart. I've had other sports cars and I have my pick of toys, but the BMW M8 convertible is perfect. The marina bay metallic blue M8 oozes sleek sports car and high-performance prestige. It is certainly flashy, but with a classic elegance that BMW impressively portrays. Other players show up with their Ferraris, Porches and tricked out Hummers, but I will take this car over any of them.

Everyone has their opinion, and even my agent provides unsolicited commentary. He wants me to have a bright red Ferrari or a loud Maserati to "enhance my image." But the persona of the modern super athlete is a caricature, and just not me. Besides, I've got much more to worry about these days.

My agent, Thomas Bader, has one purpose in life and that's to make money with my next contract. Tom suggests that "elevated fashionableness will equate to a bigger contract." I don't know anyone else who talks like that, and it drives me crazy.

He's probably right; image is everything as they say. Tom is just doing his job and I appreciate it; however, I know two things. One, I'm a baseball player, a centerfielder, and not a damn cartoon. And two, BMW knows what they are doing, and the car fits my six-foot-three-inch frame like no other.

It's not yet six in the morning, but I'm on the road early due to another sleepless night. The insomnia and odd thoughts began the previous year right around the All-Star break. Sometimes sporadic, other times unrelenting, it's quite concerning to say the least, and I need to figure out what the hell is happening before I jump off a cliff.

I hit the premium button on the pump and reflexively stare at the churning blue digits while high octane gasoline pours into the tank. I don't know if high octane makes a difference, it's probably a price gouging scam like organic food. Regardless, I find myself buying premium gas and often purchasing organic foods out of some perverted form of guilt. I suppose sometimes it's easier to comply than to question, so it's just what I do.

The ride from my Tampa penthouse at Bayshore Regency to the spring training site in Clearwater is a little over twenty miles. Particularly in the early hours, the drive is fantastic. The air is fresh and dewy with the bright Florida sun starting to provide some warmth and a peach- colored glow. I enjoy the short trip each day of spring training, and I can tell just by the weather that the end of the preseason is near. At the onset of camp in February the temperature is a lot cooler and even chilly some mornings, while in March the Gulf Coast climate shifts into tropical heat mode.

The short commute is therapeutic and helps manage my disturbed sleep patterns. On bad days, no matter when I fall asleep, I wake up at exactly 3:48 am riddled with emotion and thoughts. Most often I wake up at the conclusion of a realistic dream, sometimes so lifelike and frightening that I am panicked. Other times, I wake up bombarded with melancholy and helplessness, panting to catch my breath.

Although the despair and loss of sleep is emotionally draining, I manage to function even though the sensations are consuming and the disturbances are unlike anything I've known. It's like being at the top of a roller coaster about to soar down a decline, then realizing the tracks are gone and nothing is going to stop the fall.

Often, the feelings are of extreme loss like someone close to me is dying. What's worse is that I'm supposed to do something about it, but I am helpless because I don't know what to do or who to save. There's an element of good versus evil to all of it, and my anxiety compounds each day of confused thoughts.

The glaring question is almost always, why is this happening to me now? I am the reigning Most Valuable Player in the league, and the timing is perfect to head into my free agent year. I'm about to cash in on a huge contract, maybe even a record breaker, so my career path has never been better. Sure, a contract year and the clamor from fans who assign lofty expectations can add a degree of pressure, but the demands of the game have never gotten to me before. Besides, I'm most at ease when I am on the baseball field, so there's got to be another trigger.

I struggle personally, though not anything that is out of the ordinary. Like most, I have a speck of anxiety derived from the lunacy of the recent COVID pandemic. Certain events and political personalities have forced me to question the path of the country, and I'm likely more of an ideologue than before. Once apolitical, I can't help but notice things going on in the world, and I live in the free state of Florida for a reason. I pay enough attention to have some concerns, though soon I'll have enough personal wealth to live life on the outskirts of society making none of it matter much to me anymore.

I have a hard time dealing with trust and commitment. My relationship with my girlfriend causes some angst, leading to changes in the way I view my personal life. Cultivating the relationship while focusing on my career is a challenge, but it's not something that should put me one step from the loony bin.

I don't think alcohol is a trigger, and I never take drugs, rarely even an aspirin for a headache. I drink occasionally and maybe I've tapped the bottle a bit more than usual of late, but the drinking helps when there's nowhere else to turn. Besides, the fog created by good whiskey helps me think outside of the box. If I thought cutting out drinking would help, I'd do it. But, a little whiskey from time to time settles my mind while I search for an epiphany.

I'm not suicidal, although on occasion I've had the passing thought that I'd rather be dead than continue living through my current state. Sleep deprivation is awful, and the emotional swings suggesting impending doom are harrowing. Still, I have no thoughts of grabbing my gun to end it all. Luckily, the peculiar feelings are ephemeral so at least for now I'm able to function.

I call these early hour occurrences *episodes* because, well, I don't know what else to call them. The word episode provides a better mental image for me than hallucinations, delusions or haunting, and I try to leave out schizophrenic or paranoid as an antecedent. Those words seem to fit, but it's best to trick myself into labeling the events episodes, so I leave it at that.

Thankfully, I don't have an episode every day, but when one occurs, I instinctively drop a text to the clubhouse manager, Chief Daley. Chief is like a father figure and the closest thing I have to family. He's nearing eighty-five years old, yet I don't think he has ever considered retiring from the game. Once a player in the league many years ago, baseball is the source of his vitality. He's been managing the clubhouse for decades and I've been fortunate to have him as a fixture in my life since I entered the league.

A little after four this morning I sent him a simple text. *Morning Chief. Another great day for baseball.* It usually doesn't take long for him to write back, no matter what time I text. Like clockwork, he immediately sent back, *Yes it is, TC. Hit 'em hard today.*

Our little ritual has gone on without fail. Chief can be a bit ornery, and each time I expect him to curse me out for texting so early, but he never does. I hope he doesn't figure out that my texts are designed to check if he is still alive and kicking. After an episode it's something I do to set my mind at ease, and at least for now he does not seem to care.

Once Chief acknowledges he is still breathing I am usually able to shake my thoughts and move on with my day. Instead of ruminating on my emotions, the best course of action is to shower, have breakfast and get out the door. At least when I have one of my obscenely early days, I get a few hours to myself by being away from the crowds and doting fans.

There are few people on the road at the early hour, and driving away from Tampa, heading west out of the city avoids rush hour traffic. The solitude makes even small tasks like filling up the gas tank more peaceful as the private wee hours allow for an escape from curious fans. Publicity and attention have become a part of my life as my baseball stardom has grown. Consequently, I have learned to value the few moments of seclusion since the rest of the day wouldn't be mine.

I know many would kill for the notoriety, but it's not something I favor. Unlike many players, I don't crave the limelight and never look to use success in the sport to garner admiration. My focus has solely been on the game for as long as I can remember, and I can do without the honking car horns and yelling fans. I simply prefer to play baseball and be the best that I can be.

Nonetheless, here I am, *the next* baseball idol with the masses seeking greatness from TC Hunter. The fans irrationally worship, and the sports reporters hound while I constantly remind them that all I am doing is playing a kids' game. That clarity helps me cope with the external suggestions that the game itself rests on my shoulders. Although I try not to succumb to pressures, perhaps it all contributes to my mental woes. Given my current state, the reasonable conclusion is that the fanfare, the records, and the constant attention may be taking a toll.

My parents named me Theodore Cobb. My folks said they both agreed on the name, but I'm sure it was a small fight, and my father got his way. Theodore Samuel Williams, the "Splendid Splinter" was my dad's favorite player. He said Williams was the best pure hitter to ever play the game, and I must agree.

More consciously than subliminally, I mimic his hitting style by concentrating on the same lower half load that starts my swing. But even with the mirrored style, it is a sacrilege to draw comparisons like many of the baseball commentators and pundits often do.

Stylistically, I suppose it can be said that we have the same approach, and my long, athletic frame kind of matches up with Williams'. However, I have a long way to go before I accept those comparisons, and I know even my father would take umbrage.

"Even more important than baseball," my dad would say about his idol, "Ted Williams was a Marine." Williams served in World War II and learned aviation. He did not see combat in WWII but flew thirty-nine missions in the Korean War in the early 1950s. In fact, his F9F Panther jet was shot down on one of his operations. Williams landed the plane on its belly and escaped off the wing. I often get nostalgic in my wee hour restlessness, and damn if I can't still hear my dad telling the story of Williams as he did repeatedly in my youth.

Theodore Samuel Williams was named after Theodore Roosevelt, and I in turn was named after him. *Teddy Ballgame* as he was also known won the Triple Crown in 1942, leading the league with thirty-six home runs and 137 RBI's while posting a .356 batting average. He then spent the next three years serving his country. He returned to the league in 1946 to help Boston win the pennant and went on to win another Triple Crown in 1947, just missing a third Triple Crown in 1949! A nineteen-time All-Star, he even compiled a .316 average with twenty-nine home runs in his final season at the age of forty-one.

If he did not miss those five seasons during his baseball peak, he would undoubtedly own most of the league's hitting records. Ted Williams was not just an elite baseball player; he was a legend, a military hero and a mythical figure.

"Anyone paying attention knows he was the greatest hitter to ever live," Dad would say, using the label that Williams himself coveted. I don't know that I ever felt compelled to be as great as Ted Williams, but Dad certainly wished that upon me. Finding the balance between brash confidence and humility was the key to success, and the lessons I learned from my father were invaluable in helping to carve my own path.

My middle name, Cobb, creates an interesting comparison.

Juxtaposed against Williams, Cobb too had legendary talent, though a very different persona. Like Williams, Tyrus Cobb is considered one of the greatest baseball players in history. My father puts him ahead of most, even Babe Ruth, as he noted that Cobb could do just about anything on the ballfield. The *Georgia Peach* as he was nicknamed played in the early 1900s, a significantly different era in the game.

Cobb played centerfield the bulk of his career. He was a decent defensive outfielder, but his forte was offense. His career batting average of .366 was unprecedented. He held the league stolen base record until 1977, and still maintains the steal-home record at fifty-four. A crazy stat when considering modern day baseball, he also stole second, third and home in succession an unprecedented four times. His career hits record of 4,191 was broken in 1985, but it took Pete Rose over 2,500 more at bats to collect the record.

Cobb was a groundbreaking player by all accounts, but his image was tarnished by accusations of racism and violence. My father would declare, "Bullshit!" when he heard suggestions that Cobb was a racist. There is certainly evidence of language used by Cobb that would not be acceptable today, and uncorroborated stories of unprovoked attacks by Cobb are part of the lore. Contrarily, he is also on record as being one of the first players to support minority integration into the big leagues.

Violence on the other hand is not so debatable. Cobb had many clashes with heckling fans, and even climbed into the stands to beat an unruly few. Over the years, his violence was embellished. One thing was for sure, Cobb was an ultimate competitor who would play the game hard and defined intensity for his time.

"You want that son of a bitch on your team," my dad would say. "You have to play the game with a little bit of red ass like him if you want to be great." I can attribute some of my aggressive play on having that edict pounded into me as a kid, though I wonder what my father might say about the balance I've found between being son of a bitch and sportsman.

To complete the triumvirate, Hunter is our surname. There is no relation, but my dad would talk about baseball great Jim "Catfish" Hunter as if he was a long-lost cousin. Catfish entered the baseball scene in the mid-1960s and garnered instant idolization from my father. Hunter was amazing and became the highest paid free agent pitcher in baseball in the 1970s. Above all else, he was a competitor and a winner who passed away too early in life from a battle with amyotrophic lateral sclerosis (Lou Gehrig's disease).

My last name wasn't chosen, but my father certainly used it to mold me as a player. All three players, Williams, Cobb and Hunter, were fierce competitors. Williams was laser focused on hitting, Cobb played with ferocity, and Hunter pitched with an immeasurable will to win. In many ways I had no choice but to emulate all three.

The gas pump clicked indicating a full tank, and I snapped out of my wandering thoughts. I replaced the nozzle, tightened the gas cap and checked my pockets for my wallet. For no good reason I have an irrational phobia of losing my wallet and having my license, credit cards, and other personal items blasted across the internet. Funny, I don't fear someone taking my cash; I'm more concerned with someone upsetting my life and rummaging through my personal property.

I hopped back in the car and zipped out of the lot heading west on the Courtney Campbell Causeway. I hit the media button on the console to get to my country music file. As a member of No Shoes Nation, my playlist is heavy on Kenny Chesney, but also includes quite a bit of Jason Aldean, Dierks Bentley, Kid Rock and Jon Pardi. Lately, I also favor Morgan Wallen, an artist I need to see in concert. Wallen never planned a music career, instead pursuing professional baseball before injury changed his path. It's funny how several famous country stars played baseball in high school and college. I suppose the pain and struggles of the game translates well into the emotions of a country song.

The tunes help me relax while driving the scenic causeway toward Clearwater. The mangroves below the highway are filled with tropical plants and wildlife. Perhaps in another life I might be an ecologist, but as a novice bird and wildlife researcher of the area, I like spotting the egrets, pelicans, herons, and plovers common to the area. My favorite is the great blue heron, which I find both graceful and glorious. Birds in flight represent freedom and solitude, bringing peace to my unsettled thoughts.

The crystal clear Tampa Bay water below teems with wildlife. Fish are easy to spot, and the flora and fauna of the area is amazing. In the distance I notice a pod of dolphin frolicking about and I keep an eye out for manatee, another favorite. The morning ride to the field is more conducive to finding wildlife than the ride back to Tampa when boats and fisherman tend to scare the creatures away.

My morning drives provide a great time for contemplation. Peering below I noticed a fast-moving fish dart into the reeds in pursuit of a kill. I thought it might be a barracuda or a small shark, but it moved too quickly out of my line of vision to be sure. The glint off the Gulf made the landscape difficult to view, adding disappointment to my otherwise peaceful morning.

Forced from my distraction, an article about elite athletes developing acute insecurities popped into my head. An information junky, I recently read a column suggesting a growing number of superstar athletes are faced with eccentric thoughts and anxiety as life's demands persist. Social media is somewhat to blame, as some start feeling they are living in a fishbowl and forced to meet unrealistic standards.

Secure in my own skin and never falling for the trappings of social media, I brushed the idea aside. Williams was brash and confident, Cobb was self-focused and a little bit of a prick, and Hunter was a determined competitor. I emulate the trio, in that my tendency is to focus on my performance on the field and brush aside the distractions off the field.

Self-analyzing is not my forte, though I have no choice but to consider the moving parts of pending free agency. I'm the main topic of conversation in the media and the demands for my time are unrelenting. Whether it's the team, the ownership, the league, my agent, and even the players' union, they all want a piece of me. Where I play out the rest of my career is relevant to the entire league, and the decision will also impact my position in history. I prefer not to think about a legacy, but it's unavoidable given the constant talk about records and comparable players. Yet, in the pit of my stomach I have a hard time believing there is a direct correlation between these factors and my current mental state.

Perhaps, like a plethora of athletes who now speak about their mental health problems, I could look for help. It would not be easy for me, but maybe I could overcome the stigma and seek professional guidance. At the very least, I need to consider the option.

I once lived a life devoid of episodes, so I try to remain optimistic that my woes are temporary. If I remain carefree and determined to do my job on the diamond, my agent will handle the business end, and all will fall into place. Conquering the business hurdle may just be enough to jar my psyche from conflict to harmony.

The tune on the sound system changed from Kid Rock's *Born Free* to Jason Aldean's *Try That in a Small Town* just as a few clouds block the sun's glare. Setting my bipolar tendencies aside, I crank up the song, sink back in my seat and continue my ride looking for exotic fish and birds.

CHAPTER 3

THE TEAM LOT is nearly empty. Staff and players might trickle in over the next couple of hours, but the full team is not required to arrive until nine. It promises to be a long day, so I planned to relish the fleeting moments of calm.

Tony Ferrante, an older, white mustached security guard ushered me into a spot. A gentleman and huge baseball fan, Tony loved his job. "Good morning, TC. The best spot for you like always," he said with his thick New York accent. Like so many residing in the area, Tony was a Northeast transplant with little intention of ever going back.

"Thanks Tony. How's the family? Everyone good?" I asked. I often struggle to create chit-chat, and I've learned over the years that some take my social awkwardness as conceit. That could not be further from the truth, so I try to be better at small talk. Clumsy with my conversations, at least Tony appreciates me and never notices my struggles.

"Yes, yes. Everything is good TC, everything is good. Another great day at the park," he says, his wide smile glowing in the early morning light.

"You love baseball, don't you Tony?"

"I don't care what anybody says, it's the greatest game on this planet."

"I'm not going to fight you on that one, Tony."

"You know, it's the only team sport where the defense has the ball."

"Never thought of that, but you are right," I said. I paused for a moment to consider the oddity before continuing. "You get back to New York much, Tony?"

"Nah, barely get back anymore. It's better here. Brooklyn ain't the same," he says, "not much family left up north. They either moved down here or kicked the bucket."

I laughed along with Tony while considering how the older folks in Florida prefer to consider death a topic of good humor. Tongue-tied again, I struggle for a retort, so I instead wish him a great day and am on my way. It's my sixth spring training with the club and Tony has been the morning security guard from the onset. He's such a solid guy that I make a mental note to do something special for him before spring training ends. He drives an old Buick that he parks in the far corner of the lot. Maybe I'll park a new car next to his and flip him the keys on the last day of camp. That would be a fun surprise, and I'm sure something he'll appreciate.

My spring training regimen is consistent no matter when I arrive. Even on days without an insomnia episode, I tend to get to the ballpark before any other players. I typically grab a protein bar and drink, get dressed and click the remote for the huge, eighty-inch player lounge television. Being regimented is something I learned early on in my athletic pursuits, and it has served me well throughout my career.

The shelves in the kitchen area are freshly stocked, and I notice a new supply of Fit Crunch energy bars. I favor whey protein milk and cookies flavor, so I grab two, one for now and I throw another in my locker for later. I chose a hard stool instead of the inviting couch nearest the television in order to trick myself out of considering exhaustion. Particularly when I have a night of restricted sleep, I consciously limit my lounge time and never misuse the many amenities.

As I click through a few channels, nothing catches my eye. The news seems more pessimistic than usual as they report on the foul state of the country. I pause for a moment on a news channel to watch a reporter lament about a politician's claim about inflation. The previous day it was the same pessimistic tone, but the topic was the open border. No matter the subject, it's always hollow talk without any action or progress.

I click on the baseball channel, which only adds to my frustration. The reporter is talking to a league official about the season's new rules changes. The bureaucrats passed rules for bigger bases, a pitch clock, a limit to pickoff attempts, and a regulated defensive shift. They also implemented an automated ball-strike system to have pitches called electronically, relaying the calls to the home plate umpire via an earpiece. Cumulatively, the changes threaten the very fabric of the game, yet the guy from the league is parading like a peacock over the new adaptations to cut twenty minutes off the average game.

Watching the interview, it occurs to me that only media types and league officials complain about the pace of play. The fans appreciate the drama, and not having a clock differentiates baseball from other sports. If I were to guess, it has something to do with money and television productions since the proposed rules are not for the betterment of the game.

The league administrator reminds me of the politicians on the other channel. They claim to be doing something for the benefit of the people, yet each has ulterior motives. Personal agendas take precedence under the auspice of welfare, when in reality they will cause ruin and perpetuate further issues. Disgusted, I turn off the television and opt to start my training for the day.

Ending my lounge time, I move onto the weight room for a strength maintenance workout. Most players prefer to lift after baseball activities, but I like hitting the weights first. Besides, being the early bird allows me to leave the ball yard much sooner after each spring training game. My teammates brand me the afternoon phantom for my penchant to disappear while they linger about. I'm okay with the label because I know nobody outworks me no matter the time of day.

The workout area at the facility is state-of-the-art. At the back wall of the large room sits a series of weight stations. Each cubby is complete with ample weights, a weight bench, and a squat rack, as well as a computer tablet that trainers use to post suggested workouts. The tablet is anchored at the corner of the individual station and players punch their names to get their personalized daily tasks.

I work closely with our team trainers to develop a lifting routine, and my workout encompasses a wide variety of movements. The computer system monitors my progress and keeps a record of every repetition. In the technology age gone mad, the tablet also videos each movement so the trainers can monitor form to spot potential injuries.

My on-season exercises are designed for maintenance, unlike off-season strength workouts that take twice as long. It still takes about an hour to complete my training and another fifteen to twenty minutes to do a yoga-like stretching routine that I perform each day. If I still feel tight or achy, I opt for a whirlpool bath, a deep tissue massage, and chiropractic treatment to really loosen up the joints and muscles. Brute strength without flexibility is counterproductive.

Massage is just what I need, and I'm already done with a good part of my daily regimen when several team members arrive. I make a bonding session with my teammates a prerequisite for each day, so after a second sports bar and an electrolyte drink in hand, I sidle up to Trent Evans at his locker. Evans, a top-notch closer, came over in an off-season trade and we immediately struck up a friendship. He is a six foot five inches tall, big Texan with arms so long he looks like he can scratch his knees without bending over. His long arms and wide shoulders help him generate a fastball that consistently reaches a hundred miles per hour, and his long, brown hair and goatee give him an intimidating look.

On the mound he appears aggressive and maybe even a little crazy, but in the locker room Trent is soft spoken and gentle. I think he gets a kick out of the duplicity and uses his on-field alter ego to his advantage. The big righty has interesting perspectives, and our conversations usually veer toward topics outside of baseball. This time the topic is the absence of faith, patriotism, and family in the younger generation.

Disrupting our discourse, a couple of locker stalls to our right, is one of our designated hitters, Gus Fallon, holding court with pitchers John Miller, Billy Campbell, and Jim Gast. Trent and I pause to listen as Gus talks about some girl he had met in Orlando during an off day. Apparently, he had to shave his entire body to remedy the severe case of crabs as a result of his tryst. Gus was colorful and told a good story, even one about pubic lice. Sophomoric tales are part of clubhouse banter, though I can only take it in small doses and opt to excuse myself from the group.

Heading out of the locker room I hear more bursts of laughter, but don't turn around to consider the source. Instead, I head toward the batting cages, determined to complete my work for the day. I tend to take extra swings most days during spring training and I only reduce my swings if my hands are sore. Extra work is a badge of honor and provides a level of internal confidence I need to succeed.

Fans mill about the complex, so I pose for a few pictures and sign autographs after completing my rounds of hitting. Ownership encourages players to be extra accessible during spring training, and I try to oblige. After all, a picture or an autograph takes a few minutes, but the typical fan spreads the story all over cyberspace making fan encounters invaluable in contributing to the health and popularity of the game.

My promotional duty satisfied, I walk back to our baseball headquarters and hear music blaring from the locker room. Fights over control of the music ended when the players agreed a schedule among themselves to pick room tunes. Rookies had no say, but the veterans wanting a place on the schedule were on a rotation to command the music. This day it's heavy metal cranking over the speakers, so it had to be our second baseman and resident hard rocker's playlist.

Ancillary issues like music in the clubhouse often fester into a major problem. With players from around the country and really from all over the world, the individual taste in music is quite eclectic. A solid percentage play country music, but at least we have a civil approach.

Entering the building from the field, the locker room is straight through the corridor. The facility is modern and pristine, newly designed to keep up with the expansive spring training sites throughout the league. The weight room as well as the training area is to the right while offices for the manager, coaches and administration are down the hall.

I pause and reluctantly turn left into the hall toward the offices. At the onset of spring training the team is introduced to the resident sports performance psychiatrist. Sessions with the psychiatrist were not mandatory, but they are highly recommended to get ahead of any sports-related anxiety and stress. Not only does the organization recommend counseling, but both my manager and agent suggested I try a few sessions to mitigate the inevitable pressures they foresaw from my rising stardom and free agency year.

No one had an inkling of my true problems, yet my manager and agent often display real concern about my temperament. I am prone to outbursts, and perhaps they think my personality deficiencies might amplify when under further duress. I think they are off base with their assumptions, and any incidences from my past have been justified. Whether it was charging the mound after a pitcher threw at me, or cursing out an umpire, the acts came out of raw emotion and not some sort of mental breakdown. I only flare up when it is warranted, and I have never done something that Williams, Cobb, Hunter or any other competitor of the past did not.

My manager wants to keep me on the field, and my agent wants to make sure I don't do anything to jeopardize contract negotiations. I get why both suggest I give counseling a try, but even with my combustible emotional state I remain reluctant.

I tend to be a perpetual skeptic when it comes to doctors in general. Whether it's a medical doctor or a psychiatrist, my life experience has shown that doctors are as full of shit as everyone else, and my general distrust for humanity does not allow me to attach to them any special status to a degree. With my feelings in conflict, I approached the psychiatrist's office door. The hallway is empty, and I stand by the door for a moment considering the next step. I sense someone approaching and stand still, hoping to go unnoticed. A tap on my shoulder spins me around, but oddly there's no one in the hall. I take it as a sign to make a quick exit. The doctor's focus is to help players with their mental state to improve on-field performance, and my problems went well beyond that scope.

I turn to leave just as the door swings open. It's as if the doctor sensed my reluctance and knew I was looking to escape. "Well hello TC, this is a surprise. What brings you this way?"

"Hey, Doctor Nelson, I usually don't head down to this side of the building," I say. Extending my arm to shake his hand, he was not buying my effort to play it cool.

"Please, call me Joe," he said. "Why don't you come on in and have a seat?"

Dr. Joseph Nelson is in his mid-fifties and seemingly harmless. He recently sold a successful practice and took on the team gig while in semi-retirement. His welcoming smile has me trapped, so like a moth heading toward a bright light with no choice but to bang into the glass, I step into his office to avoid looking like a loon.

Dr. Joe motions to a seat adjacent to his desk and closes the door. The office is small, and the walls adorned with placards baring inspirational phrases and interesting sayings. Directly in my sight line is a picture of Johnny Bench with a quote that reads, *"Slumps are like a soft bed, easy to get into and hard to get out of."* To the left, another poster says, *"Never let the fear of striking out get in your way. –Babe Ruth."*

"So how is your spring going?" he asks as an ice breaker.

"Spring has been good. The weather is great, and I like that I live just up a way in Tampa. No complaints." There's nothing like engaging in small talk about the weather and lying to a shrink.

"Right, you live here in the off season. How long have you been here?"

"I've been in Florida for about seven years and bought my place in Tampa, oh, I guess four years or so ago."

"You really like it here, don't you?" he asks.

"Well yeah, low taxes, plenty of fishing, guns, and scantily clad women everywhere. What's not to like?"

"I think I'm with you," he chuckles. "I'm thinking about getting a place down here as well. Do you have family down here?"

"No. No family," I say. I stopped short of telling him details. Perhaps another time I'd tell him how my mother and father died early in life at the hands of a drunk driver, and how my grandparents more recently died from the COVID-19 pandemic because of the New York governor's reprehensible nursing home policies. No, I'll entertain him another time about how I hope drunk drivers and certain politicians would get syphilis and die a slow death.

"Do your parents live elsewhere? Any brothers or sisters?"

"No, I, uh, I don't have any family. No brothers or sisters, and my parents and grandparents are all deceased." I tend to draw inferences from television shows, and I thought I saw the doctor forcibly suppress a reaction. I expected him to dig in, grab a notepad and start scribbling.

"I am very sorry to hear that," he said. "Where were your mother and father from originally?"

"The Northeast. I was born in the Bronx and grew up on Long Island."

"Ah, I think Tony the security guard is from that way."

"Yes, Tony is from Brooklyn," I say with an exaggerated New York inflection. I don't think he picked up on it.

"No siblings?"

"No brothers or sisters, no." I'm growing uncomfortable with the direction of the inquisition, so I point to an antique looking display on the wall. Next to an advertisement for *Ted's Creamy Root Beer* and *Red Rock Soda* was another sign showing Ty Cobb promoting Coca Cola. "Did you know that Ty Cobb's mother shot his father?"

"Cobb's mother shot his father? No, I didn't know that," Dr. Joe says as he looks over his shoulder at the poster sized piece of the Georgia Peach.

"Sure did, she shot and killed him a few weeks before he made his baseball debut in 1905," I blurt, wondering if he knew my attachment to Cobb.

"Really?"

I know something about family tragedy, and I continue with the story that my father often told. "Apparently, Ty Cobb's mother was rumored to be having an affair. His father, W.H. Cobb, often went out of town on business and she supposedly used those opportunities for her trysts. Cobb's father faked a business trip by packing the car and hitting the road as he often did. He circled back later that night in an attempt to catch his wife in the act. While climbing on the porch in the wee hours, Bam, Bam, she shot the old man twice."

"No shit?"

"He died that night, and nobody is truly sure what happened. Amanda Cobb claimed she suspected a burglary was taking place and she accidentally shot her husband. Other stories would of course emerge. Somehow, I think she should have been the one to take the bullet."

"So, you think the wife was cheating and did it on purpose?"

"I can be a little jaded, but that's my read."

"That's an incredible story," Dr. Joe says. "Family catastrophe often molds the survivors. It probably had a lot to do with who Cobb was as a player and a man."

That's probably true. "All I know is it's pretty fucked up," I mumbled.

"So somehow, Cobb was able to channel the devastation to become a great baseball player and icon. You know, people are capable of incredible things in the face of despair. Some blame God, some get angry, and some use tragedy as a unique form of motivation."

Dr. Joe shifts into shrink mode, as I expect. "I suppose so," I say. Well played, Doc. He's talking about me as about Cobb.

He continues. "It's absolutely true. I'll bet for Cobb, he emptied his emotions into his game. Sometimes, the emotions spill over, and in his case he had some displays of anger and rage from what I know of him. Although for the most part, he likely used his misfortune as a motivator. Maybe as a way to get the affirmation that he lost when his father died."

"That's some deep shit, doc," I half joke. I always thought of my similarity to Cobb as a result of my father pushing me to play with an edge. I never thought of any further similarities, but I can see how the search for affirmation and an approving voice might account for some psychological issues. My parents never saw me play professionally, which irks me to this day.

Am I longing for my parents? Well, yeah. But I've been feeling this way since they unexpectedly died many years ago. That emptiness is not something new, and the ominous feelings of despair I get in the wee hours of the morning are very different than that grief. I certainly didn't expect to get real answers from a brief conversation, nonetheless, it doesn't hurt to search for that eureka moment.

"The humanity in athletes is often overlooked. They have problems and issues just like everyone else."

"Amen to that, Joe." If the good doctor only knew the half of it.

Sensing we had veered off the path, Dr. Joe maneuvered the dialogue back to baseball. He may have dealt with serious mental health issues while he is running his practice, but he's now employed to deal with sports performance. Even if he senses more significant issues lurking beneath, he veers the conversation back toward his new sphere.

The conversation shifts to the inevitability feelings of inadequacy that baseball players get as a result of playing a game where even the best hitters fail twice as much as they succeed. Fortunately, I've taken my game to a level where I have avoided prolonged slumps, but the game has a way of bringing even the best players to their knees. If there's anything that helps performance and consistency, I'm interested.

Dr. Joe references purposeful techniques he calls *coping mechanisms*. Unknowingly, I'm already using one of them. He directs players to write a mantra or calming saying inside their ball cap. They pause to take off their hats to read the inspirational words during stressful points in the game.

I've been writing things inside my hat well before it became fashionable. Even though the sayings are not exactly inspirational or something he might suggest, the conscious act of taking time to distract from the pressures of the game is a positive. I sweat a lot, so I change hats often, constantly changing my private message. *"Piss on the fastball"* and *"Let's Go Brandon"* are my most recent ones, the latter both a political statement and something that makes me laugh.

Happy that I use one of his techniques, Dr. Joe suggests others. Taking a piece of grass or a handful of dirt and tossing it away after a bad at bat or an error is an interesting one. Tossing the particles away is a symbolic gesture of casting off negativity. Come to think of it, I've noticed many players tossing something aside and utilizing the technique. Giving that one a shot might be better than my current coping method of cursing and punching my own face.

I like Dr. Joe's demeanor. Our discussion provides practical methods to help my game. He is a professional and anxious to help. Yet, even though he is a licensed psychiatrist with years of experience, I don't think I could discuss my insomnia, or my true concerns with him. Even if I want to talk about my episodes, my subconscious won't allow me to broach the subject. A lot is required to break down that wall.

I peek out of the door, looking both ways before sneaking out of Dr. Joe's office. Awkwardly self-conscious from my visit to see the sports shrink, I also cherish my privacy. There's no need for questions or rumors about my personal business.

The hall is clear, although a few men gathered inside a meeting room adjacent to Dr. Joe. Hoping to go unnoticed I sped by and viewed the trio out of my periphery. Each dons a suit which I find odd since even team executives and media personalities dress casually during spring training.

Although curious, I didn't dare to look when over my shoulder I hear the catcalls. "Hey kid, baseball is ninety percent mental, the other half is physical," one of the men taunt. "Baseball ain't no pink tea, mollycoddles better stay out," harps another. "Forget the tea, pour me a cup of truth and maybe some Mr. Coffee," a third player says, sending the group into a loud cackle.

They reminded me of old-time baseball players hanging out in a dugout and chirping at an opponent. "Hey kid, if you see a fork in the hallway, take it," one of the men calls out, alluding to a famed Yogi Berra misspeak. That one seemed to really crack the group up and I spin around as they hoot their appreciation...

Assholes, I think.

Whipping back toward the meeting area I expect more barbs. Instead, I recoil after hearing the short burst of magnesium powder of an old camera flash spread through the air. The blinding burst is temporary, leaving me alone and dumbstruck in the hallway wondering how my imagination got the best of me.

Staggered and standing alone, another voice shouts my name. Hesitant to look, the voice grows like a crescendo, finally snapping me out my funk after the fourth or fifth holler. Team Manager Billy Law sits behind his office desk. His door open, he waves me in, "Did I catch you daydreaming, Ts? Get your ass in here. I wanna talk to you."

Billy Law is the best manager in the league. My manager for the brief time when I was in the minor leagues, he was promoted to big leagues a couple of years into my career. We've always maintained a professional distance, but I consider Billy a good friend.

Billy is a dying breed, not yet extinct but on the endangered species list. A solid baseball man, he has learned how to effectively marry the intense analytics infiltrating the game with old- school baseball philosophy. In an era of organizations that stress statistics and probabilities, he manages with his eyes.

Billy has thirty years in the game as a player as a coach and manager, and he uses the instincts accumulated over that span. Probabilities and statistics have their place, but he knows how to discern the odds provided by analytics from the true chances for success. Instead of robotically constructing lineups, he relies upon guttural intuition, often walking the line between what the organization administrators want him to do and what his baseball experience dictates.

Willing to buck the trend, he puts his job on the line. "If we were playing a video game, then going by what the computer says would be fine," he often says to his critics. "We decide things on the playing field, and that's how I manage."

Billy wins, so he's able to tell his detractors to pound salt. In a league that favors low batting average power hitters that strike out two hundred times, Billy prefers all around players who approach the game in a more traditional manner. "Don't tell me about exit velocity and launch angles. Give me a player that drives in the runner home from third with less than two outs, or a player who can win the game with his legs!" he often declares. Home runs are great, but winning baseball requires more than the occasional home run.

Through the office glass I see my skipper's smiling face as he waves me into the room. Billy is the ultimate player's manager and stands from his desk to greet me. It's a simple gesture that makes players feel like they are on equal footing instead of looking across the desk from a superior as if being sent to the principal's office.

Our team made the playoffs three consecutive years, but since we did not win a championship, the pressure is building on Billy. His resistance to statistics and probabilities has a faction within the organization looking to replace him with a *yes* man. However, due to leverage from my pending free agency, and I have made it known through indirect media channels that if Billy Law goes, I go. Billy knows I am in his corner, and he in turn provides me with certain freedoms within the game. It's a wonderful symbiosis fortified by a profound respect for one another.

"Morning Billy," I say. No matter the day or what might be going on, he always appears content and happy.

"Good morning T. Another great day at the ballpark."

Billy often called me *T* instead of TC. Sometimes it sounds like *Tees*, which might have been his way of saying *TC*. Originally from Louisiana, Billy has a Southern drawl and an engaging habit of making up words and names.

At fifty-two, Billy is a fitness nut with a firm grip who often jokes that if I was not careful he'd start playing again and steal my position in centerfield. He is a fixture in the weight room, and his runs on the treadmill are legendary. The example he sets, particularly to young players who often think they are impenetrable, significantly impacts the team. Baseball season in the majors is a grind, and Billy's concentration on work ethic and proper nutrition helps the squad remain healthy.

"What can I do for you Skip?" I ask, hesitant he might ask me about my session with Dr. Joe. Fortunately, he ignores why I might be walking down the hall.

Already dressed in his standard coach attire of white baseball pants and a short sleeved warm up jacket, he looks slightly concerned. "Two quick things," he says. "First, I am going to DH you today and keep you out of the field. You look pretty locked in already, so just take a couple of live at bats and then we will take you out of the game."

I nod to indicate I'm firmly on board. It's not uncommon for veterans and star players to have limits on their spring training action, particularly toward the end of camp. Limited action means limited chance for injury. It also gives management a chance to get more looks at some of the other young players. "I'm not going to fight you on that one, Skip," I say, "and the second thing?"

"The second thing is about the rookie Bobby Mitchell. His bat looks real good and we can use him at third base, but management wants to send him down to the minors. The kid is immature and he's spending most nights carousing at the clubs."

"Yeah, that's what I hear too."

"I asked management to give us a chance to reel him in. I need you and the other veteran players to have a talk with him and maybe show him the way. Scare him if you have to, but get him in line."

Baseball teams are held together by an intricate web of relationships and circumstances. Team chemistry is as important as talent level, and Billy is a master at gauging talent with personalities and manipulating a squad's overall morale.

"I can do that," I say. "I'll get Sammy and Johnny involved." Sammy Taylor and Johnny Baugh are no-nonsense veteran players who come off as a couple of bad asses. Taylor is our first baseman, and Baugh, our starting catcher. Their sole goal is to win a championship before they retire, and they'd hang the kid off a balcony by his ankles to get him in line if it advances their chances.

"Good, you know how this type of thing can play out if left unchecked. Drunken bar brawls, sex assault allegations. I can see it all coming, and we need to stop it. We need Mitchell at third, and maybe coming from you he will get straightened out in time. The last thing we need is any controversy or a cancer in the locker room, and I don't want him sent to the minors."

"I agree. I'll get on it right away. Anything else, Skip?"

"No, that's it. Get your work done today and get out of here early. We got that thing tonight over in Tampa."

Toward the end of spring training the organization hosts promotional events. This evening is a meet-and-greet for snowbirds living in Florida for the winter and who would soon head north for the spring and summer months. The perennial season ticket holders appreciate the perk, and it was part of the job to be accessible to loyal fans.

"Hey," Billy says as I head for the door. "Are you still with that lady friend of yours? Ain't my business, but she seems fantastic."

I glanced over my shoulder and took a few steps into the hallway. Calling out playfully, I answered, "Yup, she is fantastic, and you are a hundred percent right. It ain't your business." Billy respects the boundaries I tend to create. He never pries or plays angles, yet he'd prefer if I were settled.

"Don't let a good one slip away. Over thinking ruins happiness, that's all I'm saying," Billy exclaims through a hearty laugh.

"All good Skip," I respond as I make my way to the field, anxious to get to the place that represents my only true comfort zone.

CHAPTER 4

MY AGENT CALLS as I get in my car to head back to Tampa. He has a knack of catching me as soon as I leave the spring training site, as if he has a tracking device on me. His timing is truly uncanny, although I did expect his call since he intends to meet me at the evening event at the Marriott to snap publicity photos.

I know he is right about the public relations battle being relevant to getting the most out of my next contract. Logically, being a fan favorite puts pressure on management, which in turn should increase the dollars in any offer. Social media has become an effective way to measure popularity, so I go with the flow as my agent does his thing.

My agent is detail oriented and sometimes a little stuffy, but I am always confident he is covering all angles and contingencies. Rightfully so, he views my pending free agency as an opportunity of a lifetime for both of us. There is huge money at stake, and a player in my position gets one bite of this apple, so I tolerate my agent's often obscure scenarios and what if propositions.

"TC Hunter, this is Thomas Bader." He consistently opens every phone conversation with the same introduction. He probably thinks it is part of being professional, but I find it odd and extraordinarily annoying.

"Hello Tom. I got out of Clearwater early and I'm heading back to Tampa." The preseason game was still going on, so I was fishing a bit to see if Tom has a source with the team who fed him information of my whereabouts.

"Yes, I figured you would have an early day," he says, not willing to divulge his mole. "I will meet you on the outdoor terrace at the event later tonight. I'll probably get there around eight-thirty, and I'll snap a few pictures and maybe a quick video to post on your fan page."

Tom enjoys being elusive and vague. I contemplate asking who might have tipped him off, but what does it matter? I suppose he could have been following the game on the radio and heard they took me out of the game after a few innings.

"Sounds good, Tom. The event starts at seven, but I'll probably get there around the same time you arrive." I'm not looking to be fashionably late; rather I'm following instructions from the team's publicist who prefers I make a grand entrance an hour and a half into the event.

"Perfect," he says. "But we have some business to discuss. The team upped their offer to ten years for three hundred million. The offer added two years from their eight-year, $240 million initial deal."

"Okay, so what do you think?" I ask.

"A better offer, and the owner made it clear that he wants to be proactive to get something done before free agency kicks in. But it's still not close to what we can get in the open market. I told him you are worth four hundred and fifty million over twelve years."

The numbers being thrown around are like Monopoly money to me. My current one-year deal pays sixteen million, which is more money than I could ever imagine. I live well and I try to do some good charity work, and it's still more than I will ever need.

"What did he say to that?" I ask.

"Honestly, he did not say much. I took that as a realization of where the market is, or he would have barked at the figure."

"So, what does that mean?"

"It means that if you want to stay put, I'm sure there is more room than their ten-year offer. I don't think they will come up to the four-fifty figure, but I'll bet the next offer will be in the three-fifty million for ten territory."

Stopped at a light, I noticed the driver of the car behind me trying to get my attention. I give the fan a wave and a thumbs up and he appears satisfied with the interaction. "Let me chew on that Tom and maybe we talk a little later."

"Just remember to be patient. And I still want to have our strategy in place to not negotiate publicly once the season starts. The union likes that idea as well as it will keep the pressure on ownership," he says.

I'm being used to set the market, and the union is keeping a close eye on my path. I'm not exactly comfortable that the union is so involved, but my contract could impact pay to other players for years to come.

"I'm taking your advice, so yeah, that's the policy. I'm following your lead and I will tell the media the same when they ask. We've been negotiating, and I won't entertain any further offers after the season starts."

If I don't sign and end up in free agency, some of the bigger markets will likely come in with figures that could prove outrageous. I did not want to live and play in certain cities, but nobody needs to know that right now. As long as I have another great season, I control the leverage, and I'm confident my agent knows how to use it to our advantage.

"Good," Tom says. "I know you understand. I will see you a little later tonight. Thank you, TC Hunter."

Thank you, TC Hunter represented the end of each call. Like Tom's introduction, he ends every conversation the same way. He's a great agent, but so very quirky.

⚾ ⚾ ⚾

The Florida afternoon sun is strong, but it doesn't deter me during my drive home. I'd rather be a little hot and keep the car's top down than to close up and use the air conditioner. Fresh air is better, and there's something intoxicating about the smell of the Gulf.

The tropical scenery is something I always wanted in my life. I could really piss the union off and sign a contract with Philadelphia so that I can keep attending spring training so close to home. Or maybe I'll sign with a Texas team and become a Gulf of Mexico commuter of sorts. Either way, spending my time where I want to live while still sitting on a pile of money makes sense.

Tom's plea for patience is a reminder that I am in the driver's seat. Although there is something noble about maintaining the status quo and playing for one team for an entire career, I can't let it cloud my judgment. From a traditional sense, playing for one team used to be a badge of honor that Cobb or Williams would appreciate. But times have changed. Even Catfish Hunter capitalized on free agency during his career. There are so many variables, but my goal is to not let it become overwhelming.

The remainder of my drive home is uneventful. No manatee, no dolphin, no great blue heron. I'm sure they were there to be found, but the sun is so bright off the bay that all I see is a blinding reflection for most of the drive.

⚾ ⚾ ⚾

I spot Jennifer in the parking lot as I pull into the condo complex. It isn't uncommon for her to stop by unannounced, so I figure she might want to continue our recent conversations. We've been dating for about half a year, and our relationship is at a crossroad since I'm about to depart for the season. She parked in the main lot and positioned herself so that she could wave me down as I pull in. With my dirty blond hair waving in the convertible-induced breeze, and the music cranked up, I'm a little hard to miss.

I met Jennifer Vivino in late October upon returning to Florida from the previous season. I was trying a new restaurant in the Hotel Haya in a historic part of Tampa called Ybor City. Reviews on the Flor Fina restaurant noted "great food and a private bar setting for an upscale clientele." I was hoping that I might add the new restaurant to a short list of establishments where I feel comfortable having dinner and maybe a drink or two without drawing a crowd.

I was only at the bar for a short time when one of Jennifer's friends recognized me. Out of my periphery I had noticed the group of a half dozen women at the far end of the bar. One of them was inconspicuously gesturing to point me out while another broke from the gaggle to move toward me. When it's a group of attractive women, I tend not to mind the attention, and I tried to play it cool as I saw her approach.

I turned my head slightly to see who was coming my way and it was like being struck by a lightning bolt. I first noticed the face of an angel who wore makeup sparingly. What makeup she did have on accented her bronze, Florida tan and her long, brown hair had sun baked blond highlights that shimmered like gold.

I tried to avoid being caught giving her the once over, but my eyes were drawn to her long legs and fit body. She was wearing a form fitting dress and she looked perfectly proportioned. The black dress was sexy, but also perfectly restrained, leaving much to the imagination. She carried herself with confidence, but without the self-importance of some women I have known.

In my travels as a professional baseball player, I have dated actresses, media personalities and models, but I have never seen someone so stunning. When she smiled, her glowingly white teeth accented her natural beauty, and her face was warm and inviting. When she asked if the seat next to me was taken, I was tongue-tied and stammered before asking her to join me.

I bought her a drink, the house special martini, and we chatted for a bit before I asked if she would accompany me for dinner. I figured she was either there for a girl's night out or she was meeting someone, so I was surprised and thrilled that she said yes. She said her friends would understand, and I ditched my plan to grab dinner at the bar, instead seeking out the hostess to arrange a private table for two.

I don't think I am too bad in the looks department, but I felt out of my league. The waiter that night commented that we made a fantastic couple, and I guess that's what we became. I do not tend to seek out women to date. They just sort of enter the picture and in this case, I instantly fell for Jennifer.

A young, red-blooded man I am drawn to gorgeous women. I'm a sucker for a pretty face, and Jennifer checked all of the boxes in the looks department. However, there is much more to her. Jen is smart, kind, compassionate with a personality unlike others that I have dated. She challenges me mentally and our conversations are often fun and uplifting. I can be a tough nut to crack, yet she gets something out of me that I don't offer to others.

To go along with what I can only describe as a fulfilling friendship, our sex life is outstanding. Being compatible in the bedroom department is important, and our physical relationship is matched by emotional companionship. When I am with Jennifer I feel exhilarated, yet at the same time I feel vulnerable and emotionally exposed.

I've had a few relationships in my life, and when I became a baseball prospect it undoubtedly increased my appeal to the opposite sex. Thinking everyone is a gold digger might be a bit cynical, though I would be kidding myself to think that isn't a factor. An easy life and the prospect of rubbing elbows with stardom can be alluring, and it has been a noticeable part in previous affairs.

I broke up with my first girlfriend, Jillian Sansone, shortly after heading to play in the minor leagues. I was living in New York and attending high school when I was drafted in the third round of the league's amateur draft. Even though I was rated in the top ten high school players in the country by the national scouting bureau, Perfect Game, I didn't get selected in the first or second round. At the time, I didn't know what I wanted to do. I had a scholarship to attend a university with a powerhouse baseball program and I initially thought I would go that route.

The baseball scouts knew of my inclination so selecting me did not guarantee that I would sign. However, after some soul searching, I realized I was considering going to school because it was what my teachers and counselors were encouraging me to do. Finally honest with myself, I knew that I wanted to get into professional baseball as soon as possible.

So, I hired an agent who happens to be the very same one I have now. Tom used the leverage I had with having a college scholarship lined up and forced the organization's hand. That was my first contract negotiation, and Tom handled it perfectly. He had a signing bonus number in mind and even though privately, he knew I wanted to sign and move right into professional baseball, he let the team know that I would go to school if I did not receive a certain figure.

Tom was masterful in leaving the door open just enough to have the team think I might forego school. He taught me that we needed to be very patient, which became harder to do with each day that went by. It was like playing a game of chicken, but Tom knew that the team desperately wanted me to sign.

In the end, my agent was able to squeeze the right amount of money out of the Philadelphia organization and I walked away with a seven-figure signing bonus. Tom knew that the team viewed me as the steal of the draft with one scout telling management that they needed to sign me at any cost. That scout, George Martin, came out smelling like a rose and parlayed the success into becoming the head scout and lead talent evaluator for the organization.

After signing my first contract, I was assigned to the team's affiliate in Clearwater. They also had a minor league team in upstate New York, and I thought they might send me there. Instead, I was off to Florida where I began my love affair with the Gulf of Mexico.

Subsequently, I broke up with my first girlfriend, leading to a pattern I've continued with all my relationships. Realistically, I did not want to have anything that might distract me from my career. Jillian was a fantastic girl as were some of the others. It was not always easy to split up, but it was the right thing to do. I needed to throw myself into my work, and that focus helped me to quickly climb the ladder within the organization.

I've had relationships in the off season, and I've even had a tryst or two with baseball groupies during the season, but I don't allow myself any diversions. I've always been very careful about that, and I think it has served me well throughout the years. Now, I have Jennifer who I connect with on another level. She's smart, she's drop-dead gorgeous, she's fun to be around, and a part of me can't envision being without her.

I will always maintain proper attention to my craft, though recently I've been thinking of ways to strike a balance. During the season I am unrelenting in my work and as such, can be moody and basically miserable to be around. I knew immediately that I would need to find a way to make sure Jen always feels like a priority while also making sure I never lose my edge as a player. I know I love her, but if I can't get myself to go all in, she would not be getting what she truly deserves.

Jen has not put any pressure on me, and she thinks she can manage the situation, although I don't think either of us can fully understand the potential complications of a long-distance relationship. Our regular season baseball schedule puts me on the road often, sometimes for weeks at a time. That alone creates a logistical nightmare and makes trust a factor. It's not my style, but baseball players are known to have a girl in each town. She should never have to wonder about anything like that, yet even the thought can be enough to spoil a relationship. Frankly, I tend to have inherent trust issues myself that I would also need to work through.

Even if we found a way to overcome some of the obstacles, I am most fearful that I will never be able to resolve my psychological issues. I fear that she will bolt out of the door if I level with her about my insomnia and frantic episodes. I have a whopper of a problem. In many ways, I am living a lie.

Curiously, I do not have episodes when Jen stays the night. We both have busy schedules, so she does not tend to stay overnight each time we see each other, but the sample size is large enough that I know for sure my head is in a different place when she is around.

When Jen is in my bed, I seem at peace and emotionally in check. She has a calming influence that provides me with a feeling of normalcy. Selfishly, it's a pretty good reason to keep her in my life.

The last time we spoke our relationship felt in limbo. With so much going on professionally while also dealing with psychotic dreams, I can sometimes be a poor companion. Often, frightening thoughts push my outlook toward pessimism, and the worst part is that I can't tell her why I am so off. She knows when I have things on my mind and suspects I will revert to my pattern of breaking up with women for the season. I have tried to assure her that I want things to be different with us, but Jen is rightfully skeptical.

I park the car and walk down the ramp from the parking garage toward the main lot. The sun beams down and Jennifer looks fantastic as usual. She dressed casually, wearing a black halter top with white shorts. Her hair is in a ponytail, and she was sporting Chanel sunglasses that fit her face perfectly. Jen has many different looks, from sophisticated to casual, and she makes them all work. Still, it's her smile that lights up my world no matter how she is outfitted.

"Hello Jen," I say as I walk toward her. Given our last conversation, I search for a sign that her attitude toward me might have changed. With enough life experience in the relationship area, I approach her with caution, but all I see is my Jennifer, smiling and cheerful.

"Hi, Ted. I hope you don't mind me popping over today."

She never calls me TC. It's always Ted or Teddy, which is kind of our thing, and it's okay with me. "Don't be silly, no problem at all. How are you? You look great?" I give her a quick kiss to put her at ease.

"Great, I know you have plans for tonight, but do you have some time for me."

"Of course, come on up. I always have time for you."

We walk side by side, holding hands through the parking lot and to the lobby. Her hand fit perfectly in mine, and her grasp seems a little tighter than usual, squeezing so that I won't let go.

The lobby is empty besides a maintenance worker buffing the

floor with a large rotating machine. The worker doesn't notice us, focusing only on his task and listening to music through earphones. The marble tiled floors sparkle as the machine eliminates the scuffs from everyday traffic.

The elevator door opens and a curious looking older gentleman steps out. The man tips his fedora toward Jen who appears not to notice him. He looks like an English gentleman from the 1800s. *Odd*, I think, as I have never before seen him.

"Interesting looking fella," I say.

"What fella?" responds Jen.

Really odd!

I hit the button for the penthouse, and we ride up still clutching hands.

We reached the top floor, and the elevator opens into the vestibule. A huge window in the hall displays a breathtaking view of Hillsborough Bay. It is one of those days where the water shows more green than blue, and the sun hits the sea just right. From the penthouse floor you can see for miles clear across the bay to Davis Island, and Jen pauses for a second to take it all in.

I hold the door open as she steps into the foyer. Down the hall into the main living space is a huge sectional couch facing a window with the same spectacular vista. She likes a squeeze of citrus in her drink, so I cut up a lime and add it to a glass along with sparkling water and ice. When I hand her the glass she's still smiling, although she looks anxious to talk. I sit adjacent to her and absorb the view of the fishing boats and luxury yachts in the shimmering inlet below.

Jennifer sits gracefully, her tan, athletic legs crossed. She looks stylish and elegant as usual, and I think about how many times we sat in the same spot enjoying the scenery and each other's company. She sips her drink and places it gently on the cocktail table. With her gaze fixed upon me she says, "I'm glad I got the chance to see you. I have not been able to get you off my mind."

I smile and give her a comforting nod to indicate that I too was thinking of her. I didn't like the way we last left off, and I can tell she didn't either. I truly wish there was a way to make it all work without angst. I have been battling the reluctance of thinking our relationship might get in the way of my performance and have been working on being less irritable after bad games, and on making her feel like a priority.

The bigger issue is my state of mind and how I can cure myself without getting Jen involved or hampering our relationship. I fear not coming to terms with my mental health will likely bring doom to our relationship. Out of fairness, a big part of me wants to fix myself prior to allowing Jen to move deeper into my life. She should not have to live with my burden, and a few days ago I was pretty sure we needed to cool things down. Selfishness pushed me in one direction—making me guarded and aloof—while love pulled me in another.

"This is hard, Teddy. I never want to be a hindrance, and I know how much you value your career," she starts. Her eyes are normally fixed on me when she speaks, but she looks away, struggling to find the right words. "I want to find a way to make us work, but I need to know that you are all in."

"It's hard for me to explain what goes on in my head," I say. I stare out the window as I too have a hard time elucidating. "Above all, I want to be fair to you. I may not be able to give you what you deserve, and I know I can't make you understand."

"But I do understand. You are scared, and you think I'll be an obligation. You think I will be someone that you are required to set aside time for. But I don't need that. I don't want that. I just want us to take it as it comes, and I understand where you are in your life and career."

"I'm scared that I can't live up to what you want me to be. What if I fall short?"

"You won't fall short. We will grow together and share life together. I know you feel like life is better when we are together. You can't deny it."

I have no doubt about that, but I'm hampered by other concerns.

"What if we give it a go and I disappoint you? What if things in my head end up too tough for you to deal with?" I ask.

"I've seen glimpses of what's in your head. Besides, I can say the same thing. Nobody is perfect."

"I'm far from it, Jen. I'll always be true to you, I can tell you that."

"And I'll be true to you. You can take that out of the equation if that's what you are worried about."

Cheating doesn't top of the list of concerns but makes the top five. I have never been a hound like some of the players I've been around, but I was cheated on once and I hated the feeling. It wasn't the act, but the deception that impacted me.

Jen isn't at all like the woman who fooled around on me. That one was living in a Tik-Tok world where social media dictated her every move. She was more interested in popularity from a virtual community than anything else, and she used the idea of dating a professional baseball player to that end. Living in a world of networked communities she was more interested in status, and in hindsight, I should have seen it coming.

"No, I'm not worried about that. Just promise to always be honest with me. If I end up not what you want, then just tell me. I don't think I could ever take feeling like something was done behind my back."

"It's a non-issue to me Ted. We can promise to be true together and that'll be that. I trust you and you trust me."

"I know it to be true, but thank you for saying it out loud."

"Then what are you afraid of?"

She leaves the door open for me to explain everything. How I'd rather be dead than fail. How I don't want to fail in baseball or in our relationship. How I've never allowed myself to be emotionally invested in a relationship during the season and doing so would be a huge leap. How my head pushes me into dark places and how in one sense I am motivated, while in another sense, I'm completely frightened by the prospect of not living up to an ideal.

Frenzied nightmares and odd thoughts push me in all directions.

I was reared to play the game and to be the best. Forces drive me toward that legacy. At the same time, those forces haunt me and make me feel like I've got more responsibilities than one man can handle. My mental instability is a riddle. The same feelings that irk me also motivate me, and I don't know if I am uncontrollably unstable or if I'm running through some phase where there is an eventual solution. Either way, the quandary is whether Jen should be dragged into my vexing world.

Instead of providing any real explanation, I simply say, "I'm not afraid. I can be eccentric and ornery, but I think I can be better."

"And I'll be patient and understanding. Let's build a life together. I don't know much, but I know we are supposed to be together."

"You think we can do this?"

"I'd run through hell and back to be together," she says.

I stare at her for a moment and notice a mist in her eyes. Jen is normally graceful and stoic, and her vulnerable side is the reason for my reluctance. If I could somehow place her in my fucked-up head, maybe she would understand my fears. Letting her in might be the only way to truly understand my apprehension.

"I know we can do this," she continues. "We will take it all as it comes and we'll deal with every episode in life together."

Did she really just say episodes in life?

Our embrace is warm and wonderful. Jennifer fits inside my arms perfectly and I want the moment to last. I'm not much for looking for signs, but I can't help but see optimism in Jen's words. Yet, countering the incredible emotions is entering something completely foreign and unsettling.

Jennifer leaves to head back to her house in Sarasota. I asked her if she wants to accompany me to the team event and she declines. She keeps some clothes in one of my closets so she could have made a quick change, but I think it's her way of demonstrating she can keep distant from my professional life. We have much to navigate, so I appreciate the sentiment and we promise to spend more time together in the coming days.

There is much to consider if we are going to make a relationship work, but for now, Jen made it very simple; she will continue living in Florida, pursuing her career while I do my thing in Philadelphia. We will spend time together, but we would avoid the feelings of obligation that can get messy. We agree to strip away the pettiness that can creep into a relationship, so at face value, it's a great step forward.

I'm sure she would accumulate plenty of frequent flyer miles, but I wanted her to do things at her own pace and make sure she was diligent about her own career. She is involved with some amazing charitable endeavors through her work, and it was very important that she continue. Hopefully, we'll find a way to strike the right balance.

I threw in a dip of tobacco and poured a shot of a single malt Irish whiskey that goes down smooth. Whiskey is my drink of choice and takes the edge off. I keep a tin of Skoal around for rare occasions. It's a terrible habit, and I'm glad I reserve it for particular times like when I have a terrible game or when my head is spinning.

I wonder what Jennifer will think about the tobacco habit. Like my borderline schizophrenia, it's probably something I should have confessed to her in advance. Maybe I'll quit dipping before it turns into a problem.

My phone buzzes and a text from Jennifer reads, *Being deeply loved by someone gives you strength, while loving someone deeply gives you courage. – Lao Tzu*

I sip my drink and take a few deep breaths. If I can come up with a strategy to address my mental anxiety, perhaps everything will fall into place. There's an old baseball saying that goes, "The key to success is to keep your highs low and your lows high." Even keeled is the key and perhaps I can use the adage to manage my turbulent existence.

CHAPTER 5

I THROW ON a collared shirt, black slacks and Salvatore Ferragamo Oxfords. It's not my thing, but shoes are something that my teammates talk about and compare, so I make sure mine are fancy enough and in style.

My mind askew, thoughts bounced between Jennifer and my recent hallucinations. The disappearing men from the meeting room earlier in the day are etched into my head as is the gentleman in the condo elevator. Dreams are one thing, seeing things is quite another. The thought of adding more pieces to an already unsolvable puzzle makes my head spin, and I hoped to use the fan event as a distraction.

The JW Marriott is off Bayshore Boulevard on Water Street and less than ten minutes away. The proximity to my condo is a big plus, and although I don't typically enjoy large team-sponsored social gatherings, I'll put on a good face.

I get tired of the same conversations and questions, but I know it is part of the job. Are you ready for the season? Are we going to win the championship this year? You are going to stay with the team and sign a contract soon, right?

Of course I'm ready for the season, and of course we want to win a championship. I offer cliché answers and remain courteous. When they ask about my contract extension and free agency I provide a typically vague answer when I really want to say is, *"Do you have access to ownership to get them to pay me fair market value?"* I can only imagine the ensuing havoc if I answer their questions honestly, so I take the high road instead.

As planned, I arrive nearly two hours into the event, fashionably late to create a buzz. The fan social is set on a beautifully decorated terrace overlooking the water. I walk in and high-five a few of my teammates looming on the outskirts of the party. It's crowded, but there is room to move about, and my eyes dart around the space seeking a niche. The goal is to find a corner spot where fans remain in my sightline, and nobody can ambush me from behind.

Waiters and waitresses scurry about with drinks and hors d'oeuvres. Off in the distance I see a couple talking with Billy Law. Stan and Lois live in my condo complex and are fervent fans. Sometimes I feel like they are stalking me, often popping up in the condo lobby to engage in conversations or to invite me to a party. They are nice enough, but a little overzealous, and although Billy will keep them occupied for a bit, I'm sure they will seek me out.

I scan the masses for the old man in the fedora or the mystery trio from earlier in the day. I have no reason to believe they're here, yet my mind won't purge the images from my head. There is something oddly familiar about those old souls, and I shake myself as I head through the crowd to find my perch.

I locate a spot to my liking and notice a rising clamor as the party goers became aware that I have arrived. Johnny Baugh and Bobby Mitchell enter the terrace at the same time and are also part of the grand publicity stunt. Baugh is a fan favorite and Mitchell is a rookie sensation. Fans appreciate rookies since they are a fresh team commodity and bring a sense of anticipation. Baugh assigned himself to Mitchell for the night to keep the kid from drinking too much and hitting on the female guests. The shared spotlight helps disburse the crowd, so at least I'm not getting immediately mobbed. The attention is flattering, and once I get over my initial social anxiety I do start to enjoy myself.

"Hello, it's very nice to meet you. Sure, I'll autograph the baseball that you found in your purse. And a photo? Certainly. Yes, of course I remember you from last year. You were the one who yelled what at the game? No, I didn't hear you. Sign this for your kid? No problem...."

The conversations are monotonous, but the fan excitement makes it worthwhile. Television revenue and game attendance pays the bills, and players sometimes lose sight of the importance of the promotional side of the business. Work stoppages and stylistic rule changes threaten the very existence of the game, and I never take the fans for granted.

"Do you think you can break the home run record?" a fan asks as he makes it to the front of the line. The middle-aged man dressed in a blue sports jacket and khakis is someone I recognize from previous events. The jacket makes the fan sweat, and he uses a handkerchief to wipe his brow. He's a passionate fan with an array of questions and strong opinions. He never holds back and his thoughts on the state of the game often entertain.

"Well hello, Ivan. Good to see you again. You know I don't worry about those things."

Without skipping a beat he says, "You hit sixty-one homers last year and everyone knows that tied the real record."

"I just try to be the best player that I can be. Some things aren't in my control."

"I think you can do it. You missed a dozen or so games due to injuries last year, too."

Such optimism is great, but my only recourse is to deflect the thought, *Geez, a lot of things have to happen to hit that many. Staying healthy is just a small part.*

Ivan is unrelenting and opines, "If there's anyone who can do it, it's you. I think you will break the record someday too. Breaking both records would be great for baseball."

"Easy now, let's take one day at a time, one at bat at a time. God willing, we will win some games," I say in rehearsed form. "Are you getting season tickets again this year?"

"Yup, always the same seats, four rows up from the dugout and a little to the right. I'm on the aisle. You know where. You always see me there."

"That's right. You are a great fan my friend," I say as I reach to shake his hand. Ivan is not an autograph seeker and prefers a few pictures. He hands his phone to a nearby fan to snap a few shots as I pose with my hand on his shoulder. Tom joins the photo session, snapping images to plaster on the social media page he manages on my behalf while a short distance away a few brighter camera flashes fill the room. The bright flares are odd, but I keep my attention on Ivan who basks in the attention.

As Ivan happily walked away, a young boy dragging his mother desperately tries to break her grip. He breaks free from the human leash and makes a beeline for me. I can hear his mother shout out "Ethan!" and I give her a reassuring look to let her know it's okay.

"I think you can break the record too Mr. Hunter!" the young boy says, panting as he races toward me.

"Well, who do we have here? Ethan, I think your mom said?"

"Yes, my name is Ethan and I'm a huge fan of yours." Ethan Colbert looks like a miniature version of a sports reporter. He wears a dark jacket with pens and markers sticking out of the pocket and he is holding a notebook. He dons a team ball cap to hide his bald scalp and a face covering to shield germs. Ethan is just ten years old.

He attempts an apology and I raise my hand to assure her that no apology is needed. I introduce myself and she says her name is Jane Hanover. Her boy is a spitfire and keeps her on her toes.

"What do you have in your hand there, Ethan? Is that a notebook?"

"No, well sort of, I call it my logbook, Mr. Hunter. I tend to jot things down a lot. You know, interesting things I see or sometimes people I meet."

I stoop down on a knee to get Ethan on eye level. "Well, the first thing you are going to have to do now, Ethan, is not call me Mr. Hunter. That was my dad. If we are going to be friends, you need to call me TC."

His eyes sparkle and he smiles ear to ear. "Well, can I show you something TC?"

"Of course, what do you want to show me?"

He edges next to me and offers his logbook. Jane starts to protest as if it is an imposition and I again shoo her off. Finally, she relaxes, and I begin to enjoy the moment.

"Well, this is my book that I write down really cool things. I have a page in here where I talk about wanting to meet you. I have it folded over and didn't think I'd ever get to use it."

"Can I sign it?"

"Yeah! I brought a sharpie just in case!"

The young boy opens to a blank page adjacent to a quote he penciled in that read, *"Life is not a spectator sport. If you're going to spend your whole life in the grandstand just watching what goes on, in my opinion you're wasting your life." – Jackie Robinson.*

The boy beams with happiness and I notice camera flashes from multiple spots in the crowd. Ethan is digging the attention. As I eagerly sign his logbook he blurts, "Do you like snakes, TC!"

"Actually, no, they kind of freak me out," I say, handing his prized book back.

"Me too! I'm not afraid of much, but I can't stand snakes. I once came about six inches away from stepping on a coral snake," the young boy exclaims. He flips through his book and shows me pictures. He was in the high grass of a park adjacent to his home in Fort Myers and stumbled across the snake.

"My friends said it was probably just a Florida crowned snake, but it was definitely a harlequin coral snake. Very venomous," he continues as he flips through other snake pictures. There's a black mamba, pit vipers, cobras. The notebook is Ethan's snake research book as well as his keepsake. He leafs through the book whenever waiting at the doctor. It helps him ignore the sounds, sights and smells of the medical office.

Ethan continues as if hanging out in his living room. "Hey mom," he shouts. "Remember the time we went to the Everglades?"

Jane sheepishly nods as Ethan continues. He's going a mile a minute, keeping everyone in the vicinity amused.

"Mom was freaked out about the Everglades and all the gators. They call the strip in the glades where we were Shark Valley. I have no idea why it would be called that when all I saw was gators and snakes. I try not to get scared much, but I think snakes frighten me more than alligators. What about you, TC?"

The kid's energy and excitement captivate everyone as if he is holding court. "Hmmm, that's a good question," I say. "I don't think I'm a big fan of either, but snakes bug me out a little more than alligators."

Satisfied with the answer, he changes the topic. "I think you are the best player around. Maybe ever! I think you could break all the records someday!"

"I don't know about that. I really don't look at that stuff, but I appreciate your endorsement. I just enjoy playing and meeting fans like you."

"Hey, would you mind signing my hat too?" Ethan asks. Showing no signs of self-consciousness, he whips off his cap.

"Of course, kid." The boy flushes with excitement as I sign his hat with the same Sharpie. Fans of a team or a player are provided a sense of identity and a distraction from life. Some fans take it to a different degree, but for Ethan, being a fan provides this boy the ultimate diversion from his medical battle.

I summon Ethan's mother and pull her aside. Jane, temporarily at ease and basking in her son's happiness, tries to hold it together. With misty eyes she thanks me repeatedly even though I tell her that it's my honor to get to know her son. I smile broadly when she mentions Jennifer and the Arnold Palmer Children's Hospital Charity. Jen set up the encounter, but never mentioned it and wanted no credit for the moment.

Still milling about, I call Tom over for favor. I whisper to Ethan that my agent provided his mom with my direct phone number so he should contact me any time. I also tell the young boy that I will treat him to front row seats at a Tampa Bay game when we come down from Philly later in the summer. His embrace nearly brings me to tears.

At my request, Ethan stays by my side throughout the night. I greet hundreds of guests and the little boy intriguingly gets involved with each conversation. He acts like my personal usher and makes the night go by in a flash. At least my long, odd and eventful day has a magnificent ending.

CHAPTER 6

THE CLOCK ON my nightstand blinks 3:48 am. It's only the third time I have had an episode in back-to-back nights, and so far I've never had three nights in a row. Sleep deprivation alone is torturous, but I'm even more concerned about the acceleration in my delusions.

With each episode I try to think of a trigger. I can sometimes go a week or two without one of my fits, so it's definitely not something predictable. There must be a reason for each happening, and I look for something that might be consistent for both days. Did I drink, eat or do something out of the ordinary? Was I feeling something each day to cause a reaction? Could it even be an interaction? So far, outside of noticing that I don't have episodes when I am with Jennifer, I have not found any patterns, and the insomnia episodes continue at random.

Lying in bed exhausted and distraught, my mind spins with overloaded thoughts. As usual, I'm in hyper-drive, and trying to fall back to sleep would prove futile. Whether I remain in bed or get up and walk around, I am filled with emotions and provocative thoughts that I can only describe as acute nervous energy.

I keep a notebook in my nightstand, and I jot down my emotions immediately after each episode. On some days, I've written down words like *isolated, helpless, lonely* and *haunted*. Other times, I've written down *anxious, scared* and also the word *weighted* to describe the pressure I feel. This morning the feelings are different, and I write down *anxious*, but also two new words that I have not used before—*hostile* and *exhilarated*.

The morning episode was another dream sequence, but very different from others. On occasion, my nocturnal thoughts swerve from the harrowing to the banal, often centering on baseball. This time the visions were very specific, right down to the exact game situation and pitcher, as if I was visualizing a specific at bat.

I am facing Greg Thomas, a lefty pitcher from Detroit. In my vision, I survey the field before stepping into the batter's box to analyze the defensive shift. The shortstop is playing up the middle and the third baseman is in the shortstop hole. But, more than that, the outfield is completely shifted toward right field. Thomas does not throw hard, so both the infield and the outfield are playing an extreme pull shift, counting on me to hit the ball to the right side.

The details are unambiguous. It's the sixth inning and I'm up with the count of two balls and two strikes. Thomas is pitching from the stretch eyeing my teammate, Jerry Hamlin, who is on first base. I pick up the rotation on the curveball and I let the ball get deep into the zone, smacking the pitch down the left field line. Sprinting hard out of the box I round the bases and slide into third for a triple. I pop up from the slide and I exclaim a profanity to my third base coach while fans go wild.

I use visualization techniques often to prepare for a game, and I've even had dreams that help me visualize a particular pitch. I don't know how many times I've envisioned a fastball or a hanging curveball and planted that pitch into the seats. However, this dream went well beyond, being so specific that it felt more like a baseball prophecy. Unlike a dream, it was more like a baseball highlight reel, already etched in the baseball archives.

I consider sending Chief an elaborate text to see if he has any suggestions on how to handle the oddity. I think better of it, realizing I'd have a hard time explaining the obsessive baseball clairvoyance. Instead, I send him my perfunctory hello, are you alive text, and I receive the usual affirmative response.

Befuddled by the episode, I draw optimism from potentially being able to distinguish between the real and the imagined. By approaching this episode pragmatically, there might be a way to unravel the illogical and finally set my mind at ease. The dream felt like a harbinger of my next game, but I was in control. What might happen if I disrupt the vision by not playing along?

◈ ◈ ◈

Amped up at the prospect of discovery I'm anxious to start the day. I jump out of bed and head to the kitchen. The fancy coffee machine on the counter makes lattes, espressos, cappuccinos and virtually anything imaginable. I toggle through the menu and hit the button for a mocha latte, one of my preferred selections.

The early morning temperature feels perfect for the balcony, so I choose my favorite chaise lounge and recline as I sip the chocolate flavored brew. In the far distance I see the lights of a few fishing boats out early for the day. A fleeting thought of dropping everything and spending the rest of my time fishing on the sea below provides a degree of comfort. If my mental state becomes too intolerable, I suppose I can walk away from it all and change gears. I doubt my competitive drive will ever let me do that, but at least I have an escape plan.

Down below, the streets are empty. Looking for another individual who might also be suffering from insomnia, I don't even find an occasional car headlight of another early riser. Misery loves company, and isolation can be just as bad as sleep deprivation. When one of my favorite coffee shops opens, maybe I'll make a run to the Blind Tiger Café for another shot of caffeine and more importantly, some human interaction.

I scroll through my phone for a few social media sites to see what my agent might have posted from the previous night. Tom uploaded a collection of photos from the team promotional event and achieved his goal of cheap publicity. With all of the likes and shares at the bottom of the screen, clearly he achieved his goal of exponential fan impact.

A picture of the little boy, Ethan, makes me smile. He made quick use of my phone number and texted a quick note of thanks as he drove home last night. I shot back, *"See you soon, kid,"* which received an emoji thumbs up response. The picture reminds me to send him some baseball paraphernalia, knowing he'd love to have autographed jerseys, baseballs and bats. I planned to send him a crateful, and Jennifer might have his address.

I finish my coffee while reviewing articles from a few of my favorite internet news sites. By 5:00 am I've read all the interesting articles from Breitbart and The Bongino Report, so I decide to take a morning jog. The weather is perfectly warm, yet there is little humidity and I throw on a pair of shorts, a T-shirt and my favorite running shoes. Grabbing my wireless earpiece, I crank some music before bolting to the elevator down to the Tampa streets.

The early morning run flanking the harbor fills my lungs with fresh, salty air. A welcome kick start, and with endorphins flowing, I temper my pace, conscious of the long, potentially interesting day ahead. Still, I run five or six miles on the empty streets before returning to the condo.

To kill some time, I make my way to the marina to peruse the selection of yachts. An array of extravagant vessels lines the dock, though nothing is blowing me away. I prefer to charter a boat when I head out for a day on the water but intend to make a purchase when the time is right. Eventually, I want something big enough to travel anywhere I might choose, but not utterly ostentatious. Sleek, yet practical is how I describe it, and I know it will hit me when I see something that fits.

Still unreasonably early, I head to the baseball complex to prepare for a road game. Particularly toward the end of spring training, the veteran players generally don't travel. However, I tend to go on more road trips in spring training than most. Another one of my quirks, I don't like getting used to one batter's box and one batter's eye, so traveling to different fields equates to better performance on the road when it counts. At least that's my perspective and particularly today, I insist on making today's trip to Lakeland.

A simple way to disrupt my premonition would be to march into Billy Law's office and ask him to skip the trip. Avoiding the game entirely and defying the episode is simple, however, curiosity isn't going to allow me to back away. Without question, I need to see how the details of my latest episode might play out.

⚾ ⚾ ⚾

On the bus heading to Lakeland, Billy Law announces that the starters of the game would get two or three at bats each. He will then make substitutions to spread out the playing time, a typical practice for late spring training games. The idea is to balance getting the regular players their needed at bats to stay sharp, while getting them out early to avoid injury. So, in theory, there's a good chance that I won't even be in the game by the sixth inning even though my premonition told me otherwise.

Detroit was throwing a pitcher who they anticipate being one of their five starters for the regular season. This was important since starters get stretched out to eighty or ninety pitches to prepare for the upcoming season. The pitcher in my episode was Greg Thomas, a lefty reliever, so it makes sense that he might enter the game around the sixth inning. However, there are no guarantees he's even slotted to pitch today, and if he is scheduled, it's quite possible that the starter could throw six innings given the extended pitch limit.

I go about my normal pregame routine and try to distract my thoughts. I have a solid batting practice and I feel consistent with my rhythm. After batting practice, I shag fly balls in the outfield as per my routine. Even though we're on the road, I sign a few autographs down the left field line. It's a weekday afternoon game, so I assume the kids in attendance are on spring break. I try to accommodate as many as I can with a signature or a quick handshake.

I jog back to the dugout and raise an eyebrow at the lineup. One of the key figures in my dream, Jerry Hamlin, is not in the lineup. For the specifics of the premonition to be true, he would have to be inserted.

TC Hunter is penned into the second spot in the batting order. A conventional baseball lineup used to have the best overall hitter on a team batting third, but that recently changed. Analytics suggest the best hitter should bat either first or second to get more at bats per game. A traditionalist, I'd prefer hitting third, but I've grown comfortable in the two hole.

With the start of the game, I shift into concentration mode, barely considering anything besides the game. I line one out to right field. Then, in the bottom of the first, I make a nice running catch, covering a ton of ground and snaring a ball in the gap. Some pundits suggest I could serve the team better in right field due to my strong arm. Thankfully, the organization disagrees and places me in the iconic centerfield position where I belong.

The game moves at a fast pace. The starting pitcher for Detroit, West Rekeda, deals a good fastball and a sharp slider to keep our team off balance. He's mowing our lineup down and I don't get another at bat until the fourth inning when I walk, steal second, but am left stranded on base. There's no score in the game, and it's doubtful I'll get an at bat in the sixth inning.

Rekeda gives up a walk and a hit in the fifth inning, but the game remains scoreless, and his pitch count is at seventy, which means he'll likely throw in the sixth. If I get a third at bat, I'll likely face Rekeda, and not a reliever to end my day.

Floyd Graber leads off the top of the sixth. I'm in the on-deck circle concentrating on Rekeda but take a quick glance into the Detroit bullpen. There's activity, but I can't tell if it's a lefty or a righty. Graber walks on the twelfth pitch, having fouled off a few.

As I approach the batter's box, I hear the umpire yell, "Time!"

as the Detroit manager approaches the mound to make a pitching change. I return to the on-deck circle to stay limber, and as I add pine tar to my bat, I hear the PA announcer say, "Entering the game, number forty-three, pitcher Greg Thomas."

While the relief pitcher warms up, I hear scuffling in our dugout and half hope that I'm being replaced by a pinch hitter. But then I hear Billy Law shout from the dugout to the first base coach, "Bring Graber in." Looking over my shoulder, Billy waves Floyd Graber off the base and replaces him with a pinch runner Jerry Hamlin.

Well, son of a bitch, now Hamlin is on base just as I dreamt. Even though I hope that some of the details of the episode might get spoiled naturally, I'm not completely shocked at the turn of events. Still, I have a premeditated plan to spoil the outcome, just to confirm I am in control. One simple solution is to jump on the first good pitch and not wait for two strikes. I'm going to nail the first good one that I see, and that will be that.

When Thomas completed his warm-up pitches, I survey the field and walk with determination to the batter's box. The shortstop shifts up the middle and the third baseman fills the shortstop hole. The second baseman has his heels on the outfield grass, and the entire outfield shifts as anticipated.

Thomas is going to pitch me inside to get me to pull the pitch into the defense, and my goal is to crush the first pitch, no matter the alignment. Thomas, in the stretch, glances at the runner on first base. He hurls a blazing fastball to the inside part of the plate, right where I was looking. Off the bat, it's a tape measure homer. But as I start my jog toward first, I see the first base umpire raises his hands while the home plate umpire shouts, "Foul ball!"

I gather myself and walk back to the box. I crack a wry smile and shake my head, pissed that I yanked the offering foul. If he throws the same pitch, I'll make sure I keep the next one fair.

The next pitch was a curveball in the dirt. Ball one. With the count one ball and one strike, Thomas delivers the third pitch. I hear the first baseman yell, "He's going!" to indicate the runner at first is attempting a steal. I'm still thinking inside fastball, but Thomas hangs a curveball that I plastered down the right field line. The ball likely travels four hundred and fifty feet, a homerun, for sure. As I start my trot the ball hooks right of the foul pole for another long strike.

Again, I return to home plate, kicking myself all the way. All I had to do was take the pitch, and the foretelling of the at bat would have been broken. The catcher would have made a play on the base runner and there would either be a runner at second base from a stolen base, or the runner would be out, and I would be hitting with the bases cleared. Instinct takes over, and I swing at the fat breaking pitch and the bizarre morning forecast remains intact.

Determined to break the predetermined chain of events, I look to simply put the next pitch in play. With the count at one ball and two strikes, all I must do is stick my bat out at any pitch and the episode would be spoiled. Regrettably, the next pitch is a fastball at my ear. I hit the dirt hard to get out of the way and angrily glare at Thomas who shows no remorse. Instead, he yells, "That pitch wasn't that close. Stop the drama and get in the box."

When a pitcher throws one near your head, purposeful or not, you get pissed. And this guy not only threw one close to my dome, he has the nerve to pop off. Instantly, my thoughts from the morning drift away and I dust myself off. The guys in our dugout razz the pitcher, so I let them do the shouting while I consider charging the mound. Instead, I keep my cool and take a moment to gather myself before stepping back to the plate.

"You know what to do now, TC," screams a woman from the stands. She's a couple rows above our dugout. The strange woman is dressed in black and has several tattoos adorning her arms, neck and face. She looks out of place, and her voice echoes over the rest of the crowd.

"Blast the next pitch. You know you've got 'em!"

The woman's display is distracting and a bit odd, but I step back to the plate, barely beating the pitch clock requirement. New rules dictate that the pitcher is required to deliver a pitch within fifteen seconds with nobody on base, and twenty seconds with runners aboard. The penalty for noncompliance is an automatic ball, while the penalty to a batter who is not in the batter's box within eight seconds is an automatic strike. I hate the rule, but there's no way I will allow it to get the best of me.

I admonish myself silently for the distracting thoughts and gather into the box, determined to scorch a ball off the cocky pitcher. With Jerry Hamlin on first base, Greg Thomas fires. I pick up the rotation and instantly recognized the curveball. Unlike the hanging curveball he threw earlier in the at bat, this one has bite and I let the ball get deep, driving the pitch down the left field line.

Hamlin scores from first base, and I sprint around second, sliding feet first into third. Fired up and without thought after a pop-up slide, I yell, "That's how you fuckin' do it!" as I pump my fist and stare down the pitcher.

We take the lead and I'm replaced after the half inning. In the dugout, I sit dazed for the remainder of the game wondering what the hell just happened.

⚾ ⚾ ⚾

The remainder of the week on the ball field is relatively uneventful. I continue my spring training routine in preparation for the season and try to put the surreal game in Lakeland behind me. I certainly can't chalk it up to a fluky coincidence. My dream foreshadowed very specific actions and there simply was no way of denying that an extreme visualization magically came to fruition.

I consider telling Billy Law about the peculiar chain of events but opt against it. My manager or a teammate wouldn't believe the tale anyway, and as ballplayers, we've all had premonitions. If I tell Tom Bader, he'll likely order immediate psychological evaluation.

Preemptively, I could offer details of my troubles to Dr. Joe Nelson. However, he'd view things on a clinical level and would recommend further therapy and probably medication. The idea of medication, even if it's meant as a sleep aid, conjures images of depression drugs like the ones they show on television. *"Taking such and such drug may increase suicidal thoughts."* No thanks, doc.

Chief is a logical consideration given his vast experience. Although, telling him how I had seen events before they had happened would likely draw an incredulous response from the old man. From a baseball standpoint, he'd likely chalk it up to the intense homework I do on pitchers, leading to an anticipation of a pitch or an at bat. The rest of the tale he'd consider an embellishment. He might understand my insomnia since I text him at all hours of the morning, but he won't buy into any of the other stuff. I trust Chief wholeheartedly, yet even he wouldn't understand.

Maybe I can find a fortune teller or a damn gypsy or something; someone who believes in tarot card readings, crystal balls, and reincarnation. That would be a hoot if I were discovered summoning the spirit world to get things off my chest.

Thankfully, Jen meets me at the condo after the Lakeland game. She intends to stay over for several nights until I head north for the regular season. Although our sex life isn't exactly conducive to getting lots of sleep, at least with Jen in my bed I know that I'll sleep through the morning uninterrupted.

After our first blissful night we wake up about 10:00 am, perfect since I have a night game and don't need to be at the park. Jen fits perfectly in my arms and waking up with our skin entangled provides comfort and an inner peace that replenishes my being. Our physical connection is undeniable, but I also love how Jen's mind works. She knows what I need to fill my core and I gladly oblige her suggestion to start the day late. Negative thoughts are supplanted with feelings of belonging when we are together.

We spend the next several days in the same manner, focused on our relationship and enjoying our time together. The theory that I would not have an episode while with Jennifer once again proves true. It's like she provides a protective ring around my psyche.

Additionally, our extended time together further verifies that I have room for both Jennifer and my baseball activities. Even though we start our days on the later side of the morning, I'm still able to get in all my baseball preparation. I fulfill every obligation without skipping a beat. The only change in my regimen is a slight decrease in bullshit time hanging out with the team or watching the baseball network in the morning. Neither is a big deal as the benefits certainly outweigh any negatives.

Notwithstanding the intense anticipation I feel when starting the season, I'm also conflicted, since the last several days have been so enjoyable and without mental anxiety. Though the season promises to be like no other, leaving my current state of affairs is tough. Just the anticipation of further episodes torments me.

I give Jen a key to the condo and make security aware that she may come and go as she pleases. My agent and his management team take care of the logistical issues of my relocation, and Tom assures that all my creature comforts await in Philadelphia. The team charter flight is scheduled for the Tuesday afternoon prior to the start of the season. There are team workouts in Philadelphia on Wednesday and Thursday in preparation for the opening game Friday afternoon. The west coast of Florida is my home and it's where I want to live the bulk of my life, but there is something exhilarating about heading north to start the season that makes me temporarily forget about the Gulf Coast.

Business considerations are also a welcomed diversion from my moving angst. I expect a call from Tom regarding new offers. Since we made a point of stating that we would not negotiate a contract during the season, the Philadelphia organization will likely make a last-ditch effort to secure a contract prior to opening day.

Using opening day as a deadline is a ploy to force the team's hand. Tom could strategically deviate from the plan during the season, but at least from a public standpoint we made our position clear. It's a common technique for athletes on their walk year, and I have all the confidence in the world in Tom. He expects an improved offer but warned that I should temper my enthusiasm. He doubts an offer at this juncture will be one to veer us from dipping a toe in the free agent waters.

Even with everything covered, I can't help but have a touch of unwarranted anxiety. No matter how I frame it, leaving Jennifer behind makes for a tough exodus. We spend one more night and morning together, and we both make it a point to enjoy each other's company instead of getting emotional about the departure. Our relationship on solid footing; we promised to see each other soon, confident that absence will in fact make the heart grow fonder.

CHAPTER 7

FOR FIVE CONSECUTIVE years I've leased the same condo unit in an area called Society Hill, a historic neighborhood in Center City, Philadelphia. It is about ten miles away from our home ballpark and on the Delaware River that separates Pennsylvania from New Jersey. The location is ideal, with several hoity restaurants nearby and other upscale amenities within walking distance. I tend to stay in a very tight circle near the condo, my niche isolated from tourist traps and urban decay.

A prerequisite is a water view, although nobody is going to mistake the Delaware River for Old Tampa Bay. I don't get to seek out a pod of manatee or exotic birds; however, the water provides moderate tranquility and makes me feel I am outside the concrete jungle of the city.

A few teammates own properties in the neighboring suburban towns, and a couple live over the bridge in the New Jersey suburb of Bellmawr. Living out of the city is ideal for a player who has a wife and kids, but it's not for me. The majority of bachelor teammates reside in the nicer areas of the city, a few in Society Hill, and several others in an area called Rittenhouse Square. Although there are shoddy areas sprinkled in the vicinity, there is plenty of upscale housing with twenty-four-hour security surveillance to placate a player's safety concerns. Like so many cities in the Northeast, the crime rate is tangible, and athletes are unfortunately a target. Along with fame comes risks, so I take precautions by limiting my time out in the public space and paying extra for a private, covered parking nearest the condo entrance.

Up north, I forego the hot sports car look preferring to drive a less conspicuous vehicle. My Range Rover SUV is still a luxurious ride and comes with all the bells and whistles, but it does not draw attention like the BMW convertible. Being inconspicuous is a security advantage, and I take as many precautions as possible. Unfortunately, a car dealer told me that bullet proof glass is not a safety feature offered as an option.

Anxious to get to the stadium I speed out of the garage, accidentally chirping my wheels on the garage floor. No matter how many years I play, the feeling I get when I step onto the field of any one of the big-league baseball cathedrals is indescribable. Our home stadium is even more inviting and provides a sense of belonging. It's where I fit, and I'm humbled and honored each time I walk through the doors.

The phone rang only a few minutes into the trip. Once again demonstrating the uncanny ability to catch me in the car, the console displayed *Tom Bader – Super Agent,* a label that I created in my contact list.

"TC Hunter, this is Thomas Bader."

"Hello, Tom, how are you doing this fine morning," I responded, wondering if he might sense my eyes rolling at his consistent introduction.

"I take it you are settled in and that you have everything you need."

"Yes, Tom. Back in Philly and headed to the stadium."

"Excellent," he says. "Hey, a delivery is coming to the condo later tonight. Some staples to stock up your fridge, and I made sure you have your nutrition bars, your supplements and all of that stuff."

"Thank you, Tom. Not necessary, but appreciated."

"Only for you, TC. I want you to be happy and comfortable."

You also want me to keep you as my agent since you are about to make tens of millions of dollars in commission. I appreciate Tom's effort, but I'm also a realist.

"So, what's up today? I have a sense that you aren't calling to say hello."

Tom snorts, or maybe it's an excited chuckle. I don't know how to describe it, but it's a sound he makes when he's about to talk money. He's a good agent, but he's very predictable.

"Well, the club has made another offer. It's significant, but I want you to chew on it for a bit."

"Go ahead."

"The club has offered thirty-four million per year for ten years, which is pretty close to what I was thinking they would do."

"Yeah, I remember you saying that. And they would ink that right away?"

"Yes, they would TC. But I want you to consider a few things."

"What's to consider? I stay put and they pay me a ton of money. I finish my career right where I started, and I'm comfortable. I don't have to uproot, and I can just play baseball."

"All great points TC. However, I have to note a few items. Now, listen to me for a second before you respond."

"Okay, I'll listen." It's difficult to describe, but Tom's tone changes and his cadence slows when he talks data, statistics, and money.

"First, you deserve to be the highest paid player in the game. Trout got over four hundred and twenty-five million for a twelve-year term. And you are a better player now than he was when he signed his deal." Recalling my vow of silence, I stop from interrupting. Tom continues. "In actuality, I don't know that you shouldn't be the highest paid player in all of sports. Mahomes in football signed something like a five hundred-million-dollar contract, albeit it's not all guaranteed. Your status as an athlete should matter, and I think we could use that figure as leverage."

Tom pauses for emphasis and to take a breath. "Third, the union will have a problem with any contract they deem a hometown discount. They will view it as a black eye and a detriment for players moving forward."

Three hundred and forty million dollars is a black eye?

"Four, yes, even though it's a ton of money and more than you will ever need, remember this is likely your last swipe. It's your last chance to get your slice of the pie, and there won't be any looking back."

"And lastly, if you have the monster year that you and I anticipate and you guys make a run at the championship, the coffers will open. Hell, even if you are killing it going into the All-Star break, we could open up another conversation. The threat to cut off talks prior to the season is just posturing, so we could engage anytime. I guess what I'm trying to say is that there are many reasons not to jump at what is, yes, a very substantial offer."

Pausing, I make sure he was done. There's validity to each of Tom's points and eagerness to get a deal done often clouds my judgment. "Look Tom," I respond, "being the highest paid player isn't what is important to me."

"I realize that TC. Yet, you need to look at this differently. Who should get the revenue you as the best player and entertainer, or the owners? Whether we like it or not, your decision impacts that equation."

"I understand that. If you think about it, wouldn't my contract offer be a higher number than a player getting his ass taxed in California or New York?"

"That's a legitimate point. Nevertheless, the numbers won't be looked at in that manner by the public," he said. "Unfortunately, team location only impacts the real numbers from a mathematical point of view. In the sports world, getting a contract that gets abusively taxed isn't what anyone considers, and the bottom-line number is what will be used to dictate other player contracts down the road."

"I understand."

"Good, I need you to understand. Look TC, I don't want your gut reaction. I want you to chew on it and we can talk tomorrow. We have all the leverage here."

"Okay."

"In the meantime, this is how we play it. I will tell the owners that you are thinking about the generous offer, but it's probably still out of market. I will play it up so that they know you are appreciative, but

I'm going to make sure they realize there are outside forces in play. In the meantime, we invest in an insurance policy that pays should you have a career ending injury."

"That makes sense. Go on."

"Next, I'm going to contact the media. The baseball channel has been up my ass to get an interview with you, and now's the time to do it. You don't mention anything about the offer if they ask. You just tell them that you are hopeful a contract extension gets worked out before the season opener. I will call you back with a time for tomorrow's interview."

"Thanks Tom." Before hanging up and with much to consider, I ask, "If you were in my position, what would you do?"

Pausing briefly to contemplate, Tom carefully answers. "Look, I just want you to be happy. I'm going to make a ton of dough on this either way," he says with a chuckle. "But if you are asking me what you should do, I think you should be patient and not jump at this offer. It's significant, and I know you prefer to stay put, but be patient. This isn't about greed, it's about your true value."

"It's a lot of money, Tom. It's a stupid amount."

"I agree. And you can do some great things with it to enjoy your life. You could do charity work, build schools, sail around the world, buy a small island. You could do virtually anything with that type of money, but let's get you paid what the market says you are worth."

Some of my teammates obsess over their market value. Maybe they are right; maybe I need to change my perspective.

"One more thing," Tom continues. "Movie stars are sometimes paid thirty, forty, fifty million per film. Some make over a hundred million in a year, so don't feel like it's too much."

There's little reason to attempt to make him understand how putting the business end to bed as soon as possible might help in other ways. Hell, all this contract stuff may be why my anxiety has been overflowing. But Tom's right; I should not rush into anything for the sake of ease.

Approaching the ballpark, Tom calls within five minutes to advise that the television interview is set for noon. He works quickly, and I appreciate how he's always a couple of steps ahead.

⚾ ⚾ ⚾

I lower my window to greet the new security guard. He smiles to overcome his nervousness and exclaims, "Welcome back to the stadium, Mr. Hunter. We are all looking forward to a great year!"

He looks to be in his mid-twenties and referring to the name tag on his jacket, I say, "Corey, please call me TC."

"Why thank you TC. I'm new here. It's an honor to meet you."

"The pleasure is all mine."

Corey sheepishly fumbles to find the knob to open the gate. I pretend not to notice and instead wish him a good day and toss him a wave when he finally finds the right button. He'll settle in eventually.

Several cars line the lot indicating I'm not the first one to the yard. I'm not surprised to see Chief Daley's old, white Cadillac Seville in the far corner. As clubhouse manager, Chief has his hands full at the start of each year. After I hit the locker room and put things in order, I'll make a beeline to the bowels of the stadium to chat with my old friend.

The locker room is attached to the player's lot by a short hallway. I open the glass door and am greeted with the familiar aroma of the hall. A burgundy rug with our team logo adorns the hallway and whatever they used to clean the rug gives the room its distinct smell. Up ahead through the vestibule another glass door etched with the team logo and *Players and Coaches Only*, my home away from home.

Offices for the manager, coaches and a few office administrators sit directly in front of the entrance. Down the hall and to the right, an expansive player's lounge connects to the even larger locker room. Each player has his own private locker space that most decorate with pictures of their family, girlfriends, and other personal items. A padded chair sits in front of each cubby while a batting practice jersey and uniform pants hangs in each stall.

Most veteran players keep the same locker each year. The other cubby spaces are interchangeable and used strategically to place certain players among others. Rookies and the more free-spirited individuals are typically placed next to seasoned players in order to keep them in line and as a constant reminder to focus on the game. My locker is a preferred aisle locker with just one neighbor, Johnny Baugh.

The far end of the locker room connects to the lavatory and shower area. Adjacent to the lavatory is the training room, complete with rows of medical and chiropractic tables. An assortment of medical devices, including electronic stimulation machines and physical therapy contraptions, are strategically placed throughout. A couple of ice machines along with moist- heat-hydro collators are plugged in by the back wall next to several soaking tubs and a small pool that is set up for aquatic therapy. The trainers have all the bells and whistles at their disposal to treat injuries and keep players on the field.

Busy taking inventory and making sure all the machines worked properly, I quickly greet the trainers, careful not to interrupt their work. Thankfully, I've had a relatively injury free career, but I still maintain strong relationships with each trainer. They work extremely hard, and inevitably I will need their help to take care of the bumps and bruises of a baseball season.

Opposite the training area and near my locker is the tunnel entrance leading to the home team dugout and ballfield. Midway through the tunnel, a door on the left leads to indoor batting cages and the team weight room. Each cage is equipped with the latest high-tech pitching machine that can throw up to a hundred miles per hour, giving players the opportunity to hit during games or when there's inclement weather.

The weight room is state of the art, complete with a computer system similar to the one at the spring training facility. Workouts are monitored and technique is filmed, all with the goal of maximizing results and preventing injury. Nothing is left to chance.

A heavy metal door to the right of the tunnel leads into the stadium innards. The hallway leads to several different rooms where equipment is stored, and uniforms and other laundry is cleaned each day. A side office near the equipment room is where I knew I'd find my good friend and confidante, Virgil "Chief" Daley.

The office door was mostly closed, but I see cigar smoke wafting. There are no smoking signs all over stadium, but Chief makes his own rules. I give the door a couple of taps and push it slightly forward. Chief mutters, "Is that the grim reaper?"

I push through the entrance to see the familiar grin, complete with the Arturo Fuente Robusto cigar in the corner of his mouth. "Sorry, to disappoint, it's just me."

"Well goddammit TC, ain't you one in the same? Fuckin' horse's ass."

Chief looks great, though cantankerous as ever. He is slight in build and probably about five foot four. He contends he is shrinking an inch each year, but even in his advanced age he still somehow looks like an athlete. Dressed in his standard Chief uniform, an old school light blue team T-shirt and gray sweatpants, his scruffy beard makes him look scraggly. If I mention his unkempt look, he'll likely joke that the facial hair keeps the hordes of interested women away.

Chief pushes down on the desk to help rise from his chair and curses at me when I put my hand out to help. Being called a fuckin' horse's ass is a term of affection in his book. Even at eighty-five years young, he's razor sharp and full of piss and vinegar.

"How are you doing, Chief?"

Chief gives me a bro hug and asks, "What are you checking up on me in person now instead of by text?"

"What do you mean?"

"You keep texting me early in the morning. It's like you want to make sure I'm still alive or something. You do it more often now, like you think the grim reaper is heading my way."

I deny the accusation. I think the politicians call it plausible deniability; of course I'm checking on him."

"Nah, I text you because you pop into my head. I miss you sometimes, old man."

"Yeah? Bullshit. I know why you were texting. Well, I ain't dead and I don't plan on kicking the bucket any time soon. I'm as alive as you leave me, probably smoking one of them cigars you sent me for Christmas."

"Are they good? You need more?"

"Outstanding, but I have plenty left. You sent me four cases for chrissake. You trying to kill me or something?" Chief laughs heartily at his own joke.

"Old man, you might live forever," I say to my closest friend. "You better because who else would I talk to? We have a lot of catching up to do."

Chief flicks his cigar ashes and smiles. With his left eyebrow raised and a funny grin, he says, "You are damn right we have some catching up to do. Like always, I got some things I need to show you. Gonna be an interestin' year!"

"You've got that right old friend. You've got that right."

Chief and I talked for the better part of an hour until I have to get on with my day. Emphasizing he had many lessons to teach me, he seems to have more on his mind than the usual nostalgia. Chief's stories about some of the old-time baseball players are classic, and I never miss an opportunity to learn from his tales. He promises to have some whoppers ahead, along with things that will further my baseball education.

My old friend is quick to interject anecdotes as a means of tutoring me on baseball as well as life. Yet, I notice exceptional urgency in his tone. It's as if he has accounts that need to be applied immediately in an effort to mold me before it's too late.

I head to the field for the team workout. The northern weather early in the season is often challenging, but today looks workable with temperatures in the low to mid-fifties. It's not exactly spring training Florida weather, but at least it's not one of those raw, rainy, thirty-degree days common to baseball in the Northeast.

After an extensive stretch and a progressive throwing routine, the position players begin with infield and outfield defensive work followed by a short round of hitting. With the roster defined, players are set into batting practice groups used throughout the season. The groups modify with injury or when someone is replaced, but the groupings help maintain daily efficiency.

Pitchers work separately doing long-toss and bullpen sessions depending on each pitcher's individual schedule. During spring training, our staff lengthens the workload of our starters. By the addition of key relievers, we should win even more ballgames this year.

The practice blueprint marks a professional efficiency that allows for a vast amount of work completed in a relatively short time. A variation of the same plan is used throughout the country by professional and amateur teams alike. Yet, a certain excitement fills the air when a team with lofty expectations gathers. The rookies and younger players feed off the seriousness and maturity of the veteran players. Despite being one of the early favorites, our team has a certain vibe, ready for the marathon season with no chance of resting on our laurels.

The workout wraps up just before noon, perfect for the arranged interview with the baseball channel. The camera crew sets up behind the large portable batting practice backstop and begins filming as I approached. Shedding any self-consciousness, I smile and wave at the camera crew as I near.

Rodney Harris, a former big-league player with an electric smile, drew the assignment as the lead interviewer. He does a great job for the network and has parlayed his playing experience into a nice broadcast career. Rodney takes a few steps toward me and gives me a bro hug as one of the crew members hands me a microphone.

They also provided an earpiece to receive questions and comments from Rodney's cohort, Kevin Vernon who is back at the television studio. He too had an exceptional baseball career before heading into broadcasting. Kevin is more of the jokester while Rodney plays the straight man, but both men have a blast doing their job. The network masterfully cuts Kevin into the screen in a separate box on the side monitor, visible to Rodney and me.

The television shot displayed the field and the few players milling around for extra practice makes for a good background. Rodney guides me to where we need to stand and begins.

"Hello everyone. We are delighted to have with us today the great TC Hunter, centerfielder extraordinaire and the talk of the town here in Philadelphia. Welcome TC and thank you for taking the time for us."

"It's my pleasure. Great to be here," I lie. I like Rodney and Kevin, but I'm doing the interview only because my agent told me to.

"Ladies and gentleman, we have here the best player in the game. This man can do it all," Rodney says, playing to the camera. The guy is bubbly and almost too exuberant, but it works.

"Thank you, Rodney. I don't know about all that. I just try to play the game hard each day and look to help my team win."

"And he's modest, too! You guys are favored to win the pennant this season, any added pressure on you?" Rodney asks.

"Oh, I don't know. Any good player puts pressure on themselves to perform. Is there something added because of expectations? I don't think so. If you need expectations to put added pressure, then maybe you aren't approaching the game the right way to begin with."

"Now that's a great answer. Maybe it's your approach to the game that makes you such a great player."

I start to say something but hear Kevin Vernon chime in over the earpiece. "Yeah, yeah, I like the modesty and all. Face it, you are the best player in the game, so let's move on. Let me ask you this. You were very critical of the recent work stoppage. You were kind of critical to both sides. Did you get any heat for your stance?"

Throughout recent baseball history, the game was plagued by several work stoppages. There was a strike in 1972, lockouts in 1973 and 1976, more strikes in 1980, 1981 and 1985. Then another lockout in 1990 before a long strike that impacted the 1994 and 1995 seasons. After that long strike the fans were more than pissed. The 1994 playoffs were canceled and even though the 1995 season was only shortened by eighteen games, baseball almost did not come back. The league lost much of its fan base, and some teams were hemorrhaging money. In 1994, it was all about the owner's requirement for a salary cap. The recent work stoppage stemmed from a luxury tax imposed for exceeding the salary threshold. Competitive balance was a mess and things had to get worked out, but I never understood why the result would be a stoppage in play. Couldn't negotiations just start earlier prior to butting up against a wall? Intentionally vague, I regurgitated the basic premise.

"I don't know about taking heat. My only point was that both the union and the owners knew we had to work out issues for a new collective bargaining agreement, so I questioned why the two sides couldn't start talking sooner."

"I get that, I get that," says Kevin. "So, you weren't saying that one side was wrong and one side was right. You were just saying, you know, get it done!"

"That's exactly it. I'm just a ball player, so I leave those things up to others. But we have to stop getting to a point where games are in jeopardy. Baseball fans deserve that from us."

"And that's why this man right here is not only a great player, but he's a fan favorite," Rodney says.

"That's exactly right," Kevin echoes. "TC plays the game the right way and puts the priority on the right things."

Rodney is up next, and I know he's going to press me on my pending free agency. "So, from what I understand, the club has made an offer to extend your contract. Is there any movement on that?"

"They've made a substantial offer that we are considering. I try not to worry too much about the outside stuff. I let my agent handle it."

"So, the offer is substantial, but you aren't sure just yet if you'd prefer waiting and becoming a free agent."

"Yeah, like I said, there's a lot of moving parts and my agent is handling that with ownership. I can tell you that I would love to stay put and be with one team my entire career." The answer was rehearsed and effective.

Kevin chimes in from the studio. "And from what I gather, you aren't going to negotiate once the season starts. Is that to put pressure on ownership?"

"No, it's not to put any pressure on anyone. I just want to focus on the game and my teammates once we start the season. I don't want the business end to be a distraction."

"That's understandable," says Rodney. "Well, look. Can I get you to make any predictions? Any goals you want to hit as a player? I mean, you've got crazy talent. You may have broken the home run record last year if you didn't get hurt."

"I don't know, I mean a lot has to go right to break records. That's for you guys to talk about. My only goal is to win and to help my teammates."

Intentionally controversial, Kevin cleverly asks, "So, TC, I was wondering, so what other towns do you like to play in?"

I could see where he was going and stalled. "There are a lot of great venues with outrageous stadiums."

"How about New York? You like New York at all?"

"Sure, I like playing in New York."

"What about Atlanta?"

"Great place and great baseball venue."

"San Diego?"

"Awesome weather. Great stadium."

"Boston? Chicago? Miami? Arizona?"

He continues to name all of the organization cities rumored to have interest in me.

"All great cities," I say, implying I'd leave the door open to all options.

"You live in Tampa, right?"

I laughed and reply, "Yes, I love it in Tampa. It's where I call home."

The duo got what they wanted and shift the conversation. Back to baseball, they finish by asking about rivals and try to pin me down for statistical goals for the season. After some more generic answers, both Rodney and Kevin thank me for my time and we exchange pleasantries. They asked if I would be on again and if I'd consider being miked up for a game. I tell them yes to both, although I'll never wear a mike while playing. I curse too much.

As soon as the interview ends I check my phone and see a thumbs up text emoji from my agent. Another text from Jennifer says I looked great, followed by a bunch of hearts and some XOs. My new young friend, Ethan, also sent a text saying he saw the interview and thought it was *AWESOME!*

Mission accomplished. Just one more day of practice and then the season would finally be here.

CHAPTER 8

SOMEONE YELLS INCHES away from my face, "We stand for the national anthem, goddammit!" The crystal-clear voice booms, "We fight for freedom, and we respect our flag, you fuckin' shit!"

Pushing aside the fog I scan the room. Leaping off the bed I reach into the top drawer of my nightstand and grab my .357 Glock pistol. A security consultant I hired several years back strongly suggested I become a licensed gun owner for moments just like this. With so many challenging the right to bear arms, I am glad I suffered through the state's red tape.

The room is dark, so I search for movement. Nobody stirs, and the blackened images of the room look normal and in place. Holding the pistol in firing position I slowly creep toward the far end of the room, using the wall for protection to make sure nobody is behind.

Slipping by the condo security guards is a challenge, so the intruder in my home is likely a professional thief. I click the pistol safety off and plan to stand my ground. Hopefully, it won't come down to it, but my general strategy is to shoot first and ask questions later.

I hit the light switch with my right hand while pointing the gun forward with my left. Still no movement, though I anticipate an ambush. It takes a moment for my eyes to adjust to the light, and I see the room is empty. I check the closet; nothing appears out of place.

Leaving the bedroom, I peruse the main space of the condo. The open floor plan helps the situation and the thin living area shades emit a small amount of light. The television is on, providing some light. *Did I leave the television on? Is that what I heard?* The theory makes little sense once I notice the volume of the television is set low compared to a voice that was thunderously loud.

I checked my flank and slowly walk into the main living area. I again used the wall for protection and ease over to a main bank of light switches. Using the same technique of reaching with my right hand while holding the gun at the ready with my left, I cover ground deliberately.

Turning the lights on, a few hiding spots remain. I expect to find someone crouched behind the kitchen island. Darting to my left with gun drawn, the kitchen is clear. Next, I check the entryway closet; still nothing. With one unchecked area, I quickly move to the second bedroom.

Convinced the intruder is in the room, I carefully open the unlocked door to reach inside. Hesitant and expecting a surprise attack, I move swiftly, turning on the lights and yelping slightly out of nervous tension. Nobody's there.

I head back through the living area to the front door. The door is locked and there's no sign of forced entry.

Lowering the Glock, I shake my head to clear the cobwebs. My heart races. I extend my arms above my head. I don't know if the technique works, but out of habit I mimic what I do when out of breath from a workout.

More calm, but with my mouth bone dry, I head to the kitchen for water. Grabbing a glass, I used the refrigerator dispenser and replay the last several minutes. I could have sworn there was someone in my bedroom. The voice was loud and distinct and woke me from a deep slumber.

The recent spike in crime in Philadelphia has been all over the news, so maybe the nightmare was a reaction to what I had been seeing and reading in the media. Briefly, my thoughts are on my collection of guns in Florida. If this would have happened in Tampa, would I have grabbed a pistol or the AR-15 rifle? The pistol is probably the better choice to confront a burglar.

Chugging more water, I scan the kitchen. The microwave's digital clock flashes as if the power had gone out. The blinking display reads 3:48 am, and if there's any doubt, I'm certain there was no intruder.

It is opening day and I've been rudely awakened by another early morning episode. I've got to hand it to my polluted brain; I come up with some crazy shit. Disturbing and lifelike, the latest installment again feels pointed. With old glory waving across the screen, I search for reasoning, though expecting no answers.

Although composed, my left hand shakes. Still holding the gun, I release my grip and the Glock drops to the counter. The clanking snaps me out of the stupor. Thinking more clearly, I realize that whether I have a schizophrenic disorder or some other mental issue, I have to find a way to come to terms with the situation, or the next time I might very well end up dead—or, possibly someone else by my hand.

CHAPTER 9

CHIEF AND I walk through the locker room toward the tunnel. A few players receive preventative treatment in the training area. Starting pitcher, Jim Gast, lie face first on a massage table getting a rub down while nearby, John Miller, gets his right ankle taped. Outfielder, Trevor Gill, lie prone on a table in the rear of the room getting heat applied to his lower back. His headphones on and his eyes shut, he looks to be taking a quick catnap.

Billy Law, already in full uniform, discusses injury protocol with the head trainer. Reinforcing the line of communication necessary to keep injury information in house, his animated motions suggest he will take the brunt of the responsibility. The media likes to poke and prod, and Billy disseminates information as he sees fit. Chief gives Law a quick wave saying, "Go get 'em today, Skipper." He receives a quick wave back along with a smile, but Billy is absorbed in his important conversation.

Making our way through the tunnel toward Chief's office I hear the unmistakable sound of the heavy duty commercial washers and smell open detergent bottles. Chief checks the washing machine timers and mutters something about taking the clothes out of the washer right away to avoid getting musty.

We turn into his office and Chief demonstrates his excitement. "I'll make it quick," he says. "Got something for you." Rummaging through an old metal locker next to his desk he reminds me of a kid going through a toy chest. The locker looks fifty years old, maybe something he moved to his office to preserve the relic. The metal door cabinet is sturdy and unlike the flimsy metal used today.

Seemingly out of place and taped to the inside of the locker is a poster from *The Rocky Horror Picture Show* with the caption, *I would like, if I may, to take you on a strange journey.*

Reaching toward the back shelf and pushing aside Ayn Rand's *Atlas Shrugged* he declares, "Here it is!" as he pulls out an old MacGregor baseball glove. The leather is dark brown and stained by glove oil. It's flat as a pancake and looks like a right-handed outfielder glove from back in the day. "I want you to have this," Chief says.

"Well, take a look at that old glove. Was it yours?" I ask. Virgil Daley was a solid professional baseball outfielder with a ten-year big-league career long before he was called Chief. Examining the glove, I notice the laces are old with some fraying, but mainly intact. One of the laces at the front tip of the thumb has the unmistakable look of chewed leather. My glove has the same as I sometimes chew on the lace out of nervous energy when I'm in the outfield.

"Not mine, no," he says. "This glove, TC, belonged to the great Henry Aaron."

"You are kidding?"

"Why the fuck would I kid about that? It's one of the gloves Aaron used during his career. He used it in Milwaukee. I played beside him one year and I remember him using this very glove."

"So, it's got to be at least fifty years old. Where'd you get it?"

"It's closer to sixty, and never mind how I got it. It's yours now to keep for another sixty."

I shake my head to suggest there's no way I'll accept the glove, but he's having nothing of it. Chief looks around to make sure nobody's listening. "Son," he says, "because of my age, it's time to pass it along. You see, it's much more than just sentimental value. You have an enduring love of the game and I know you understand the significance."

"I don't know what to say, Chief. Thank you. You can't imagine how much this means to me. How much you mean to me." I couldn't protest. The man fills a void in my life, more than he'll ever know.

Hiding his misty eyes, he exclaims, "Let me tell you something about Henry Aaron. Not the baseball player, but the man." Moving to the edge of his desk he sits and points at a folding chair for me to do the same. Sitting with the glove in hand, my eyes are glued to the old man.

"Henry was one of the best baseball players to ever play the game, which goes without saying. That ain't nothing compared to the man he was." Taking a deep breath, he gathers his thoughts. "That man had more character and courage in one finger than anyone else I knew. You know he got death threats as he was approaching Babe Ruth's home run record?"

I was familiar with the story that Aaron received numerous threats and felt like someone was going to kill him as he rounded the bases the night he broke the all-time career home run record. The threats were racist with the premise that a Black man shouldn't break the record of a prominent White player. I nod.

"FBI said the threats were credible and Henry was really concerned. But you'd never know it. That man never complained, never said a goddamn word, and you know why? Because he knew how significant he was, not to baseball, but to mankind. His character rose above all, and he wouldn't allow himself to be intimidated. He wasn't just important, the man transcended the sport. As a Black player at that time he and some other players went through more shit than you could ever imagine."

I consider myself a baseball historian and I read as much as I can about the players of the past. I knew some about Henry Aaron, but Chief's personal connection is captivating.

"I was honored to play alongside that man, and even more honored after he retired. The charity work he did to help underprivileged kids… man. Nobody knows about that stuff, but he had the biggest heart. Henry had so much to be pissed about. He could have been bitter, but he never was."

"How'd he handle it all, Chief? I mean, all he went through must have been mentally draining, no?"

"Well, yeah. I know he didn't sleep well. He once told me about nightmares he had, people chasing him, trying to set him on fire, crazy dreams. He was definitely haunted by some of that stuff."

Crazy, haunting dreams hit home. "How'd he deal with the mental stuff? I mean, how'd he cope?"

"You know TC, that's a good question." Chief rubs his chin, seeking his next words. "I think he was chosen, you know. At some point, he realized he was selected to be the one to endure and to make things better. Guys like Hank and Jackie Robinson understood they had a bigger purpose. Jackie wasn't just part of the Civil Rights movement. No, Jackie was chosen as the trailblazer. He led the way and the country followed!"

Chosen? Chosen by whom?

Clearing his throat, Chief continues. "When faced with daunting issues, you can curse the darkness or be like Henry and lift the candle. He was the epitome of class, and he knew he was important. I miss the man. Do you know he was awarded the Presidential Medal of Freedom?"

Although I vaguely remembered something about that, my tendency is to pay little heed to things outside of my realm. Chief gets angry that I disregard things he considers important, but I shake my head no, anyway.

"You really need to start paying attention to things, son. George Bush gave Henry that honor. Didn't matter that Henry was a Democrat and Bush was a Republican. None of that mattered then like it does now. Man, things have changed, and it's really not that long ago." Chief pauses a short while. "Do you know how much that man did for race relations for the league?"

"Just what I've read," I say. Not living in that time period, there was no way for me to fully understand the prejudice.

"He could have ridden off into the sunset, but after his career ended, he continued to work against racism and bigotry in the league. He made a tremendous impact, and was unrelenting in that regard. But, you wouldn't even know it because he didn't grandstand. He didn't look for credit. He worked to implement change, not draw attention to himself."

"The man was legendary," I say.

Chief's eyes grow wide. "Certainly a legend, but he was much more! That's what I'm trying to tell you. There are legends, and then there's beyond legend. Life ain't important unless you make an impact on others. That was Henry. That was Jackie."

"I am honored to have this glove, Chief. I take it with the thought that maybe it helps me be some small fraction of a man that he was."

The old man nods and pinches his lips in a knowing smile, content that I understand the message.

Hope springs eternal for all baseball teams at the onset of a season. The hurried anticipation of opening day exemplifies that phrase as each team starts the season with youthful optimism. Opening day is a celebration of the beginning of a new baseball marathon. Fields are immaculate and stadiums shine like a new car as the first of 162 games is elevated with unique grandeur. Players pace, fans cheer, and the media buzz with unbridled excitement and anticipation.

Nervous and eager, I set my focus on the opposition pitcher. Video of the thirty-two previous career at bats against the Chicago veteran pitcher, Jeff Daulton, indicate a discernable pitch pattern. Daulton likes to work his changeup away and, as a right-handed pitcher, he also throws plenty of back door sliders to get ahead in the count, particularly against lefty hitters. Through visualization and study, I'm fully prepared.

The festivities began with the stadium announcer presenting the opposing team's coaches, players and starting lineup. Next, he announces our squad, and the crowd roars raucously with each name. By the time he calls out the starting lineup, the crescendo grows to a deafening hum.

Upon hearing my name announced as the second hitter, I rush out of the dugout to high-five my teammates and coaches, before taking my place on the first base foul line as is customary with the ceremony. The stadium is packed with fans ready to cheer; the game appeared to be sold out.

In traditional manner, both teams remained on their assigned foul lines as the public address announcer asks all to rise and remove their hats for the playing of our national anthem. The American flag is marched out by the Army Color Guard, and the formal gesture ignited my patriotism and reinforced the symbolism of each color. Red symbolizes hardiness and valor, white is for purity and innocence, and blue represents vigilance, perseverance and justice.

The anthem is performed by a popular singer and actress from Philadelphia. I close my eyes in calming mediation as the familiar words ring out over the loudspeaker. The diminutive singer's voice is powerful yet angelic, and I stand in joyful amazement.

Breaking my mediation, I hear a group of fans in the lower section reacting. Initially, I chalked the noise up to fans who already had a few too many beers. But the voices grow more strident, forcing me to open my eyes to find the cause of the uproar. The young performer continues to sing despite the noisy interruption, and my attention moves to the yelling fans above the dugout.

Johnny Baugh sees me searching for the source of the disturbance and taps me on the shoulder. He points toward the opposition dugout where Chicago first baseman, Jamie Cunningham, is kneeling alone in the dugout with his back facing the flag.

Cunningham, a ten-year veteran in the league, stands about six foot four inches tall and at around two hundred seventy-five pounds, nobody is going to miss his protest. Crouched on one knee, but with his torso erect and chest puffed, he lifts a fist in the air as if mimicking Tommie Smith and John Carlos who raised their fists during the anthem at the 1968 Olympics in Mexico City.

I contemplate charging toward the opposing dugout and

knocking him on his ass. Instead, I opt for self-control, and I let him continue his grandstanding. The flag, the anthem and the liberty they represent give one the freedom to protest, but a guy like Cunningham could opt to do something meaningful instead of acting with irrational self-importance. His public display will only rouse divisiveness. I think the country is tired of such antics. I am.

A Ben Franklin adage pops into my mind: *"We are all born ignorant, but one must work hard to remain stupid."* Those eloquent words described Cunningham perfectly, and at some point I'll set the guy straight.

Boos continued to rain from the crowd after the anthem, along with beer cups and what looked to be hot pretzels thrown in Cunningham's direction. Stadium security hustles to the area while the young lady who had just sung a wonderful version of our national anthem sprints from the field. She likely understands the booing is not directed at her; still, she did not get the accolades she deserves. I made a mental note to track her down at some point to make sure she knew how much I appreciated her singing.

Interrupting the moment, our leader, Billy Law, shouts, "Let's go boys. It's game time. Forget about that, forget it." He's right; it's time to get back to business.

Cunningham struts up to bat in the first inning to a new round of vociferous boos. I take some joy from the fans' reaction and can tell that our catcher is giving him lip service. From my perch in centerfield, I can tell that Johnny Baugh is providing more than a colorful civics lesson.

After retiring the opposition, it's our turn to hit, and my first plate appearance could not have gone better. With our leadoff hitter on second base after a single and a steal, I work the count to two balls and one strike. Through my pregame preparation I anticipate a changeup and guess right. The off-speed pitch was up in the zone, and I plaster the offering into the right field seats to give us an early lead. Damn it's great to get off to a good start.

After doubling down the line on a back door slider and scorching a line drive that was caught by the centerfielder, I was up again in the eighth inning. The game is well in hand and the team is on cruise control when I barrel a ground ball through the left side of the infield. I beat the third baseman who had shifted to the hole to compensate for the shortstop playing up the middle, an alignment I expect to see throughout the year. The league legislates rules for defensive alignment, but if teams still want to be cute and shift as much as allowed, I'll keep abusing them until they go back to playing a standard type of defense.

Now on first base and with the game no longer in doubt, it's a perfect time to have a little chat with Mr. Cunningham. "What's your problem, douche bag?" I say. Cunningham probably outweighs me by a good fifty to sixty pounds.

"Fuck you, Hunter."

"Don't you think your little display is a slap in the face to the country and to all of the veterans out there that fought so you could play the game and make millions?"

"That ain't why I did it. That ain't the point."

"You know Ted Williams was a war hero? You know Yogi Berra was at Normandy beach for the D-Day invasion? You know how many other players at that time put down the bat and picked up a rifle to fight for our country? Guys like Bob Feller. And you piss on them like that?"

"Man, you don't know shit. Ain't about that. It's about oppression and cops killing Black people."

The like-think stemming from politicians and the media is infuriating. "Bullshit, you don't care about that," I say. "In your city, Black kids are dying at the hands of other Black kids every day. Are you protesting that gang violence, dickhead?"

"Fuck you," Cunningham repeats.

"No, fuck you. We stand for the anthem, goddammit. Respect the flag you fuckin' shit."

"I do what I want. You wanna stop me?"

The first base umpire yells time as my first base coach, Sonnie

Mejia, starts in our direction to calm the situation. Cunningham lifts his glove into my face, and that was it. Before the umpire or Mejia intervene, I sent a left cross against Cunningham's jaw. The punch sent him two steps back before he stumbles to the ground.

The typical chaos of a baseball brawl ensues. Both benches clear and form a mass of human beings, grabbing each other and pushing against the mob. The bullpens come running in from the outfield and join the melee while the crowd roars.

I expect opposition players to come after me, but they really don't. There's a typical masculine posturing that goes on in these types of melees, however, no punches are thrown. Through my career, I have been in plenty of bench-clearing brawls, and this one feels different, almost like some on the Chicago side thought Cunningham got what he deserved. Let's see if they throw a pitch at me in retaliation later in the series. I sensed they won't.

I'm grabbed from behind by Mejia and Sammy Taylor while I continue shouting an array of obscenities in Cunningham's direction. "We are one nation, mother fucker!" and "People died so you could play this game you piece of shit."

The skirmish ends relatively quickly. The home crowd cheers with appreciation as I walk toward the dugout en route to the locker room. I assume I've been tossed from the game.

Stepping down into the recessed dugout I look into the crowd. The fans immediately above our dugout cheer loudly. Amid the applause I hear a distinct voice say, "Way to go kid." I notice an old man with a fedora sticking out among the throng, the same odd guy from the elevator back home. Before I can study his face he disappears into the mob.

Taking a seat at my locker I immediately reflect on the episode from the morning. I had no regrets for my actions, but I now wonder whether I had reacted out of rage or because of the strange occurrences preceding the incident.

What I do know is that I nailed Cunningham with a solid punch.

Although he deserves it, I hope I didn't hurt him too bad. I also know that, predestined or not, I'd do it again if given the same circumstances.

○ ○ ○

My cell phone rings and I expect my agent to be pissed. Tom might consider the brawl as a negative toward contract negotiations, but instead of lecturing, he simply takes the facts at hand and lapses into agent mode.

"We are going to get ahead of this, and it won't be a problem," he says. "Hell, it might even help us in the long run after I get through with it."

Tom constantly reinforces why he's gained my loyalty. His mindset is to go on offense, and he'll spin the incident into my favor. I like the strategy because there's nothing to be defensive about.

"I will have a statement prepared shortly. When we get feedback from the league, let me address it. I will have the commissioner kissing your ass in Macy's window by the time I get done with this."

Relieved, I agree to review his official statement before he sends it out. I then hang up and call Jennifer. Once she discerns that I'm okay, she laughs, having seen it all unfold on television.

A text from Ethan makes me smile. *"Nice left uppercut,"* he texts. *"It was a left cross and violence is never the answer,"* I text back.

Within the hour Tom sends me the publicity statement:

Today, I had an incident on the field with Chicago player Jamie Cunningham. I reacted to Cunningham's pregame display of disrespect to our flag and national anthem. It began when I let Cunningham know the flag is a symbol of strength, hope and peace around the world and the conversation escalated into a physical altercation. Cunningham began the assault by shoving me in the face and I reacted in self-defense with a punch. Although I regret the incident, I do not regret standing up for our country. We stand for the national anthem. We fight for freedom and we respect our flag.

I read the last two sentences a second time, the words glued in my head.

Texting, *"Great. Use it."* In turn, Tom sends the statement to his sources in the press and also plasters the text all over social media. To get in front of things even further, he sends an email directly to the commissioner's office noting how Cunningham was the antagonist with his pregame events and also by throwing the first blow.

My phone is on fire with texts flying in from everywhere. Teammates as well as other players from around the league thank me for taking a stand. I even hear from professional athletes from other sports. I have no regrets anyhow, but the support bolsters my stance.

I typically pay little attention to social media, though in this case I want to see if Tom's strategy is effective. As he often explains, public perception is important, so I'm glad to see the overwhelming responses to the social media posts were positive. There were a few trolls trying to pick a fight and suggesting my actions were racist, the usual drivel from the fringe, but they were quickly dismissed by public sentiment.

I call Jennifer back before going to sleep, asking if she could carve out some time to fly up to Philly for a few days. Opening day was exhausting, both mentally and physically, and even though it was only a few days I need her emotional support to add some normalcy to my thoughts. I'm thrilled when she agrees to head up right away. I desperately want to see her to calm my mind and to sleep normally absent strange occurrences.

There's no way to top this opening day. When my head hit the pillow I'm spent and could only pray I get a night of uninterrupted sleep.

CHAPTER 10

SLEEPING THROUGH THE night should not feel like a luxury. I did get a full night's sleep and it felt like I was on vacation and woke to the opulence of a hotel room somewhere in the Caribbean. My head is clear, and I feel the revitalization that only a killer night of slumber can provide. Refreshed and determined to engage in a normal day, I'm thankful for the reprieve.

Still in bed, I notice over a hundred texts to review on my cell phone. There are also a dozen voicemails that I'll listen to on the ride into the stadium. The only one I play immediately is from Jennifer. Fantastic news! She'll land in Philadelphia later tonight.

Famished, I crawl into the kitchen to grab a protein bar and a Greek yogurt. My mind is clear, and I feel oddly unburdened and lucid. Although the previous day was a circus, I feel good about my actions. When given the responsibility of standing up for the flag and demonstrating patriotism, count me in.

A message from my agent says that he already heard from the commissioner's office and they were reviewing the event. They plan to take my account into consideration and get back to us quickly. Tom also said that if they levied a suspension we will appeal, and according to what he's seeing we're winning the publicity game on this one. "So don't worry about anything and just play," he says. *Just play*, two words I happily live by.

There are plenty of cars in the player parking lot. I say a quick hello to the security guard, Corey, and back the Range Rover into a spot. It threatens to be one of those colder, damp Northeast games. At least we're scheduled for another 1:00 pm start, and with any luck the sun will break through and bring the temperature up a few degrees.

I put on a pair of shorts and a T-shirt before heading to the trainer's table. Particularly with cold weather games I require a deep tissue massage and heat artificially pushed into my muscles. Analgesics the trainers use make my legs and back feel warm and less susceptible to cold weather muscle pulls. I have no idea if there's any proven medical value to the heat cream, but when applied in conjunction with a massage it sure feels good.

Prone and with my face resting in the hole of the chiropractic table while my arms wrapped around the side, I toggle through text messages. Attempting to answer each, I limit my response to a fist bump or electronic laugh for most. A few of the messages are particularly amusing and warrant a brief quip, but with so many to review I limit personal replies.

After the massage, I put on my uniform and head down the hall to hide from the press. I'll deal with the reporters at some point after the game, and Chief's workplace provides the ideal refuge. Chief is making sure all of the cold-weather gear is being distributed to the players and coaches. Many players are particular about what they wear under their uniform, and Chief takes the task seriously.

I sit at Chief's desk while he runs errands. I grab a pen and paper. I have about a half hour to kill so I jot a few notes to create a loose timeline of my episodes. I try not to dwell on my mental issues, especially prior to a game, yet secluded and with time on my hands it seems a good time for reflection.

My very first episode occurred the morning of the previous year's All-Star game. The game took place in the third week of July, and I don't recall anything unusual about the occurrence. I remember waking up at that god-forsaken hour emotionally spent and I chalked it up to anxiety about the game.

The initial episodes were subtle. Mostly, I recollect feelings of unease and panicked anger, but there was nothing that I'd consider bordering on the paranormal. I took probably the first half dozen or so episodes as simple insomnia until I realized they were occurring at exactly the same time of the morning.

The All-Star game was the usual fun event, highlighted by the interaction with the other great players from the league. I was voted in as a starter and I ended up with three at bats, a walk, a double to right and a strikeout.

The game had a disappointing ending, and for the first time the gala felt more like an exhibition than a real game. A thunderstorm interrupted play just as we were heading into extra innings. Instead of a rain delay, league officials decided to end the game in a tie. Both teams were running out of pitching, and it was not worth risking a player getting injured on a wet field. Given the history of the game, it was an obscene decision and I recall being quite pissed at the outcome.

The mid-summer classic, as it's labeled, historically has been a grudge match between leagues. The players take great pride in their effort, and managers play to win. For the baseball purist, it hurt that the game was reduced to an uncompetitive spectacle.

I jot down feelings I had after the game, those I remembered when I woke up so early the following morning. I did not realize it at the time, but even the first episode may have been an omen to a game that left me dissatisfied and confused.

The next episode occurred several weeks later. I don't know the exact date, but it was sometime in mid-to-late August, and we were on the road in Los Angeles. Like the first episode, the second was benign and there was no significant dream or haunting.

That morning, I couldn't sleep, feeling angry and so antsy that I left my room and made my way to the hotel roof to get fresh air. On the West Coast at the time, my sleep pattern was out of whack and the early morning mental wakeup call screwed things up even more. To catch up on sleep, I took a nap in the corner of the visitor's clubhouse. Somehow, it didn't impact my performance as I hit three home runs that night. I never forget a big game, and I was sure the achievement was on the same day as that episode. After my third home run, the jumbo scoreboard displayed an image of a nutty LA fan grabbing my home run ball away from a little kid who initially caught the shot. He threw the ball back onto the field out of a perverted sense of loyalty for the home team, but the idiot fan didn't realize the boy was in tears after having his souvenir stripped away.

After the half inning I brought a signed baseball and one of my bats with me onto the field and handed it to a security guard by the outfield wall. He gave the items to the boy and the kid was thrilled. Now that I think of it, I had the same feeling of contentment at that moment that I feel today.

I make more notes on the other dates that I remember, and although not all episodes resulted in some form of resolution, I feel like I'm onto something. For the most part, I match the feelings I had each early morning to something that occurred later that day. Writing it all down strips away feelings of mere coincidence. However, the days of each occurrence seem random and the episodes occur a couple times a month without any pattern.

I had an episode on September 11 that matched the anger I feel on the anniversary of that day. However, my feelings of despair were supplanted by the sense of pride and resilience in playing the first big-league baseball game after the national tragedy. The country was unified then, and the overwhelming patriotism of that time helped us cope with the devastation. That episode was a reminder of how baseball played a significant part during that time and how impactful the game can be.

Subsequent episodes in October were mundane but reinforced the tandem of baseball and history. My dreams took me to the Civil War and depicted baseball being played by the soldiers as a means to stay fit and pass the time. I later researched the correlation between the Civil War and baseball and was surprised to learn that the game was predominately played by battalions from Massachusetts, New York and New Jersey, and also by Confederate soldiers. The game was popular even then.

In November, I had my first truly bizarre episode. I was asleep in my bedroom in Florida and awoke to my phone blaring out a recitation of Paul Harvey's 1965 commentary, "If I Were the Devil." Harvey, a famed American radio broadcaster, had used his pulpit to provide commentary on an array of topics. Curiously, his famous dissertation begins with an ominous warning of the prince of darkness engulfing the world including the "ripest apple on the tree, the United States."

The text is imbued with forewarning of the devil's tactics, which include replacing belief in God with belief in the government, the elimination of traditional values, and the infiltration of evil throughout the culture. The demonstration of good versus evil is poignant, and the episode made me remember how my father played the piece to me when on long car rides.

Dad was fascinated by the prognostic aspect of Harvey's words, which rang true in 1965 as well as when he played it to me. The lessons still ring true today, and I recall chalking up that particular episode to the changing political climate from the recent election. I was completely freaked out by what felt like a spiritual visitation.

I had three more incidents in December and another two in January, all the same and quite terrifying. A being in my room had awakened me, but I was too frightened to open my eyes. The ominous figure moved upon me, resting heavily on my legs while I lie helpless in my bed. It then pinned my entire body with great force, holding me still, the combination of force and fear completely paralyzing. Though there was little sense of wickedness, I was unable to confront the form controlling my mind and body.

That was the onset of my questioning the soundness of my own existence. I assigned my emotions to the Christmas blues, though I knew it was much more than that. Tricking my mind, I used all methods to dismiss the thought of being better off dead rather than dealing with my issues. Frustration, fear and self-doubt amplified from there.

Come February, the occurrences were happening more often, and the degree of emotional strain became exponential. There were several strange dreams that month, and they became more vivid with each happening. I blamed my discontent on the fact that spring training was rolling around and I was feeling the pressures of my pending contract negotiation. It was also then that I began coping with how I might keep Jennifer in my life with the season approaching.

As I jot more notes at Chief's desk, I begin to realize that my negative thoughts and hallucinations go beyond baseball. Analogous feelings of current event issues contribute to my angst, though often framed in baseball. Thoughts of escaping the world by buying an island or a piece of property somewhere that was not accessible to others began to feel like an antidote.

Writing things down is proving cathartic, giving sequence and structure to an otherwise muddy patch of convoluted emotion. To the left side of the first page, I emphasize the numbers and darkened the times of occurrences in my quest for patterns and meaning.

⚾ ⚾ ⚾

"What the hell are you doing?" Chief bellows as he bolts through his office door. His chores were done, and I am glad he broke my train of thought.

"Nothing really, I'm having some problems and I was writing down some things to try and figure it out."

"Problems?"

"Yeah, uh, sleeping problems. Insomnia I guess."

"No shit. You've been texting me at four in the morning." Chief sees my apologetic expression and softens. "It don't matter. I'm old and I don't sleep much anymore either."

"Can I ask you something, Chief?"

"Anything."

"What would the old timers think about what I did yesterday?"

Chief squints like he always does when in deep thought. His face tightens as he looks into the distance. "You know," he says, "players from decades ago were made of a different cloth. Take Hank Aaron for example. Henry was reserved for a reason. He never wanted anyone to feel they got the best of him. He felt strongly about bigotry and racism in the league, but he never let anyone get the satisfaction."

I start to interrupt and Chief lifts his hand to indicate he's not done. "What Cunningham did yesterday was selfish. It wasn't about helping the cause. These kids today have this perverted view of life, and they've been sold a bill of goods. They've been taught to claim victimhood at every turn. Henry Aaron wouldn't go for that nonsense."

"Would he be upset with what I did?"

"No way. Times were different then, first of all. People who deserved to get punched got punched. Hit on someone's wife, end up in the hospital. Disrespect the country, dishonor a woman, you pay the price. Simpler, tougher times we lived in, and a good licking was a deterrent against assholes. There were very different guiding principles back then."

Chief is rolling so I let him go. "Nowadays, you can burn down a city if the politicians think it helps 'em, while words are considered violence to some. Common sense is gone. It's upside down and backwards, I tell you. But, Hank was old school and not about showboating. He wouldn't tolerate Cunningham's grandstanding. You did the right thing kiddo."

"Thanks Chief," I check the time and have to get moving. I consider telling Chief the real reason I was writing things down, but it would have to wait. "Gotta go, it's almost batting practice time and we've got a ballgame to win."

CHAPTER 11

THE PLAYER WORK agreement contains guidelines for player suspensions. Infractions include performance enhancing drug use, domestic violence, banned substance use, fighting, and insubordination. As Tom anticipated, the league levied a five-game suspension, the maximum for the infraction, and we immediately filed an appeal. The appeal allows me to continue playing until a forum is provided to petition the ruling.

Not only did my agent expect the league reaction, the union also anticipated the move. He explained that the powers that be would view this as more than a suspension for a minor fight. The league, which is made up of all the team owners, has an interest in painting me in a negative light. With my image sullied my value on the free agent market drops, a big boon to ownership. Some owners are even suggesting a racial aspect to my outburst. The advice I receive from Tom is simple—ignore it. He and the union will handle things. We were not going to think that this was anything more than a fight between two players over standing for the flag.

After the game it's time to allow the press to have access. My remarks are not prepared, although Tom and I did review the overall sentiment I was to portray. I blew off any suggestion regarding racism. I effectively made the reporters seem like they were the ones perpetuating racial conflict, thus making them the true bigots. Overall, I'm satisfied with the performance.

Tom says I came off great, and from what he can tell most fans are wholeheartedly behind me. We were immediately winning the public relations war and the union is determined to spin this to our advantage. I wonder if Ty Cobb's image would have been different from a historical perspective if he were backed by my PR team.

My team's owner sent out their own memo and used words like "disappointed" and "ongoing investigation," trying to pacify their fan base and, possibly, deflect why they have failed to sign me to an extension. Such posturing made me disappointed in them, and angry.

"It's all noise," says Tom who assures me that the incident will not impact my reputation or my value. He reminds me that I am a throwback type of player who approaches the game in the right way and that is why I'm a fan favorite. The slight controversy proves to be nothing, but a speed bump and we start the season 2-0. I let that be my focus.

"Control what you can control" was a mantra that my father taught me, and that type of compartmentalizing has served me well. I'll concentrate on the game and leave the rest to my agent and the union.

With Jennifer heading to town, I'm filled with anticipation. Her plane was due at eight tonight at Philadelphia International Airport, and I arrive on the early side. I make my way to the arrivals platform and tuck into a corner to remain incognito.

The travel hub is busy, indicating people are feeling more comfortable with flying. The government scared the shit out of people due to the COVID pandemic, so it's great to see travelers finally free to go about their business.

Signs were still plastered all over the airport requesting people follow social-distance guidelines, and I notice stickers on the floor in attempt to keep people in lines adequately spaced apart. The ineffective policies to combat the pandemic were based on politics and not data, and I was tempted to rip every sign off the wall. *Six feet apart* is an arbitrary notion, made up by tyrants, and it burns me that so many bought into the lunacy. The signs are likely still up as an extension of the political theatre.

Chief swears it's the same people behind the country's follies who are now running the league. Virtue signaling is the knee-jerk reaction while political-agenda-driven decisions fail to consider consequences. Chief is turning me into a curmudgeon, but he's got it right. Sometimes I think he should have run for political office. Just think of the colorful slogans he would blast to promote his world view.

The plane arrives and snaps me out of my funk. I meet Jennifer at the rear of the gate, instantly seeing her smile among the throng of plane travelers as she drew near. Her radiant glow garners the attention of every male in the vicinity, and I fill with masculine pride knowing she's with me.

It matters little that she had a long day and is departing a couple hour plane flight, Jennifer looks beautiful, and her smile lights up the terminal. It's not yet a week since I last saw her, though it feels longer. She runs to me and I grab her in my arms.

I take her bag and we walked hand in hand through the airport. The plan is for her to stay four days until the team goes on the road. I had encouraged her to pack lightly since we could buy whatever else she might need for this stay and beyond.

I don't know exactly how this is going to work as I have never had a girlfriend during the season. Yet, I'm not feeling intimidated about the novelty. Normally, I'd be hanging out in my condo thinking about the next day's game, or maybe watching a night game on television. I'm thrilled to change my routine.

Now in the car, I ask if she wants to stop somewhere to grab a bite to eat, and she quips that surely there must be something to eat at the condo. Tongue-tied, I catch her double entendre. "I am very hungry, but not for food."

I clear my throat and manage to mumble something as I speed out of the airport lot. There's probably not a recorded statistic, but I make it back to my place in record time. Two feet inside the front door, we barely control our desire for one another. Sexual magnetism is one thing; this is all of that combined with an endearing, mutual passion.

Jen gets out of bed to grab a glass of water. Her silhouette in the dimly lit room strikes me as a piece of erotic art. The dark outline of her figure is a perfect form, her long legs perfectly toned and athletic and her flowing hair draped over her strong, but feminine shoulders.

Ice water quenches our thirsts, and she crawls back in bed. Placing her head on my chest we wrap our legs around one another, both with a desire to feel skin against skin.

"So, how was your day?" she asks with a laugh.

"The day was good, but the night is better."

"Really now? So wait, how many hits did you get today?"

"I had a good day, three hits. Two singles and my second home run."

"So let me get this straight, a night with me is better than three hits?"

"The two don't compare."

"What if you had four hits? Oh, wait, what if you hit for the cycle?"

"Still no contest."

"If it's all good with you, we may have to hit for the cycle tonight, if you catch my drift."

We awake around eight feeling mentally and physically refreshed. I check my phone for messages while Jennifer showers. Several texts, none of any major importance. There were a couple of texts from a few more athletes showing their support. There's also one from Ethan saying he saw a huge python in the reeds by his house. I make a mental note to reach out to him a little later in the day.

According to Jen, Ethan is doing well. She's been in close contact with his mother who told her he's finishing up his treatment for leukemia and things are looking up. The boy's mindset is incredibly positive, particularly since we met, Jen tells me. Apparently, the small gesture of befriending Ethan is having a major impact.

I'm thrilled to hear that I lifted the boy's spirits and I pray that I would someday soon hear news that he's in remission. Jen has taken point in what we coined the *Ethan Excursion*. As soon as he receives the green light, we will set him up with front-row tickets to a game, a five-star hotel, autographs, limo rides, you name it.

I often listened to the late, great Rush Limbaugh on the radio. He' was heavily involved in charitable work, raising tens of millions for the Leukemia and Lymphoma Society, and each year I donate to the annual telethon. I miss that man greatly and my experience with Ethan makes me want to take up the mantle for that cause. Donations are one thing, but this experience has made me understand how personal impact is equally important.

The shower turns off and I prepare for what might be an awkward conversation. Not knowing how to approach Jennifer, I need to head to the ballpark for the Sunday game, another 1:00 pm start. This is unchartered territory, and I don't know how she'll spend the day.

She makes it easy and asks me to leave her a ticket at will call. "If you don't mind, I'd like to catch the ballgames while I'm in town," she says. "You just go about your work, and we will catch up after you are done."

It's a simple enough request, and Jen makes it clear that even though she's looking to attend the games, she'll be independent. Jen seems determined not to be a distraction.

One more kiss and I head out to start the day. I give the security guard in the lobby a heads up that Jennifer will need a lift to the stadium, and I ask him to keep an eye out for her. Jen is sharp and I'm pretty sure she can handle herself, but when you are in Florida mode you might let your guard down in the big city.

The dashboard reading of the Range Rover says it's forty-two degrees, and the sun's not out, but, luckily, there's little wind.

The country station on the radio plays an old song by Merle Haggard, "The Fightin' Side of Me," and it immediately places me back in the passenger seat of my father's F150 pickup. The song was directed toward Vietnam War protesters, but with an underlining patriotic theme. I recall my dad explaining the lyrics by saying, "Son, this song's about our great country that allows people to protest. But, if they disparage our great land and get out of hand, the song suggests we should kick their ass!"

I was just ten years old when he made that declaration, but it's engrained in my memory. My parents died a couple of weeks later, and in hindsight, I'm glad I learned of my dad's fightin' side before he passed.

When the song ends, I engage the car's Bluetooth to listen to two voicemails from Tom. My agent sounds upbeat. "I don't know if you are catching what is going on out there. We are definitely winning in public opinion. Call me back."

The second message was short and about an hour after the first. "TC Hunter, this is Thomas Bader, call me back."

I call Tom and this time he surprisingly skips pleasantries. "So, I'm watching the Sunday morning political shows and I've been keeping up with the talking heads, and we are killing it."

"I don't watch much television, Tom. Explain."

"Sure. The news shows are trying to twist your actions with Cunningham. So many of them are scumbags, and all they want is to be a pioneer on a topic to make headlines. A bunch of self-serving trash," Tom pauses to get back on track. "Anyway, as expected they are trying to make it a racial thing. CNN and MSNBC types even tried to attach the racism of Cobb to you because of your name. They are throwing everything at this one and trying to stoke the flames. The cancel culture crowd wants you thrown out of baseball!"

Cancel culture is something Chief curses all the time. He often speaks in vague, angry terms, and now I understand why. "Excuse me, Tom, how are we killing it exactly?"

"They are gaining zero traction, and with each attempt they get pummeled. The ridicule on social media is unreal. They are getting completely destroyed in the eyes of the public."

I stop at a light and a family in a blue sedan pulls aside. They recognize me and beep to get my attention. The husband and wife along with their two children appear to be inner-city locals, so I roll down the window as they shout how they are huge fans. The kids in the back look star struck and as if on cue, the mom says, "I like how you decked that Cunningham guy the other day."

Tom remains patiently on hold while I yell back to get their names. I ask if they were going to the game today and when they say no, I tell them I'll leave tickets for them at the gate. They're extremely thankful, and I give a quick wave, driving away thrilled that these fans would have a story to tell.

I apologize to Tom and he gets back on track. "Here's the thing. These creeps hide behind phony outrage. They attack people and try to ostracize them from their community and get them fired from their jobs. Well, it's not working when it comes to you because you are molded from a different cloth. They are trying to pile on, but it's falling flat, and they are getting destroyed."

He explains that the way we handled the situation from the beginning was important. Instead of apologizing and acquiescing, we gave no ground, nor would we ever. "It's crystal clear that they have failed to set the narrative and the country is craving for the nonsense to end. People are done with it, they are fed up. We are going to capitalize on this!"

Tom encouraged me to just do my job and leave the rest to him, which is fine with me. The people are behind us, and he reminds me to, "Never accept the premise!"

If my left cross can somehow be a conduit to a more unified country, then count me in. "All sound great, Tom," I say. He appreciates my sense of humor, so before I hang up I ask, "So, who else should I wallop?"

The final game of the three-game set against Chicago draws

another packed house. The stadium full, the fans brim with excitement. Early April games typically don't draw big crowds, so it's that our fans anticipate a special year.

I visit our team's public relations head and leave a ticket for Jen as well as four for the Middleton family I had seen on the road. Jennifer's seat is in a section they reserve for family members, and I made sure the Middleton's received great seats close up to the field.

Just prior to game time, position players head down the first base line to get the legs loose with a few sprints. On the way back to the dugout I see Jen in the reserved section, about twenty rows up and between the dugout and home plate. She's talking to a couple of the players' wives.

For a Sunday afternoon ballgame in April, the crowd is unusually boisterous. The excitement makes me edgy, and seeing that the opposition pitcher is someone I normally hit very well, adds even more pep to my step as I run out to my position in centerfield.

After the national anthem the noise died down, though there was still a buzz in the crowd. Even with a large crowd, on occasion I'll hear a single voice ring out from the seats. When playing at home, it's usually an encouraging yell from the bleachers from a fan looking to gain my attention. Sometimes, I'll acknowledge the fan with a quick wave.

In this first inning, a voice loudly bellows out above them all. "Hey, TC! Now we know why you were named after Cobb!"

I ignore the taunt, but he persists, followed by laughter and commotion from a small group. Nonchalantly I peek into the crowd searching for the ringleader and his band of cohorts. After the third or fourth time, I spot the men amid the sea of ardent fans. They're clumped together in the far corner of the bleacher seats and look out of place in their three-piece suits.

"We stand for the national anthem, goddammit," one of them shouts. Another voice rings out, "We respect our flag!" I look over at my teammate, Trevor Gil, in right field and he's not reacting. "Never shy away from the truth, that bum deserves it!" yells another.

I bark to get my teammate's attention, "Trev, you hear that?"

"Hear what?"

"You don't hear those guys yelling?"

Trevor shrugs, indicating he has no idea what I'm talking about. Neither our right fielder nor our left fielder hears the voices, and I planned to ask them again in between innings. Either they were better at ignoring the fans or perhaps the shouting is more madness conjured in my head.

I run off the field after the end of the inning and the shouting stops, but only to start again each time I return to my defensive position. I can't tell if it's two, three, four or more distinct voices, but they persist through the entire game, repeating many of the same lines. Patriotic themed, they continued to emphasize standing for the flag and respecting our country amid other colorful language. They throw in words like "white-livered rascal" and a "dirty hornswoggler" to describe my adversary, cackling in amusement. I don't know what a "mooncalf" might be, but they certainly got a kick out of words I presume are from a past era.

Despite the distraction, I have another big game and more importantly, we added to our quick start with another victory. Never unnerved, each at bat is solid and I make several stellar defensive plays.

After the final out, the team congratulate one another for the job well done in the 6-2 win. A television beat reporter pulls me aside for a few comments, and I intentionally keep the interview brief. The reporter focuses solely on my play, so I deflect the attention toward my teammates. Was I curt? I don't think so but I make a mental note to apologize to the reporter off the record at another time.

I spot Jen in the stands and she sees me. Most of the fans race toward the exit and Jen remains by her seat. She smiles glowingly and it looks like she had a great time at the game. I smile back with a quick wave before noticing a man sitting a few seats to her right. Like Jen, he's not exiting with the crowd.

Likely in his late twenties and wearing a drab, brown suit, the man looks out of place. When he pushes up and out of his seat, I notice his formidable figure, tall, lanky and very athletic. Raising his hand to his temple he calls out, "God bless you, TC. And God bless America." The voice matches one of the guys who had shouted toward me the entire game, and in a moment of déjà vu, the tone takes me back to the imaginary intruder from my apartment.

Reflexively, I give a quick salute back in acknowledgment before turning my attention to Jen. Oblivious to the exchange, Jen walks calmly down the steps toward me. We had not discussed where we would meet up after the game, so we converged at the edge of the dugout and the stands.

An usher is nearby and I ask him to show Jen to the player's parking lot. His name tag read *James from Philadelphia*. Graciously, James agrees to escort her to my car and stay with her until I arrive.

I look back towards the stands and no longer find the strange man from the encounter. Anticipating the answer, I still ask, "Jen, any idea who that guy next to you was?"

She gives me a quizzical look, "What guy?"

"He was a few seats over to your right. Nicely dressed in a brown three-piece suit?" Jen shrugs. "Never mind. Forget it, I'll meet you in a bit," I said before I headed toward the dugout tunnel.

The home stand was eventful to say the least. We start the season with five wins and one loss, an 8-6 game where our bullpen could not hold an early lead. Hey, you aren't going to win them all, but overall, our squad looks great.

The game is entering an era of computer-based models that put teams into defensive alignments that play the percentages. Although the league enacted rules to restrict the degree of shifts, they're still used, and my aim is to explode the computer analytics.

Even though the fans and our data department want me to swing for the fences, I prefer to take what the opposition gives me and slap the ball the other way, and even bunt for a base hit when the defense allows. If the defense wants to give me a free base hit, I'll take it every time no matter the situation.

Taking singles and doubles helps us win games, but it doesn't placate fans who hail me as the savior to bring baseball out of the steroid era by eclipsing the single season home run record. That expectation is both unfair and incredibly frustrating.

Much to the chagrin of the computer forecasters and homerun enthusiasts, I'm not only keeping the opposition flummoxed, my statistics over the first six games are obscene. In twenty-seven at bats, I have sixteen hits, including four home runs. My power numbers baffle opposing pitchers to question their own patterns.

Additionally, although I despise the pitch clock and the robotic strike zone, I use them to my advantage. Both are proving a distraction to pitchers who need more time to concentrate on the standard, smaller strike zone. Subsequently, pitchers are making more mistakes, and I'm clobbering everyone! Both the pitchers and batting-statistics nerds are going to have aneurysms trying to figure out how to get me out consistently.

Along with my pioneering baseball strategy, I've conducted a very successful experiment within my personal life. Jennifer visited and stayed four consecutive days. Not to scrutinize the situation, the overall conclusion is that we worked great together. I did my thing and never felt the need to change my routine. She had her own responsibilities and worked remotely while attending the ball games as my guest.

We enjoyed each other's company, and we had even grabbed a couple of nice dinners along the way, yet I never felt pressured to go outside the norm. Mutually, we aim to continue to get to know one another while navigating through our new relationship waters.

At the end of her visit, we did not look ahead to the next time we might see each other. It appeared a conscious effort on her part to allow for some space, as we are both determined to manage our relationship as it comes. We are committed to one another, and we are not suppressing the feeling that we want to see each other soon. Yet, we are not compelled to jump ahead to schedule the next date.

The ease of our relationship is, unfortunately, countered by my uncontrollable mental anxiety. Expectedly, I remain episode free when Jennifer is in my bed. However, the man in the fedora, as well as the saluting man and his crew, are clearly related to my neurosis.

I kid myself that it's become a hobby of mine, kind of like playing "Where's Waldo," but I persistently search for out of place men in old suits among those in the stands or the city streets. I don't know if there's a remedy to my problems, but seeking further interactions with the mystery men keeps me oddly optimistic. Whether they might provide answers is uncertain, but at least logically, they seem to be linked to my troubles.

Along with Jennifer, my main source of solace is the stellar play on the field. I still face repercussions from the opening-day brawl, but the incident has died down, much like Tom said it would. We hold the public high ground and that itself is satisfying. There's encouragement everywhere, yet without Jennifer in my bed, I assume it's just a matter of time before I run into even more issues.

CHAPTER 12

THE TEAM HEADS out to Atlanta, St. Louis, and Houston for the season's first road trip, each for a three-game set. Relatively speaking, the weather for the initial home stand was reasonable, but upon heading south the weather improved and even the temperature of our night games sat around sixty degrees. The uptick in temperature makes me even more anxious to get to the ballpark each day. The team is rock solid. The goal of any team is to win each series and if you can win at that pace on the road, you've achieved elite status.

Astoundingly we win all three series, even sweeping Houston. With the early surge, the press quickly moves us from the contender ranks to the favorite to win the league championship. Las Vegas odds reflect the same, moving us from a 4-1 proposition to almost even money. That shift in sentiment is premature given that we were only a tenth of the way into our schedule, but we do look impressive.

Personally, I've had a blast on our road trip. I continue to kill it at the plate, taking what the pitcher provides while waiting for mistakes. Forget exit velocity and launch angles, playing opponents who stressed such things was like taking candy from a baby. The proof was in the pudding and our team was making waves throughout the league.

Despite our winning ways, our own team's analytics department had the nerve to upbraid our manager about the team's tactics. Once, I bunted with two outs in the seventh inning of a game, stole second, and scored on a base hit by our shortstop, yet they still badgered Billy Law about the math even though the strategy worked!

To his credit, Billy listened and did a lot of nodding. He promised the analytics team that he would continue to monitor the methods, but instead confidentially declared, "Keep doing what you are doing." Luckily, we have a manager who knows how to appease the computer guys while his old-school understanding realizes the game is much more than geometry, physics, and statistical probabilities. The powers that be were using bad math, completely misstating the nuances of the game, and too pigheaded to see things any other way.

Even still, our team is on an emotional high and I find myself on solid ground. After Jennifer visited, I went hallucination free through the entire road trip. With a stable emotional state, I feel more at ease with life, so perhaps it is only when I have a certain level of angst does my brain go haywire.

It's premature to think the psychological warfare is over. However, I allow for optimism that perhaps I can eventually get over the hump. Letting Jennifer completely into my life gives me joy and hope, and our relationship provides a sense of balance that is no doubt contributing to my current peace. Combine that with glowing success on the ballfield and I've attained an overall wellness to my psyche that I have not felt in a while. Even the dreaded punch that sent the baseball world into a tizzy has proven to be a positive.

My agent was right, never respond and acknowledge the premise. Tom prepared social media posts on my behalf to bombard the public with patriotic messages and pictures of me with our troops. I visited the troops a couple of times in the Middle East, and I make plenty of stops to our military bases during the off season. In the pictures there were men, women, Black people, White people, Asian people and get this, they were all smiling. We had our arms around each other as we shared a mutual appreciation for the country.

⚾ ⚾ ⚾

I can't sleep on planes or buses and when you are a professional baseball player that's a terrible affliction. With so much travel it would be ideal to catch a few Z's while en route from one city to another. Unfortunately, it just doesn't happen for me, and it has nothing to do with the movement of the bus or airplane. I simply can't sleep when I am not in the prone position no matter how tired.

Heading back to Philadelphia I notice most of my teammates fast asleep. Johnny Baugh has his head scrunched by the plane window and Sammy Taylor is curled up in a ball, both completely out. Bobby Mitchell is seated straight up with headphones on, his mouth open and drool forming on the sides of his lips. His snoring forced a piece of gum to fall on his chest, and his eyes appear somewhat open, despite being knocked out.

Teammates, trainers and managers all look to be getting their rest, and I feel a tinge of jealousy. Only one player a few rows back has his overhead light on. Brian Cole, a newly acquired lefty reliever, has his overhead beam focusing down on the latest Nelson DeMille novel. Since he is new to the squad I don't know if he suffers from my affliction or if he's simply caught up in a great story.

I only spent one full season in the minors and found myself utterly dejected when dealing with the constant bus rides. I often reflect on that time in my career when we were forced to drive through the night in order to arrive at a host town for a series. Even if I was exhausted from a full day of play, I could never sleep a wink on those marathon bus trips. My only recourse was to take a nap as soon as I could lie flat. I do not miss those days of functioning on a few hours of sleep, sometimes even napping on a dirty locker room floor before a game.

At least now my issue is limited to plane rides and the flight from Houston to Philadelphia is around three hours. I typically use the flight time to review previous at bats as well as pitchers that I will face during the week. With all of the data a computer click away, I start with the organization's advanced scouting report of the upcoming opponent pitchers. After that, I'll review my at bats and go through any catalogued information that I deem important. At least I'd use the time to be productive.

With the distinct drone of the jet plane engine in the background, I watch every one of my at bats from the last dozen games. Overall, I'm satisfied with each plate appearance. There was one at bat in the St. Louis series where I remember thinking I could drop a bunt for an easy base hit, however, the pitcher is someone I've had much success against. I swung away and lined hard to the centerfielder.

Next, I review each starter and reliever for the next two series. I punch up my at bat history, looking for patterns from each hurler. I also watch at bats from each pitcher's latest games against other opponents to decipher their pitch selection.

Knowledge is power, and I learn a lot from the videos, sometimes even noticing a pitcher tipping off his pitches. Like a bad poker player, certain pitchers have movements or tics that give things away. With velocities sometimes reaching over a hundred miles per hour, identifying habits provides a much-needed edge.

Focusing on the computer screen, I don't notice Billy Law heading toward me. He moves down the aisle like a zombie, clearly disturbed from his sleep. He hands me a slip of paper without saying a word before trudging back to his seat for some more shuteye. The message reads, *Suspension appeal zoom meeting, noon tomorrow.*

League commissioners tend to represent the interests of team owners over the welfare of the players. Barry Schilds, entrenched as the league commissioner for over twenty-five years, tries to come off as evenhanded, but it is clear where his allegiances lie. He plays both sides of the fence and on occasion will say the right thing, but his job is to drive revenue for the owners.

Schilds has a track record of questionable decisions, but the sports media props him up, even crowning him the architect of the infamous 1998 homerun chase that supposedly saved baseball. Personally, I think his actions did more to harm the game, and many of the current day players feel the same.

After the 1994 player strike that bled into the 1995 season, fans were disenchanted and not coming back to the ballpark. At the onset of the 1995 crisis, the owners hired scab replacements. Spring training was full of second-tier, temporary players, and the quality of the game suffered. Fans were angered, and when the two sides finally came to terms, the residual impact of the work stoppage was palpable.

Then came Barry Schilds. He was hired as the new league commissioner as the answer to the fans who had sworn off the game. Schilds apologized for the work stoppage and promised a more exciting product, and to that end he did deliver. Steroids ran rampant throughout the league and the commissioner turned a blind eye. Tape-measure home runs were hit at an exhausting pace as several players blew through historic marks, rewriting the record books.

Many feel Schilds engineered the home run chase by further aiding the behemoth players by using baseballs that were wound tighter and traveled farther. Baseballs were being hit harder and longer with highlights of the home run chase plastered all over the media. The hype was something that baseball had never seen, and the marketing was magical.

The steroid pollution in baseball would not come to light for quite some time, with several players eventually admitting to rampant use. The storyline then shifted, with the tabloids littered with stories about steroids in the game, serving as a marketing ploy equal to the home run chase itself.

The media would display the words of sympathizers who

used phrases like, "Steroids don't give a hitter the ability to hit a baseball coming in at a hundred miles an hour," and "You still have to put in the work to become great." The steroid debate kept baseball alive and in the news for years, and later, even Hank Aaron's career home run record of 755 was surpassed.

Baseball benefited. Television revenue and ticket sales skyrocketed, and the impending doom predicted for the game subsided. The casualties in the affair were players, both past and present. Past players saw their records eclipsed, and the present-day player went through years of being looked upon with a skeptical eye as fans debated who might be on the juice. It was going on in other sports as well, yet baseball history took the brunt of the controversy while at the same time endowing the league with bundles of money.

I suppose I should be thankful for those effective tactics because they helped to increase player salaries. However, even though I'm about to reap the benefit of baseball's evil genius, I am embittered about the many scars left on the great game. Thus, I'm not going into the video meeting with a cheerful outlook.

Tom agrees to take the lead, and it's a good idea that he does most of the talking. If addressed directly, I have some scripted answers, but it's probably a good idea to stay quiet whenever possible. I don't self-censor very well, and Tom's nervous I'll let loose with descriptive words, which I have used quite extensively in our private conversations when discussing the suspension and the commissioner.

I take the meeting in Chief's office because it's private. There are no players or coaches around, and I also know that as a custodian of the game Chief is anxious to listen in. He's attaching a special interest in the commissioner's ruling, feeling it's important to the health of the game. Any unreasonable ruling will be a personal affront used in an effort to impact my image and, that won't sit well with the old man.

The commissioner levies the initial suspension as a knee-jerk response, and caves to the pressures from outside groups with various political agendas. I'm also sure he fielded demands from the league owners to make me damaged goods. If they can lower my value, they in turn can lower the value of other players throughout the league.

Thankfully, the fan backlash hits heavy and hard, and by winning the public relations battle we force the commissioner to backtrack. Schilds might have his warts, but he's smart enough to read the tea leaves and should do what was right for the league and the health of the game. Tom calculates that Schilds will do the right thing, if for no other reason than to fortify his own public image.

There are five people in the zoom meeting, six if you count Chief who lingers in the background. The commissioner is at his desk, his face appearing too close to the screen. He's dressed in a blue suit with a white shirt and bright yellow tie. When he leans back, I see the league logo in the background as well as a bookshelf off to the side.

His assistant and attorney, some guy named Doug Popp, is also on screen. Popp's a stuffy lawyer with his Burberry eyeglasses perched low on his nose, looking self-important and holding a yellow legal pad.

My agent, Tom Bader, and a union attorney named Andrew Blake, sit on my behalf. I suppose I should have anticipated a union rep wanting to tie in since they have a stake in my future compensation as well. Both Tom and Andrew are dressed in attorney-wear, but Tom dons a suit jacket and dress shirt without a tie. I, on the other hand, am in my baseball workout gear, which I suppose is acceptable given the time of day. If that displays a degree of disrespect, then so be it.

Schilds commences the meeting by introducing his sidekick and by acknowledging Tom, Andrew and me. He thanks us for attending, as if our participation is optional. He then notes that minutes of the meeting will be kept for documentation, so I remind myself to not use my expanded vocabulary of expletives.

He recounts the reason for the meeting, stating that a five-game suspension has been levied for the incident with Jamie Cunningham. Schilds notes that both Cunningham and I received equal suspensions and that this meeting is to address my appeal only. I had not been paying enough attention to know that Cunningham received an equal penalty, nor did I know if he had appealed, too.

The league put out an edict at the beginning of the season addressing the national anthem and player conduct, so I wonder how this would all play out. Cunningham should get hit with a penalty for his initial actions as well as for throwing the first blow. I presume we'll never get the full story on Cunningham's end, and we'd likely learn of details only through third party leaks.

Clearing his throat as a sign he's about to get to the crux of the conversation, Schilds says, "I reviewed your appeal and I have made a determination with regard to a reduced suspension. Since there is a racial element involved—"

"Whoa! With all due respect, there is no racial element to this," Tom interrupts.

"Well, Mr. Cunningham made a statement that your client made a racial slur."

"That's been disproven, and you know it. First base coach, Sonnie Mejia, and first base umpire, Joe Mayer, both stated that there was no such incident. Video tape analysis of the conversation also shows Cunningham's lying. You know it and the public knows it," Tom bristles, rightfully. Everyone knows I never made a racial slur and the suggestion is a disgusting tactic.

"This is a very serious matter, and everything needs to be considered," says Schilds.

Both Tom and I scoff audibly and in unison. The union attorney, Andrew Blake, rolls his eyes.

"Barry, don't even try going there," Blake said. "Clearly Cunningham is an activist of sorts and is simply trying to stir the pot. There's zero evidence that Mr. Hunter said anything that could be considered racist. Some colorful cursing and some aggressive language, but the rest is fiction." Blake is Black, and his words carried weight.

"You know I have to take everything in consideration, Andrew."

"No, you have to take facts into consideration."

"I understand your position," says Schilds. Popp says nothing, scribbling frantically on his notepad. I have the feeling that Popp was behind the strategy.

"Listen, sir," Tom interrupts. "My client did nothing wrong and certainly did not say what you are suggesting. As a matter of fact, he was bringing to Mr. Cunningham's attention your own edict about standing for the flag."

Nice one, Tom, although I unquestionably was not thinking about the commissioner's rules when I confronted Cunningham. Still, a much better strategy than stating my actions might have been influenced by a ghost screaming in my face the morning of the game. I doubt that will go over well.

"Your client punched another player," Schilds fires back.

"Yeah, after the player swatted him in the face first. My client reacted in self-defense. The only thing he is guilty of is explaining your own rules to one of the players on the field."

"Oh, so he is a good Samaritan in this?"

"The fans think so. The players in the league think so. You want to make this something that it's not, we won't let it sit."

"Are you threatening me, Tom?"

"Threatening? No, no, no, there is no threat, just a promise. If you enter racism into this conversation I will reengage in the court of public appeal. If you insist on bringing fiction into your decision, I will make sure the public knows exactly what's going on."

Over my right shoulder I see Chief jump up in the air and pump his fists. I'm surprised the old man can get off the ground. I bite my lip to suppress a laugh.

Tom continues. "Let me tell you something, Barry, I am disappointed in you. I thought you'd be smart enough to not fall for some sort of illogical *woke* pressure again."

Schilds smirks and looks back to his attorney. Tom was referencing how the league had fallen in line with other companies that make political statements to appease leftist pressures. The league is sticking its nose where it doesn't belong, and the consequences are hurting the product.

"If you pull this bullshit, I assure you, we will launch a public assault against you and in support of TC Hunter. I also assure you we will sue you and the league for defamation. You can do whatever you want with the suspension, but if you continue with this nonsense, we will not stand pat."

Chief runs into the hall to stop from cheering. I want to cheer myself but opt to calmly nod in agreement.

Schilds, red with anger, is not used to being challenged so confrontationally. His face tightens as he seethes, struggling for a position. Pausing, he says, "Tom, let's not forget that your client has a lot of money on the line. I don't think you want to get into a pissing contest on this one."

Unable to control myself, I blurt, "I've got enough money, Mr. Schilds. I am in full agreement with my agent, and I am prepared to defend myself against any character assault." Tempted to say something more colorful, I instead hold my tongue. The expression on Tom's face suggests he is also thankful for my restraint.

"Barry," interrupts the union attorney, Blake, "We are done here. I am confident that you understand our position and you will do the right thing. The union is in support of Mr. Hunter, and we back the strategy that Tom has outlined. We will await your response, but there's nothing else more to say."

With that, Tom, Andrew, and I sign off. Smiling widely, Chief gives me an approving pat on the back.

In Sun Tzu's famous book, *The Art of War*, it is said that a general who advances without coveting fame and retreats without disgrace is the jewel of the kingdom. I thought of this quote when Tom texts me two hours later.

His text reads, *Reduced suspension to one game. The announcement will not come until next Saturday, so you will sit out a day and enjoy the rest. Good win here. We had the moral high ground.*

I text back, *You are the best.* Tom's the jewel of my little kingdom. He knows when to advance and when to retreat, wanting nothing, well, except seven percent of my earnings. It's well earned. We beat the establishment through a campaign for popular opinion, and it feels good.

I anxiously searched for Chief. He's busy getting uniforms and equipment ready for the game, but when he finally returns to his office, his reaction is priceless. "Yeah baby!" he exclaims. "Your agent stuck it right up Schilds's ass!" He pumps his right fist and then mimes a couple of jabs followed by a big right hook to celebrate the moment.

"Tom is the real deal."

"Your agent? Yeah he is. Shut that prick up, but quick," Chief says. "They thought they had leverage on you because of your contract. No sir. That ain't gonna work."

"Yeah, Tom's sharp and is always one step ahead."

"Good man to have in your corner," Chief says before exiting again to finish his work. On his desk is an old scrapbook he'd been leafing through. The album is brown with age, but the pictures inside are vibrant, and the slight yellow tinge adds to their mystique. The photos glued to each page are clearly the work of a professional.

The photographs are an amazing account of a different age, pictures of ballplayers posing in uniform along with action shots that captured the grace of the game. Photos of players off the field are equally fantastic. Teams of that time traveled by rail, and the photos of players riding the trains are fascinating. The men played cards, drank, caroused and generally appeared to be having a great time.

Other photos show players walking the streets, sometimes in a group and sometimes solo. In each shot, players are dressed in three-piece suits, a requirement to be properly attired whenever in public. The men look dapper and carried themselves with a sophistication that marked that era. I flip the pages carefully, noticing pictures of men donning hats. Eagerly searching, I try finding a match to the man in the fedora from the condo several weeks back.

The distinct manner in which the players wore their suits corresponds to the images of suited men I've noted in the stands at our games. I shake the thought that my neurosis had somehow conjured images of ghosts and inserted them in random places of my everyday life. Episode free of late, I deliberately expunge thoughts of hauntings.

I figure the photos were taken in the early 1900s. I quickly identify Ty Cobb, Tris Speaker, Walter Johnson, Joe Jackson and Rogers Hornsby. There's a magnificent shot of Ruth and Gehrig standing together near the on-deck circle, and others of Mel Ott, Hank Greenberg, Arky Vaughan, Charlie Gehringer, and Lefty Grove. Action shots of Carl Hubbell and Dizzy Dean displaying their unique high leg kick were perfectly timed. I'm captivated.

Chief reenters the room. "Dug that album up from a closet at home."

"Who took these pictures? They are amazing."

"My father took 'em," Chief says. "He was a photographer who covered baseball teams. That's probably where my love of the game started."

"This album belongs in a museum or something."

Chief considers the thought momentarily. "My dad was a champion of the game. Preserving America's pastime was his goal, up in Heaven it probably still is," he says with a puckish twinkle. "I'm not done with it just yet, but someday you'll be the benefactor. The heirloom needs to carry on with someone who is equally appreciative when I'm gone."

I stare at Chief in anger of another reference to his demise. He turns away before I can admonish him, so I continued sifting through the pages. The album is chronological, and when I get to the back of the book the pictures are of the early 1940s, a significant time in the history of our country.

Many of the photos show patriotic themes. Several are pictures of players holding the American flag, and two full pages of different players standing in front of an Uncle Sam placard. These pages alone are a unique slice of Americana worth preserving.

Turning back and noticing the photos, Chief comments on how baseball shined brightest at that time of significant unrest. Germany had invaded Poland in 1939 and continued to expand their fighting force. Hitler was aggressively plotting to conquer all of Europe, and the people of the United States could feel war was imminent. Baseball provided an uplifting distraction.

After the patriotic shots are a series of pictures featuring Joe DiMaggio. Exceptional and distinct, the photos have me transfixed by each detail. DiMaggio was a private person, so I was surprised to see several off-field shots to go along with the many action photos.

The action photos centered on DiMaggio's famed fifty-six game hitting streak in 1941. It remains an astounding feat that goes unmatched. The Yankee Clipper's streak began in the middle of May and ended on July 16, but for two months, the country was entertained and somewhat distracted from the turmoil in Europe and the shadow of war enveloping the world.

The 1941 storied season also saw Ted William chasing a mythical statistical figure. One of the most popular tales my father loved to relay referenced the last day of that very 1941 season. On that final day, Williams was batting .3995, which translated to .400 for the official statistics. Batting .400 is a benchmark feat, and his manager encouraged him to sit out the final day of play in order to set that mark.

"Teddy Ballgame insisted on playing in the double header," my dad often exclaimed. "And wouldn't you know it, he got six hits in eight at bats to finish the year batting .406!" No player has batted .400 since.

DiMaggio won the league's Most Valuable Player in 1941, edging out Williams for the award. But most importantly, both the hitting streak and the batting average chase inspired the country at a critical time. Soon after, the attack at Pearl Harbor thrust the country into World War II, the great watershed moment of twentieth century geopolitical history.

National pride dominated and many ballplayers traded in their bats for rifles. Ted Williams, Joe DiMaggio, Yogi Berra, Bob Feller, Pee Wee Reese, Hank Greenberg joined countless others to take up arms during the military conflict. There was unity toward a cause and baseball players were no exception, some even involved in the D-Day invasion in 1944. Ironically, I was born on June 6, the anniversary date of D-Day, and I never lost sight of the significance and baseball's link.

The last page of the album appears intentionally blank, but the final picture is what stops me in my tracks.

"Do you believe in the afterlife, Chief?"

"Yeah, kid. I believe in God and that we enter his kingdom when we are gone from the earth. Believing in eternal life is better than thinking we just go away, that's for sure."

I consider that for a second before asking, "What about ghosts and dissatisfied souls? Is that just stuff we imagine?"

"What, like from the movies? Now what are you talking about, TC?" he snickers. Chief discounts the notion yet seems interested in the conversation.

"I don't know, not like poltergeists or ghoulish stuff. Like how some people say they've received signs from dead relatives... that kind of thing."

Chief pauses for a moment and scratches his head. "Since you ask, yeah, people from our past are always around us. They keep us grounded and remind us how things used to be. Sometimes, they might even prompt us in tough times to help push us through. At least that's how it feels to me sometimes."

"Huh," is all I can muster as I look at the final photo showing Ted Williams standing alongside Joe DiMaggio. I can't tell where they might be or why they were together, but the photo is one of a kind. Ted's athletic frame made his suit hang off him in such a unique way that it immediately makes me think of the saluting man from the stadium.

CHAPTER 13

I BLOCK OUT old suits, fedoras, saluting men, and the album, and turn my attention back to the game.

I had no idea that Chief is a military veteran, enlisting in the Army right after high school. He even saw brief combat in Vietnam well before that war escalated the following decade. It explains much about my friend who demonstrates a sincere devotion to the United States of America. The battle against communism and totalitarianism is engrained within him. Chief's opinions are often unyielding, but this insight provides an understanding of his notions.

With a game to play, I'm determined to shake off distractions and focus upon the task at hand. Pittsburgh's team is young and hungry and an organization on the upswing. Although inexperienced, they have enough talent to be dangerous. Billy Law has the same inkling, warning us not to take our opponent lightly in a fiery pregame speech.

"If you think you can just show up, this team will bite you in the ass," he says. "I'm sensing a loss of focus, a lot of joking around. We aren't good enough for that. We ain't even close to good enough." Law gives the standard no-letdown speech, but we all know he's right. When a team comes back from a successful road trip there's a tendency for a letdown, and it's when you think you've got it figured out that you start getting beat. Reliant on strong veterans, our squad is less apt to fall flat, however, Law's speech serves as a reminder to set the standard high every night.

Billy doesn't take credit. Our squad picks up right where we left off and starts the three- games set with a solid 8-4 win. Even though I hit another home run and drive in three, I don't like two of my at bats. One was a weak pop up on a 2-0 pitch, and the other a strikeout on a pitch that I thought was a few inches outside of the plate.

Pittsburgh's staff is comprised of inexperienced kids who still need seasoning in the minors. Their organization philosophy is to bring up the young guns and let them learn on the job. They are often wild and certainly not precise with their pitches. I make no excuses, but it can be a tough at bat when you know the pitcher is trying to throw an outside fastball and it instead whizzes one by your ear.

Even with a couple of bad at bats, I find myself in a good mood. We win another ballgame, and I had no strange occurrences to speak of outside of a few camera flashes. The unmistakable *whoosh* of the flash powder is followed by a burst of light, but the occurrences are likely a result of my fixation with Chief's album. There are no oddly placed individuals in old suits, no catcalls, and no bizarre interactions, so my mind is in a relatively strong place.

Several teammates decide on a bar called the Standard Tap. I join them for light post- game festivities, and the older players grab the rookies for a night at the pub. Unlike the dance clubs that draw some of the younger players like moths to a flame, the idea here is to show the rookies a good time within safer and more sedate confines.

The Standard Tap is said to be the first gastropub in the United States. I'm not sure if that's true, but the food and atmosphere is great. It's usually an eclectic crowd with enough young, attractive women to keep the rookies entertained, particularly once news gets out that the squad is in the house.

We order a bunch of craft beers along with three of everything on the menu. The cold beer and food shows the rookies a different mode of partying, and they seem okay with the atmosphere. They'll be even happier once they learn that I'm paying the bill.

Team unity is important and most of the squad attends. A couple go home to their families, but even most of the married players partake. Although I'm not looking to make it a long night, I too enjoy the respite.

The night out was partially orchestrated for our third base prodigy, Bobby Mitchell. At Billy Law's request we have taken him under our wing and stunted his partying ways. The goal is to keep Mitchell out of nightclubs and to get him to the field the next day ready to play.

By midnight word was out that the team is hanging out in the bar. Throngs of beautiful women file in, so Mitchell and the other eligible bachelors have plenty of flirtatious options. All seem to be having fun.

A woman fakes tripping and lands in my lap, a signal that it's time for me to leave. A dare from a small group of friends, I see this woman's accomplice use her phone to take a picture of the scantily clad blond in my arms. It's easy enough to explain and I'll get ahead of it with Jennifer. The ladies were just having some fun, but I don't need Jen seeing the picture on social media and thinking the worst.

I play it cool and get the girl back on her feet. She tries to parlay the exploit into a conversation, and I politely tell her I'm spoken for. The blonde is quite attractive, and also quite drunk. If not for Jen, I might have taken advantage.

After excusing myself I let teammates know I'm leaving—alone. We enjoyed outstanding fare and many laughs, so I leave the bar hoping the message of moderation hit home. Baseball players are notorious for pushing the envelope, and I'm sure while prepping for our next game I'll be able to spot any players who continued to tie one on.

I limited my alcohol consumption to one drink and was perfectly fine to drive home. Typically, a ten-minute ride back to my apartment, I'm running into a string of bad luck by hitting every red light. The Range Rover windows down, the cool night air is exhilarating.

Stopped at a light I caught the wafting aroma of a Chinese restaurant on the corner. The smell of wok stir-fry, fried wontons, and sesame oil mixed with the pungent scent of the city make for a distinctly recognizable Philadelphia-street experience. Even though the Chinese restaurant on the corner is closed, several cars are in the lot as staff remain behind to prepare for the next day.

I'm only a few blocks from the condo when a commotion up Walnut Street catches my eye. A group of five young kids are yelling in my direction. One of the kids, a young boy who looks no older than ten years, bangs on a trash can with a large stick, or maybe it's a bat.

I check the clock on the dash and it was almost one-thirty. I wonder what the kid is doing out at such an hour. Where were his parents? The group waits for me, so I assume they're fans seeking attention. Waiting for the light to turn, I give them a quick wave.

Glancing in the rearview mirror I notice the block is unusually dark from many broken streetlights. There are no cars behind me or in the general vicinity. Besides the lights from a few store fronts and my own headlights, the street is completely black and instinctively I feel something's wrong.

I catch movement behind the car and think it might be one of the kids from the corner. I peer again in the rearview mirror, but it's too dark to make anything out. Screw the red light, I am getting out of here.

The adjacent street is a two-way road, so I look to the right for oncoming cars. Turning back to the left, my sightline down the road is blocked by a figure dressed in black. My first thought is to punch the accelerator, but with a pistol two inches from my face I immediately lose the impulse.

The kid is a skinny teenager, maybe a little less than six feet tall. I don't know if I'm being robbed or it's a carjacking, possibly something worse.

"Get outta the car, mother fucker," the teen says. He looks confident, like he has done this before. Luckily, he doesn't recognize me.

"Easy, pal. Easy," I say. "Nobody has to get hurt here. You can have any money I have."

"No shit, fuckhead, I got the gun. I'm going to take your money and your car. Get the fuck out. You got five seconds, or I explode your brain."

"Okay, okay," I say, trying to think quickly. There is a good chance he'll just get in the car and take off, but with a small gang of thugs with him, I fear someone might shoot me anyway. I slowly reach down to unclick my seatbelt while holding my left hand up to indicate surrender.

As I reached for my belt I glance back to the corner where the others previously stood. They've disbursed. One of the kids is a hundred feet or so up the road, so I assume they've formed a perimeter to make sure nobody intervenes. I unclick the seat belt and put both my hands up. "Take it easy, I'm getting out."

"Hurry up, mother fucker," the thief grizzles. The gun is pointed at my chest as he backs off a few feet to let me out of the car.

As soon as I open the door, he reaches for me with his right hand. The gun is in his left hand as he grabs my arm to remove me from the car. Over my shoulder I hear a loud noise that turned out to be several workers at the Chinese restaurant throwing something into the metal garbage dumpster.

The kid looks up toward the dumpster for a split second just as he was tossing me aside, the pistol waving in his left hand as he jumps into the front seat. I'm off to the side, no longer facing the gun's muzzle.

Before the thief gets fully into the car I reach for the door and slam it, first catching his left foot and trapping the left hand. The kid cries out and pulls his foot into the car when I opened the door slightly to slam it again. The kid's left hand jams inside the mechanism and the gun goes flying. The third time I opened and shut the door, I break his wrist.

His shrieks of pain bring the other assailants back. I think about reaching for the gun, but opt to reach for the kid instead, throwing him onto the pavement. One of the boys running toward the car yells, "What the fuck! Mickey!"

The kid on the pavement is writhing in pain, yelling all sorts of profanities until I step on his face and jump back into my car. "Crime doesn't pay, Mickey," I say as I hop into the driver's seat.

I punch the gas and clip one of the boys running toward the Range Rover. I didn't hit him hard enough to cause major damage, but enough to knock him out of the picture. I expect to hear gunshots behind me as I speed away. I duck in my seat, but no shots are fired.

The wheels chirp and I see another figure in my headlights to the left. Instinctively, I pull the steering wheel toward the target and then quickly back to the right to avoid the ten-year-old boy. He waves his bat in the air before throwing it at the car as I drive away. The projectile falls well short as I speed down the road.

I dial 911 to report the incident. To think a group of young kids would resort to such a desperate act makes me intensely angry. With adrenaline coursing, and with the window of the Rover still open, I take several lung-filling breaths to calm myself. Damn those kids, they chose the wrong target tonight.

The dispatcher takes the details of the attack and asks if I would come into the station to provide further information. I'm not about to go anywhere besides my condo, which is a couple blocks east. I prompt the dispatcher to send an officer to me and suggest they first pick up the piece of shit would be carjackers. When I provide my name and specifics, the dispatcher speaks to me in a different manner, promising that an officer will meet me shortly.

After I pull into the covered lot, I still carefully survey my surroundings. I know the area is secure, but I'm still shaken and cautious. I escaped the battle physically unscathed but traumatized.

I board the elevator to the lobby leading to the apartment wondering if I had just had another one of my crazy dreams. The confusion makes me nauseous. I scan the area frantically and make my way to the front door, not calming until I enter the apartment and close the safety latch. To regain composure and with no time to mess around, I pour a tumbler full of Sazerac 18-year-old straight rye whiskey. I take the shot and pause only briefly before taking a second dose, this time a double.

For the third helping I pour the whiskey over ice from a mold that makes a block resembling a baseball, stitches and all. I circle the liquid over ice and plant on the couch wanting nothing to do but drink and look out into the night. I have a few things to take care of before getting to my desired level of inebriation.

I thumbed my agent's contact on the phone and tell him what happened. Even at the early hour, Tom doesn't miss a beat. He is shocked and asks a bunch of questions, none of which I feel like answering. Once he's assured that I'm fine, he shifts into agent mode and considers what to do about the incident.

Would it benefit us to make the failed carjacking public? Or maybe it's best to squash the incident and not draw any negative attention to the city? I leave it up to Tom to make those determinations and tell him frankly that I really don't give a shit at the moment.

I suck down some more whiskey and listen to Tom ramble about some more contract negotiations. Maybe he'll use tonight's failed assault to put pressure on the team as the assault gives me more impetus to leave. Tom says something about getting an offer near baseball's salary record, but I only hear every fifth word. It's not the time or place to think about such things.

Lobby security calls and I put Tom on hold. The police arrive and I tell the guard to send them up. Taking Tom off hold he insists that he stay on speaker phone. He then put me on hold as he calls the security desk at the condo to make sure they keep the police visit under wraps. Tom is very convincing, and the guard pledges silence.

A detective shows his badge and introduces himself. Brian Young looks to be in his mid-forties. He has a barrel chest and his tightly cropped haircut screamed former beat cop. He's friendly and does little to hide his giddiness from meeting his favorite baseball player.

Force of habit, I offer him a drink before realizing it's inappropriate to drink on duty. After exchanging pleasantries, I introduce Brian to my agent on speaker phone and he seems okay with having Tom listen in.

The police picked up the lead carjacker, Mickey Bruther, and shuttled him to the hospital for treatment of a compound fracture of his radius and ulna along with a contusion to his orbital bone. Both Mickey and his younger brother, Jason, were walking west on Lombard Street several blocks away from the incident when the police arrived. Jason was the boy with the bat and just ten years old, and neither was willing to give up the names of the others in the group.

Brian said that charges would be brought against both kids, with Mickey facing the most trouble. Mickey's only sixteen years old and the gun that was retrieved is unregistered. They would match the weapon to his prints, and they'd then use that information to try and find the source of the illegal weapon. Brian says he won't rest until he arrests the other kids involved.

The detective says that the case will likely go through the juvenile justice system, although it was possible that Mickey could be charged as an adult due to the egregious nature of the crime. Mickey has a previous record, but in Brian's opinion the case will likely remain adjudicated within the juvenile courts. Due to the progressive bent to the district attorney's office, the detective insinuated my status as a ball player might be the only way the kids don't end up back on the streets quickly.

What in the world were those kids doing? Mickey isn't even old enough to drive, yet he was involved in carjacking. Was this just hi-jinks or an act of desperation by street kids? Were they stealing on behalf of others?

Tom wants to be in the loop on all proceedings and I give Brian the okay to contact him directly. I did not have anything to add besides telling Brian I grazed one of the kids in the group with my car as I sped away. He says he'll check the local hospitals to see if any new patients matched the description and potential injury.

Tom worries the incident will go public but seems satisfied that the detective will keep it under wraps for the time being. The ideal would be to keep things undisclosed until a sentencing hearing. Brian explains that there will be an ongoing investigation. Officers will check with the Chinese restaurant as well as other establishments in the area to see if they have video that could help to identify the others. That could be difficult because the area was dark from the kids knocking out the streetlights with rocks in preparation for the ambush.

I take Detective Young's card and sign a baseball for his eight-year-old son. The detective reminds me that I was very lucky to have gotten through the incident unscathed. I could have made a mess of things.

As soon as the detective leaves, I top off my drink while Tom continues talking about contract offers. I'm in no mood. I eventually yell at Tom to stop speaking. Contracts and nonsense can wait. After an incident like tonight, it might be tough staying in Philadelphia no matter how rich the offer. I think of the tranquility of Tampa, and of Jennifer.

I'm not sure I should tell her. I don't want her to know I was out until one-thirty in the morning partying, nor her worrying about my safety living in the city.

After a few more sips, I reach whiskey contentment and recline on the couch. The last thing I feel before passing out is a rush of fear at the thought of keeping Jen safe.

CHAPTER 14

RELIEVED, I AWAKE at 10:30 am. I've been on a long streak of not having an episode, and given the previous night it would have been disastrous to have to deal with an early morning wakeup call.

Carefully, I stand expecting to have a hangover, but don't. I drink a tall glass of V8 and chase it down with a bottle of water just in case. My home remedy usually kills off any lingering effects.

Sitting on the couch, I take a moment before calling Jennifer. I contemplate what I might tell her and conclude that there's no reason for alarm. I'll tell her about the carjacking attempt maybe the next time we're together. I anticipate seeing her next week. We have two more games against Pittsburgh and then three in New York before flying to Miami, and then Tampa for three game sets. Maybe she'd be willing to head to Miami for a few days and then we could work our way back to Florida's west coast together.

"Good morning my dear," I say. "How are things in sunny Florida today?"

"It's cloudy this morning, but you know Florida it will likely be sunny and warm by the afternoon."

"Hey, we are heading down to Miami for games starting Friday, and then we play Tampa. Any chance you might want to connect in Miami?"

"Possibly, I have some things I need to work out. You do anything last night?" Jen asks.

An inflection in her voice puts me on edge. There couldn't be a leak already, could there? "Oh, I met up with some of the boys at this old-time pub. It was a good team building night. We should go there, you'd like it."

"I suppose you need a night out like that once in a while."

Something's off. "It was a late night, but not too late. Home around one and I just got up thinking of you."

"That's nice," she says.

"I'm going to head to the ballpark soon but needed to hear your voice first."

"Well, okay. We can talk later. I've got some work to do for now."

"Uh, okay. Something wrong?" I ask.

"No, nothing. Just busy, that's all."

"Okay dear. Talk to you soon."

"Okay, bye."

"Bye." No, I love you, miss you... just bye. The story must have already leaked.

I jump on my laptop and search *TC Hunter rumors*. I instantly get a hit: *TC Hunter Parties With Mystery Blonde*.

Shit! I completely forgot about that. I click the link and the picture is perfectly timed. There I am with an attractive blonde falling into my lap, my arms out catching her. The *goddamn internet*.

I immediately dial Jen and my call goes to voicemail. I don't leave a message. I looked at the clock and it's almost noon. *You know what, fuck this!* I've got a game to prepare for and I'm not going to grovel. I can see how Jen would be upset, and she likely thinks I'm hiding something from her. But can I get a little benefit of the doubt? This is exactly the kind of distraction I need to avoid.

I grab my keys and start out the door. Throwing my phone on the kitchen counter provides some satisfaction. No calls and no bullshit today. Instead, I make my way to the sanctuary of the stadium where I belong.

I drive a little out of the way to pass the site of the incident. The daylight makes everything appear normal, although I do see a police car parked at the Chinese restaurant. I hope the officers at the scene are there to investigate a generic carjacking and don't know that I'm the victim.

A county municipal work truck parked at the corner of the block and several workers survey the broken streetlights for repair. I counted five smashed lights, all with the lamps cracked by thrown rocks or other projectiles. The boys must have decent aim or at least some perseverance to have broken the small fixtures standing twenty-five feet or more above the street.

The sight of the stadium puts me at further ease. Once absorbed in preparation for the game I'd forget about Jen, the drunk blonde and the unfortunate incident on the city streets.

It's still early, yet several cars are parked in the player lot. A dozen or so players are at the stadium to get extra work, and I take it as a good sign given the previous night. My teammates showed discipline last night and are ready to go.

Bobby Mitchell struts around the locker room with no signs of impairment. He immediately thanks me for treating the boys to a fun night at the pub. As it turns out, he struck out with the blonde who fell into my lap, and he left the bar about a half hour after I departed.

He's working on drag bunting. Bobby appreciates how I can drop a bunt against the shift to get an easy base hit, and he wants to master the technique. That's music to my ears, and I tell him I'll meet him down by the cage to offer some tips.

Before heading out to the batting cage I walk by Billy Law's office. There are several reporters in the room and Billy looks to be holding court. He likes to do these sessions because it gives the press weekly time in front of the manager. Giving writers ample access prevents being ambushed at inconvenient times, at least that's Billy's strategy.

Billy jokes with the crowd of reporters that includes beat writers from the *Philadelphia Inquirer*, the *Tribune*, and the *Daily News*. Eavesdropping, I hear one of the sportswriters use the term "Billy Ball," a term coined many years ago for the style of baseball implemented by the late, great manager Yankee skipper Billy Martin. He forced a super aggressive playing style upon the league that emphasized base stealing and hustle. Hit and runs, squeeze plays, even stealing home were a possibility with Martin at the helm, and his style took the league by storm.

Similarly, Billy Law does much of the same, and he's proud of the label. By emphasizing old-school attributes, our team bucks the modern trend of computer model baseball. The antagonistic style of play is an anomaly given the current state of the league.

"How about we call it Law Ball," I hear Billy say. Out of deference to Billy Martin he prefers a nuanced label, and the reporters like the idea. I don't care what you call it as long as we continue to win.

Billy waves me into his office. "Get your ass in here, T. Our reporter friends want a few words with you."

My first thought is that the police leaked the carjacking incident, but I realize Billy would not be smiling if that were the case.

"I'm headed to take some extra batting practice, but I have a few minutes," I say.

"Great start to the season. Any comments on the team and how Billy is managing?" one of the reporters opens.

A generic question deserves a cliché answer, so I say, "Billy's the best manager in the game and the team is off to a good start. We take it one day at a time and just try to win ballgames."

The *Daily News* guy asks, "We were just talking about some of the changes in the league. Care to comment on any of that?"

"What are you referring to? Rules changes?"

"Yeah, can you comment on the rules changes as well as your general philosophy of the league and how you play?"

I've sparred with this reporter about several things during past interviews, but I find him cerebral with a deep knowledge of the game. I enjoy our back and forth. "You know how I feel about the rules changes. The game doesn't need changing."

"What specifically don't you like?"

"I don't like any of it. Look, there was no reason to limit the shift, enlarge the bases or implement a pitch clock. But keep watching. Rushed pitchers and the robo strike zone creates more mistakes. Good hitters will have teams begging for mercy." The reporters all laughed at that one as does Billy. I continue. "As far as putting a clock on baseball, that's the dumbest thing I've ever heard. Baseball is a game of incredible talent and skill, but it's also psychological warfare. The game is as much a drama as it is a sport, and to limit that aspect just might ruin the game."

Like many, sportswriters don't think, they accept. I continue. "Taking the concentration and gamesmanship out baseball fundamentally changes the sport! It really is an insult to tradition and the players of old."

"They say it will bring more fans."

"First of all, I think that's bullshit. Who are they and what's their agenda?" I ask, using logic I learned from Chief. "Pitchers throwing a hundred miles an hour need as much time as required to concentrate. I'm mean Christ, anybody ever think of that? In the meantime, look at how Billy's got us playing. We are old school, aggressive and fun to watch."

"Other teams aren't fun to watch?" another reporter asks.

I take the bait. "Frankly, no, some teams are run by people who have never put a jockstrap on in their lives. Rules changes and analytics, geez, they'll make the games unwatchable like other professional sports. Hopefully, the league someday comes to its senses."

"So you think baseball is being threatened?"

Threatened? "The game has been the same for a century plus many decades, and each time the wizards in the front offices get involved, they screw it up. Put the clocks and computers away and leave the game alone."

I field a few more questions and try to stay away from anything too controversial. Of course, they asked about a potential contract extension and free agency, but I remain elusive.

They also veer into statistics and records, already talking about the single-season homerun mark. I hate that I'm being looked upon as the savior from the steroid era, so I emphasize how I have little interest in records and numbers.

The writers want to chat more, and Billy takes a facial cue and gets me off the hook. "Although I'm sure he'd like to continue talking to you fellas, T has some extra hitting to do," my witty manager exclaims.

Thankfully, the carjacking incident is under wraps, at least for now.

Extra hitting and helping Bobby Mitchell with his bunting put me back in baseball mode. With nothing particular on the agenda, yet in need of grounding perspective, I head down the tunnel to see Chief.

"Hey, you get shitfaced last night?" Chief asks.

"Nah, only had one drink. Team bonding, that's all."

"What's your poison these days?" he asks. "You still a rye whiskey guy or have you gone pansy on me with them mixed drinks I see all over the place?"

"Straight whiskey, maybe an occasional boxcar or whiskey sour."

"Are you sure you didn't get sauced?"

"No. Had one drink at the bar." I'm not lying.

"Is your girl back in town? Maybe you didn't sleep a lot last night. I'd have trouble sleeping if I were you too."

"No, not that either. Do I really look that bad?"

Chief ponders a bit. Scratching his scruffy beard, his expression changes to concern. "Hmmm, I guess not. Looks like a bunch of shit spinning in your head though."

My old friend has a knack for nailing my outlook, although I had no interest in talking about Jennifer, nor do I feel compelled to get the carjacking incident off my chest. Instead, I change the subject.

"Those are some pictures from your dad's scrapbook, Chief."

"Serious nostalgia there, right?"

"The pictures on the field are incredible, but I keep thinking about the photos of the players when they were off the field. The players all look sophisticated and happy."

"Yeah, guess so. It was a different time back then, much simpler."

"Think those guys had problems? I mean, what kind of stuff did they deal with?"

"Problems? Everyone has problems, TC."

"Any have psychological issues that you know?"

"Psychological? I guess so. You know, many of the old greats drank too much. Ruth was a big partier and might have faced some demons. Drinking eventually killed Mantle. Your namesakes seemed like gents who had things buzzing around in the noggin. All the greats were, you know, isolated in a way."

Isolated, an interesting word. Chief continues. "I already told you about Aaron and the garbage he had to deal with. Mays, Robinson, Doby, and all the Black players dealt with nonsense that would make anyone a little crazy. As if sent from Heaven, Jackie Robinson preceded the country back in 1947. It was almost a guy named Monte Irvin instead of Jackie, did you know that? Think about it, America followed the game. I think baseball was destined to be at the forefront of the fight for equality."

No encyclopedia provides that perspective. Chief knows all the numbers and statistics, but I like listening to the other aspects. He has direct insights on some players, and roundabout information on many others. Chief knows the back stories and speaks without a filter.

"Look at Ty Cobb. You talk about a guy that had to deal with demons. Geez, his mother popped his father, you think he might have had some mental issues to deal with?"

"I'm sure he did," I say. "I'll bet most of the greats had demons. Just the pressures of being great all the time is enough to drive someone mad in this game." Chief flashes a quizzical look. He senses I'm talking as much about myself as players from the past. He tends to squint and look away when gathering his thoughts, and when he gives that look he usually comes up with something profound.

"Now, the *immortals*," he says. "Well, how could you not have issues when you are an immortal?"

"*Immortal?*"

"Well, yeah. There are greats, and then there are immortals. Some people leave their mark on the world and are legends that never die, they are immortal. If you listen close enough, past generations speak to you."

Immortals never die. The door opens to explain what I'm experiencing, but releasing my burden is something that I just can't seem to do. Instinctively, Chief saves me from myself and abruptly changes the subject.

"Hey, you know that Jennifer lady is good for you. You've changed since she's been around. Pretty young thing, too."

"Yeah, she's fantastic. But she might be more trouble than it's worth."

"Hell, TC, there's nothing good in this world that's easy. From what I've seen, she steadies you and makes you better. And I think you know it," Chief says with a tinge of anger.

"I do."

"Then don't fuck it up! A woman like that doesn't come around very often," he scolds. I'm surprised he's so invested in the topic. Chief rarely veers into my love life.

"You know I'm in mourning, right?"

"No, I'm sorry Chief." His wife died about twenty years ago and I never asked any details or inquire about other women in his life.

"Yup, been in mourning," he says, pausing for effect. "For my dick! It's been dead for ten years!" His cackle bellows through the room and out the hall. Clearly, he's been saving that one for a while.

Doubled over from his own joke, I let him have his belly laugh. My sight line falls to a plaque hanging on the wall above my hysterical friend. The saying on the plaque is from former big-league pitcher and author Jim Bouton and it reads, "*You spend a good piece of your life gripping a baseball and in the end it turns out it was the other way around all the time.*"

Chief stops laughing and catches my stare. Baseball grips both of our lives and has made us kindred spirits. I'm sure at that moment Chief understands how much I appreciate his wealth of knowledge, his humor and his friendship.

CHAPTER 15

I TAKE ANOTHER early morning jog to forget the latest imagery flowing through my subconscious. The previous day we had a very quick game, a two-hour 3-0 shutout win so I was back at my apartment by 10:30 pm. The early game gave me an opportunity to catch up on some sleep and counter the exhaustion of another inconvenient 3:48 am wake up.

This time the episode centers on being stuck in a falling plane with perished baseball players. The famed Korean War hero still piloted the plane to safety, this time with a large digital clock above the cockpit repeatedly counting down from fifteen seconds.

The man beside me introduces himself as Elmer, and he's less panicked by the ordeal than my previous companion in a previous plane-crashing episode. Every so often he glanced over, appearing to have something to say before turning away and calmly looking forward. Finally, the man beside me turns and exclaims, *"You know, she's worth saving!"*

This is about Jennifer? The plane banks hard into a final descent, and I find myself more relaxed than my initial experience. I know how the scene ends, and it takes the pilot's bark to snap me to attention. *"It's the foolhardy that ignore reason and truth. We're running out of time and teetering on the brink kid. It's time to be bold. You have to save us!"*

⚾ ⚾ ⚾

I let the brisk air fill my lungs as I jog the familiar path along the Delaware River. Although cold, there's little wind off the water, making for ideal conditions. When running while consumed by a broad range of emotions I often find myself in a dead sprint. Caught up in the bewilderment of another cryptic message, I make a conscious effort to ease my pace as I pass the many piers and storage warehouses lining the waterway. Jogging fires the synapses, sprinting just fatigues.

Immeasurably distracted, I make it all the way into South Philadelphia, stopping briefly at the Greenwich Marine Terminal. There's a flurry of activity in the early morning on the many piers as large shipping containers are loaded and unloaded. Huge barges move in and out of the port in a world that I find both fascinating and foreign.

I estimate I'm seven miles into a run that started near Penn Treaty Park and goes beyond both the Benjamin Franklin Bridge and the Walt Whitman Bridge. Given the circumstances, I have even more restless energy to burn and focus on my mental trauma instead of worrying about the repercussions of the long jaunt.

As I turn to start the trek back north, I remain distracted by the image of the pilot. As a young boy, Ted Williams was an idol, and his influence can never be understated. His iconic voice and mannerisms cemented my adoration, though it's his private side I find most intriguing.

A reporter once suggested he was just like the characters that John Wayne played in the movies, and the legend Williams confidently responded, "Yeah, I know." The brash self-confidence only contributed to his legend, and I was filled with awe each time I heard him speak. He commanded the room, and he was an unabashed patriot who demanded respect.

Now, he haunts me as do some of the others. They taunt me in my imagination from the stands or through some perverted dream. They occupy my thoughts in such a way that keep me in search of answers to rhetorical riddles.

Using a large ship dock off in the distance I sprint past the stern, reverting to a jog once I reach my arbitrary goal. Slowing the pace, but with my mind still racing, I consider Williams, Cobb, Aaron, and many other players that fit Chief's description of legends and immortals. Their spirits remain well after they are gone, and their historic exploits are mythologic.

I continue the early morning run wondering how any of this contributes to my twisted psychosis. The premonitions, the self-fulfilling prophesies, the calls to action, and the insomnia may never end, and I don't know how much more I can tolerate. Void of any incidents for a good amount of time, my mind hits back with a vengeance. Each time I feel under control, I get slapped back to this fantasy where the madness in my soul overlaps with reality.

"Teetering on the brink," I say out loud, seeing the breath from my muttered words in the cold morning air. The pitch clock above the pilot alludes to a finite amount of time in which I'm to act. As if I need more pressure in my life, I'm implored to challenge conventional truths.

Does any of this have to do with the bump in the road with Jennifer? Everyone seems to be interested in my love life, and she is worth saving. I recently saved my own life during the carjacking incident, so that might be relevant. The helpless despair spurred by the thought that I have to keep Jen safe seems a superficial explanation.

I'm anxious to call Jennifer after my run. Still too early in the morning I practice the conversation to effectively illustrate the misunderstanding. The night out and my omission about the picture in the context of the carjacking should squash any thought that I was doing something behind her back. I did hide the carjacking, but that was to keep her from worrying.

I consider again if I might be able to divulge my psychological problems, but my gut tells me it's impossible to let her into that world. *Um, hello Jen, are you sitting down? Yeah, last night I was flying with all of the baseball players who died in a plane crash. We started to dive toward the earth, but not to worry because we had a great pilot who saved the day. Oh, and by the way I dabble with clairvoyance, and I sometimes see spirits walking the streets.* Yeah, I don't think so.

After killing time showering and having breakfast, it's still early. Even though I risk waking her, I dial Jen's number. Again, the call went to voicemail.

◎ ◎ ◎

I see Dr. Joe Nelson at his desk. He's going back and forth between studying something on his laptop and taking notes on a yellow legal pad. Although he looks busy, I knock on the door and enter.

I have not sat with Dr. Joe for some time, and he stops to greet me. This time, he's even more cheerful and animated, as if he had prescribed himself some of his own medication. Nobody wants a depressed therapist, so the liveliness works. We exchange greetings and he states that I looked terrible. *Hey thanks Doc, much appreciated.*

We talk for a bit about my sleep habits, stopping short of details. He has a good grip on my circumstances as it relates to free agency and my emergence as a fan and media darling, so he attempts to explain why I might be losing sleep. He speaks of the feelings of obligation that I might be saddled with, along with the pressures of continuing my stellar performance, free agency, records, etc. He touches on some things contributing to my problems, but nothing that's news to me.

I nod at the blanket analysis and don't openly discount what he says, even if it's merely conventional wisdom. For insomnia, he suggested melatonin, and he assures me there is a natural type made from animal glands. *Well, that sounds wonderful and yummy.* He suggests a prescription if I should change my mind, which for the first time I didn't immediately discount. Putting an engineered supplement in my body is better than having a nervous breakdown so maybe there would come a time to reconsider taking a drug.

I thanked the good doctor and head to batting practice. Walking toward the locker room I try Jen once more. The call goes to voicemail and I again hang up. I have a game to play and have already allowed myself too much distraction.

By game time my head is screwed on better, and when my foot leaves the top dugout step, I'm back to business. Even with plenty of excuses I'm simply not going to allow outside influences to impact my performance.

It's the third game of the series and Pittsburgh starts another hard-throwing rookie. Marty Krank is one of the team's best pitching prospects and keeps us off balance for much of the game.

My at bats were solid and I finish with two hits, a triple down the right field line and a bunt single. As a team we hit into some bad luck, leaving a bunch of runners on base, including a two out, bases loaded line drive that I hit in the seventh inning. The left fielder made an acrobatic diving catch that saved the game. Despite losing the final game of the set 3-2, the squad played well.

Walking by Billy Law's office I pick up on a conversation that I'm certain is about me. Billy's on the phone, presumably with the general manager, or maybe even the team owner. The conversation ends something to the effect that the best thing to do is to leave me alone. The brass are once again upset that I attempted bunting during the game.

My next home run would be the 300th of my career, setting a record for the youngest player to reach the mark. I only knew about the record because my young friend, Ethan, had texted me the tidbit. Management is getting on Billy because they wanted me to hit the three hundred mark while playing in front of the Philadelphia fans.

"I'll hit a fuckin' home run tomorrow on the road," I shout through the door opening, clearly loud enough to be heard on the other end of the phone. Billy's not amused and slams the door shut.

I'll apologize to Billy later, but screw those guys. They don't have to sign me if they don't appreciate how I play. For the next home stand, maybe I'll make a point and have the public address announcer switch my walkup song from Kenny Chesney's "Summertime" to Frank Sinatra's song "My Way". I'm in no mood to deal with this nonsense.

After a quick shower I bolt from the ballpark and check my phone. No word from Jen. Though tempted to drop another line, I opt to stick to my guns; she'll have to call me if and when she cools down.

Tom left a series of texts, all contract related. *Philly sending over an updated offer. Came in stronger. They know they have no choice but to pay up. They are bitching every time you bunt. Call me later tonight to review.*

So they bitch about my bunting, yet they make a better offer? I'll let Tom figure out the negotiations. It's a cat and mouse game and he's the alpha tiger. We would be doing ourselves a disservice if we didn't listen, but I'm not sure any offer trumps my new reluctance about living in Philadelphia.

I race home and settle into my living room surprised at how enthusiastic my agent sounded. With each game, I gain more prominence and the organization is feeling pressure from the fans to lock me up with a new deal. Tom calls, exuberant over the newest offer, but with a slightly admonishing tone.

"If they like me so much, why the hell are they bitching when I bunt, Tom?"

"Look, they wanted you to hit the milestone home run at the home ballpark. They were planning on stopping the game, retrieving the ball, well, you know the drill."

"I don't pay attention to any of that stuff, Tom. You know that."

"Well, you should!"

Chief pushes me to pay more attention to such things as well, sometimes even getting angry when I blow it off. The sportswriters also focus on record books, and now Tom digs in.

"Come on, TC, you get their perspective. They need fans to be happy and you hitting number three hundred would have given them a moment of celebration."

Tom, Chief, and the writer are right, but they do not understand other worries are taking priority. Although excited about the progress of the new contract offer, Tom already declined it on my behalf. Still, he debated whether to leak the terms to the press to generate buzz. That might better indicate the pulse of the fans.

"Do whatever you feel is best, Tom," I respond, wholeheartedly trusting his instincts and judgment.

Before we hung up Tom mentions the carjacking and that there were preliminary hearings scheduled for the perpetrators. They found the other kids involved, but it was nothing I need to concern myself with. He praises the detectives working the case for keeping the story out of the press.

My head still spinning from another peculiar day, the choice is between a tumbler full of whiskey or making another call to Jennifer. I decided on the drink. Off the next day it feels like one of those nights where passing out might be the best course of action.

Torture is the only word that comes to mind. This time it feels more like an innocuous dream until I check my phone and see it's witching hour again—3:48 am. Feeling groggy I struggle from the couch and knock over a near-empty whiskey bottle on the coffee table. This bout feels mild in comparison to the previous night, yet I'm angry and disappointed for needing to manage another occurrence.

My legs are wobbly from my binge. I don't know when I officially passed out in the living room, but I remember hanging up with Tom and then thinking about Jennifer as I sucked down my favorite hard liquor.

I throw open the sliding door leading to the small balcony and cold air instantly fills the room. Horizontal sheets of rain pound the building but don't deter me from stepping onto the terrace. The rain mixed with sleet makes the deck slippery and my body nearly slides out from under me. The heavy wrought iron rail stops my slide, snaring my left arm, and I wonder if the coroner would rule my death an accident or suicide.

Off in the distance I see glowing bursts of lightning, which I find a novel occurrence in the morning's cold. The storm clouds are pitch black and appear low in the sky making it feel more like a Florida thunderstorm than a miserable Northeast frozen rain.

The cold rain pelts my face and I sit on a soaked lounge chair in the corner of the deck. Strong gusts of freezing air whip me. Drenched with rain and sitting alone in the cold darkness I fantasized that a strong squall would sweep me away, or that maybe a bolt of lightning will strike just right.

So much for remaining even keeled, I think. My bipolarity is nothing I can command. I remain at the mercy of my warped brain, again forced to review esoteric imagery from my soul.

The dream I had tonight took me to a desolate beach where I was enveloped in isolation and seeking any sign of humanity. Off in the distance I noticed black smoke from a smoldering fire and although it felt daunting, I headed directly for the blaze. Breaking into a swift jog I moved across the endless span, drawn to the only noticeable break in the barren wasteland.

Finally reaching the fire, embers beneath my feet turned the sand scorching hot. I hopped toward a small group up ahead. They were sheltered from the heat and halfway toward the foursome I recognized my parents. They were kneeling in the sand and tossing the cinders from a pile of *New York Times* newspapers.

I recognized the other couple from pictures. Jennifer's mother and father stood beside my parents, encouraging them to throw the burnt papers farther from the cluster. I awoke when I reached out to my father, desperate to contact the man that had most influenced my life.

Soaked and shivering I finally move back into the apartment and strip off my clothes. I grab a towel from the bathroom and pat myself dry before moving back to the living room. I briefly consider grabbing another bottle of liquor, but instead curl into the corner of the couch, naked and distraught. Somehow, I manage to fall back asleep.

I rise from the catnap at 11:00 am. Conscious that I had broken my pattern and slept through the morning I search my emotions. Somewhat appreciative of the extended rest, I'm frightened at my dulled emotions. Finding meaning in the dream seems futile.

Out the sliding glass doors to the balcony the sun has risen above the horizon and the storm has passed. Naked with a pile of waterlogged clothes on the floor, I feel undignified and alone. I grab the wet pile and make my way to the bathroom to wring out the clothes and take a shower.

The hot water hitting my face feels invigorating, and I adjust the nozzle so that the beads pulse. I move my head around for what must have been five minutes, absorbed in the staccato rhythm of the water. The steam rises from the shower floor and fills my nostrils as I inhale deeply. The shower lasts almost a half hour, and only then do I feel somewhat normal. Finally lucent, I dress.

A good amount of rain came in from the open balcony door, and I use several towels to soak up the puddles. A near empty whiskey bottle rests on the floor and the tumbler I used is filled with water from a melted ice cube. At some point I must have been drinking directly from the bottle; what an embarrassing display.

Back to the kitchen I chug a V8 and a bottle of cold water. I fill the bottle again and take a couple more gulps with two capsules of Advil from the side drawer. Since I use the anti-inflammatory sparingly, I know my body will snap back quickly with the two pills and rehydration.

I take my hunger as a good sign, so I fry four eggs to eat with some toast. Checking my phone, I notice a missed phone call and a text from Jennifer. She must have reached out when I was in the shower. *Good morning, Ted. Call me when you have a chance.*

It's best to not read tone into a text, but I'm cautiously optimistic.

Before I call, I rehearse where I'll go with the conversation. I decide that I'd tell her details about the woman in the picture as well as the carjacking but leave out passing out on the couch and waking up naked and distressed.

In need of sustenance, I quickly eat my breakfast before calling. She picks up on the first ring.

"Hello, Ted."

"It's good to hear your voice, Jen."

"Sorry, but I needed a little time."

"I understand." I want to hear what she says before explaining the situation.

"Seeing that picture set me back. The way things have been I never thought I'd have to deal with those types of feelings. Been there and done that, and it felt like a punch in the gut."

"Jen, I—"

"Ted, let me finish. I don't know what happened with that woman, but it doesn't matter. The disappointment is enough. You know how you say that you don't want distractions, well neither do I and where my mind took me at that moment was demoralizing."

"You know what, Jen? I fully understand. You hadn't called me back in a couple of days and I could be asking what you were doing and who you were with?"

"Now that's not fair."

"Maybe not, but why does trust go one way?"

"Ted, there was a picture on the internet of you holding someone else on your lap. I realize you are this big star, and this type of thing might happen to you all the time, but it's not something that works for me."

"Really?" I shoot back, no longer looking to hold my lip. "It was a setup, Jen. I was out with the team and a group of women were drunk and she faked tripping and fell on top of me. One of the others in the bunch clicked a picture and they all had a good laugh over it."

There was silence on the other end of the phone as she pondered what I was saying. It likely sounded like a stereotypical male lie, but I continued. "If I'm going to be held responsible for what someone else does or says, then let's forget it. I'm not about to take the blame for something completely out of my control."

"Even if what you say happened is true, I'm not sure if I can handle stuff like this."

"Even if? Let me tell you something, Jen, I actually made a mental note to tell you what happened, and I forgot because I left the pub right after and ended up in the middle of a carjacking attempt. Some punk pointed a gun at my head."

"What are you talking about? What happened?"

"I'll tell you another time. I'm too riled up and I'm sure you'll see it announced on social media at some point."

"I'm sorry, Ted. I had no idea."

"Thinking of you I got shit-face drunk last night. I sat alone in my apartment and drank myself dizzy worrying about you, worrying about us. Thankfully we have an off day today or who knows where my mind would be. I'm emotionally spent as it is, and now this?"

"Ted, I don't know what to say."

"Neither do I. Maybe we've both said enough." I did nothing wrong and didn't feel like spending more energy on the subject. My tortured mind tells me she's worth saving, but another part of me wants to consider the whole thing a failed experiment.

CHAPTER 16

AFTER A DAY off and then a three-game set in New York we're off to Florida. Losing two of three in New York, the squad is facing our first tinge of disappointment. Although we played solid baseball, we came up just short in the two losses. Road games in the league are tough, and the travel can catch up with a team, but we didn't have to look for excuses for the series. We just got beat a couple of times by a rival with each game possibly going either way with a bounce here or an inch there. That's baseball.

The team's charter flight is set for 9:00 am, so we'll be in Miami a little before noon, plenty of time to settle in and prep for the game later tonight. We have a dress code when traveling, so I throw several tailored suits in a garment bag and pack toiletries and incidentals. I'm anxious to get to the warmer weather, so with time to kill and energy to burn I leave for the stadium. The early morning jaunt is peaceful and there's something stimulating about the stadium under a rising sun.

Physical torment and extra hitting are a remedy for just about anything. I first hit the weight room and alter my routine for several higher weight sets on the bench press and squat rack. My demons abound, the lifting, straining and grunting provide primal relief and a reboot for my soul.

Clicking the main breaker, the spotlights are initially blinding. It took a moment for my eyes to adjust from the pitch-black darkness, but the familiar environs of the indoor batting cages eventually come into focus. It's time for the second phase of corporeal therapy, and I draw comfort from the solitude of the empty stadium and the explosive echo of the ball hitting the bat.

An effective baseball swing has a certain cadence resulting in perfect synchronization between upper and lower body. When my rhythm is right, my hands are back and my lower body ignites my swing, firing the bat barrel through the hitting zone with each repetition. I used a hitting tee to work on different areas of the strike zone, taking at least a hundred swings to reinforce my rhythm and balance.

Next, I set a pitching machine to throw blistering fastballs and continue in seclusion to further the boon to my psyche. Each loud thwack of the ball striking the bat reinforces the principle that carries me to prominence. *Work ethic is the one thing you can control, so don't ever let anyone outwork you!* Perfection is unachievable in baseball, but while others remain idle, each swing gets me closer to my personal ceiling.

Hitting until stains of blood are noticeable through my batting gloves is exhausting, yet indescribably fulfilling. I might have continued hitting until my hands fell off but heard, "Damn kid, you are hitting the shit out of it today. Taking out some aggressions?"

Taking a short break from his equipment duties, Chief's interruption is well timed. Removing my batting gloves reveal several popped blood blisters turning my hands crimson. Chief motions toward my hands and nods skeptically. Sizing me up, he moves his eyes up and down my frame.

"Let me guess, you're still having woman problems."

"Nothing I can't handle," I say. The old man knows me well and has an uncanny way of pinning me down.

Chief ponders that for a moment before asking, "Are you sleeping better? You haven't texted me at the wee hours of the morning lately."

"I'm doing okay. I still have my insomnia at times, but I figured I'd stop bothering you."

"Well, thanks for that, I guess. You think you were checking up on me, but it helped me check up on you!" Chief says with a chuckle.

"I'm fine, my friend."

"Would you tell me otherwise?"

"Probably not," I joke. "No, I'd tell you if something was up. Everything is fine."

Even though Chief isn't buying it, I know he'll leave me be.

The palm trees zip by as the plane touches down in South Florida. It feels great to be back in the land of the free and the state I consider home. It's near ninety-degrees as we depart the plane.

I prefer the west coast of Florida, but with its Latin vibe and high-end areas I also enjoy the luxurious atmosphere of Miami. The region has a distinct feel, not quite fast paced like New York or other cities, but with the same degree of excessiveness that I find entertaining.

Typically, the organization places us in less noticeable environs and away from the downtown areas of a city, but when in Miami Billy Law insists on the Ritz Carlton in Key Biscayne. The resort feel is conducive to team bonding and the Ritz is exclusive enough that we don't get hassled by fans.

Billy is an avid golfer and I'm sure already has plans with some of the other players to be on the links during down time. My preference is checking out the opulent local marinas and beaches; golf is just not my thing. No matter the preference, the next couple days will serve as a mini vacation for the squad, and a much-needed break from the mundane.

The team checks into the hotel, and with a couple of hours to kill the players mostly mill about the lobby, pool or beach. I walked around a bit to get reacquainted with the hotel layout before finding a seat in the lounge of the hotel lobby. The chaise I find is in a perfect spot for people watching.

I notice a business luncheon in a cordoned off spot. It looks like a fancy lunch with several trays of Dungeness crab claws, large shrimp and lobster tails on ice being carted to the area. The drinks flow, and I assume the event is more for show than for any practical business reason.

To my left I notice a vacationing family of four. Before heading to the beach, the matriarch insists everyone put on sunscreen and turn off their electronic devices. The kids ignore their mother and like drones scroll through the phones held inches away from their face.

I sympathize with the mom. Times have changed. Seeking acknowledgment from strangers on social media has replaced human interaction and becomes the mark of popularity and self-worth. Cognitive skills decline, but kids convince themselves of their value as long as their electronic approvals meet a certain threshold, replacing religion, work ethic, and human interaction. I might not have all my faculties at the moment, but I still feel better off than those trapped in the phony world of social media.

To the right, a couple walking hand in hand draw my attention. They look carefree, laughing and seemingly in love. Jennifer lives about four hours away, so I'd be foolish to think she might stop by uninvited. Still, I find myself looking toward every brown-haired woman in hope it might be her.

I noticed the team bus to the stadium is already parked out front. Checking my watch, I still have a few minutes but decide to begin gathering my personal items for the game. Standing by the lobby elevators is a man dressed in a three-piece suit looking in my direction. He has an impish face and stands about six feet tall. He smiles in my direction and bounces into the elevator car just as several other hotel guests exit.

I double time my steps in desperate effort to catch up with the man. The doors began to shut and I'm still several yards away, however I caught his stare. Smiling, he raises an eyebrow and tilts his head curiously just as the barrier completely closed.

Frustrated, I chase down backup catcher, Maddox Colfer, who was part of the small group that exited the elevator when the man got in. "Mad Dog! Did you see that guy heading into the elevator?"

"What guy?"

"The guy in the brown three-piece suit. Did you happen to see his face?"

"Sorry, TC, I didn't notice anyone."

The man's dress and look would not be inconspicuous in a Miami hotel. Anyone paying the least bit of attention would have noticed him, yet Maddox saw no one. My face shows great concern as I reassure our catcher that I'm fine. Maddox reluctantly goes about his business.

Watching the lights above the elevator door, I see that the car stops at the twenty-third floor. I double checked the jacket from my room key, and I see that I too am on that floor. Quickly, I hit the up button to summon the elevator, determined to find that man.

After some time, the elevator car finally heads back to the lobby. I watch the elevator slowly settle. The door opens and as expected there's only one person aboard. Anticipating a face to face with the gentleman, I instead stand before a beautiful blond woman wearing a long, black formal dress. For a moment, I think it's the woman from the pub who had inadvertently caused the current struggles in my personal life, but a closer look indicates a strikingly beautiful lady with sapphire eyes and classic elegance. Most certainly not the acquaintance from the pub, she looks more like a movie star from a different time and place.

Taken aback I move to the side to let her pass. Confused and disappointed, I step into the elevator and hit the button for the twenty-third floor. Sunk back and leaning against the elevator wall I watch as the woman pauses in the vestibule to look about.

Two men round the corner of the hallway connecting the elevators and the hotel lobby, one dressed in a black pinstripe suit. With his hair slicked back and a pencil-thin mustache, he too has movie star looks. He saunters over to meet his lady. Content, the natural beauty tilts her head up when she finds her beau.

Noticing my gaze, the man calls out, "Never let the right woman go." The elegant man then smiles before kissing the woman on her cheek. Offering his arm, he escorts the blonde away. The other gentleman is the mystery man. As he approaches I swear it is the Georgia Peach himself. Cobb seems friendly with the couple as the trio head off to some affair. With a wink Cobb says, "Don't matter what the cranks say, there are several things as important as baseball. But, hey, you have a great game tonight kid!"

Paralyzed and jaw agape, the last thought I have before the elevator door finally closes is that nobody else in the vicinity seems to have noticed Cobb or his two glamorous companions. And why did the elevator door remain open for so long?

We pull up to the stadium and swing around to the side of the building to dock the bus. Before deboarding, I check my phone and find no messages. The clock reads 3:48 pm and immediately changes to 3:49 pm, leaving me angry at the notion of unrelenting, wicked games.

If this isn't what going mad feels like, at the very least it must be a precursor to ending up in the loony bin. Fixated on the figures from the lobby and preoccupied with events from the last several days, I feel like I'm chasing my own tail. Throw in personal relationship drama and damn if it doesn't feel like there's no way out.

In the visitors' clubhouse I quickly dress into my uniform and settle to gather my thoughts. Music blasts from the stadium speakers as the home team finishes with pregame batting practice. Several cell phone texts from Chief provide further interruption.

Recently, Chief's been habitually texting obscure messages and provocative links. I don't know if he finds the articles interesting or if he's just pissed off, but sending current event articles is new. He's attempting to make a point, although I can't tell if he's trying to educate me or if he's simply bored.

Anytime I ask him about biased or incendiary news reports, he mutters something cryptic about the First Amendment, the free flow of information, or the weaponization of government. Every so often he throws in a tidbit about communists taking over the country, or neutered masculinity of our populous. His rants are entertaining if not informative, so I let him ramble.

I gloss over the first couple of links. The first an account of a millennial being uncomfortable with the playing of the "Star Spangled Banner," the second a *Wall Street Journal* poll indicating the decline of patriotism throughout the country.

An intriguing link about a former hockey great captures my interest. The link he sent this time is about former hockey great, Theo Fleury, challenging government overreach in Canada. Fleury describes himself as an empath who feels the emotions of others at such a deep level that he takes on the stress and anxiety of the population. With the government moving in the direction of restricting freedom, he fights for the people because their emotions are in unison.

Science is divided as to whether empaths actually exist, although Fleury is adamant, they do so because of something called *mirror neurons*. He insists the differing brain function allows him to echo the feelings and emotions of the people in a disheartened country.

Could it be that I have abnormal brain neurons too? Conflicted brain function is as good a theory as any for the cause of my trauma. Perhaps I'm reaching a bit, though I'm perplexed why Chief sent the link. He doesn't know of my issues and usually reserves his editorials for the numerous things he feels are dividing the country. Is he trying to get me to be more like Fleury? Beyond his political slant, is that what he's trying to accomplish by sending the articles?

On cue, another text appears from Chief, who is at home in Philly because he doesn't travel with the team. It snaps me into game mode. *Watch the back door slider tonight. Wynd is throwing tons of them.* Our opponent's starting pitcher was a wily veteran with over a dozen years of big-league experience. Despite his craftiness, my track record against the big right hander includes a couple of monster games.

I tend to remember my at bats with a photographic memory. Vividly, I recall a game a few years back where I smashed two doubles and a home run against the pitcher. With over fifty career at bats against Wynd there's clear familiarity with his pitches. However, his outings have been different of late, backing off his sinker and throwing many more sliders than usual.

A subsequent text from Chief reads, *I'll bet you a sawbuck he starts you with one on your first at bat.*

You're on!

Friendly wagers are part of our relationship. This one is more of a sucker bet that favors Chief since the pitcher's recent patterns suggest he will try to get me to chase an outside slider on the first pitch. Still, it was a win-win for me. If he throws me the pitch, I'll be looking for it and nail it for a hit. Happily, I'll exchange a hit for a couple bucks.

It's a bet. Now let's hope you no longer look like litter box cat shit and you have a big day.

Chief's wording is entertaining to say the least and I text back, *Double or nothing that I get at least three hits tonight.* I'll bet on myself anytime. On the diamond I feel no self-doubt and it's where I find steadiness and hope.

"Bet is on!"

The first pitch is a back door slider that I slash down the left field line. Chief was of course right and I'll bet he knew what I would do with the pitch. It's the first of four hits on the day, including a bunt base hit, a single to center and then a home run later in the game when the pitcher tried to come inside with a fastball. My bet with Chief is a wash after the double-or-nothing proposition. He's happy with the result since he maintains bragging rights while I have a great day for the team.

After going four for four, my batting average spikes to .438, and the home run deep into the right field seats extends the league lead. My supposition is playing out in real time, and I am outguessing the opposition with every at bat. Even though it's very early in the season, I'm ecstatic, effectively displaying both power and a high batting average. Notwithstanding the personal madness, the episodes, the contract negotiation pressures, the girlfriend issues, and the complete nuttiness that has become my life, I am able to play the game in a way that meets my standards.

Sitting on a bench in the visitor's clubhouse, my play had me settle with satisfaction. A text from the young boy Ethan reads, *Awesome game. See you soon.* The text makes me remember that Ethan will be at the Tampa game in a few days. Jennifer helped set him up with first-class treatment for the game in celebration of his cancer being in remission. Through my recent turmoil I nearly forgot about the grand occasion. I wonder if Jennifer will show.

CHAPTER 17

SEEKING A RESPITE, I make my way down to the hotel bar. The lounge at the rear of the Ritz Carlton property is luxurious. The large bar is adorned with hanging crystal fixtures with lights that reflect off of the many gold-accent pieces filling the room. The bar spans the open space and the mahogany wood contrasts perfectly with the dark marble counter.

A dozen or so tables are strewn about, each with immaculate, perfectly creased table clothes and place settings. Waiters wear white shirts and black pants, vests and bowties, and they zip around the room making sure the clientele are well attended. With a number of players and coaches prepared to consume a vast amount of food and alcohol, it promises to be a good night of tips for the staff.

I follow my standard plan in mind—show my face and mill about for an hour or so and then go to bed. With the way the guys consume liquor they won't notice me slip away.

Moving about the room, I see Billy Law and Johnny Baugh sitting at the far end of the bar having an animated conversation about golf, or maybe fishing. Billy's gesticulating energetically while Johnny smiles, looking entertained.

Taylor, Colfer, Gabriel, and Graves stand together at the opposite end, and I notice Mitchell, Stanyek, and Griffin hitting on some of the local women. The ladies, all very attractive and dressed to the nines with a particular look that screams Miami vixen, gravitate to the young players. I know the type well and figure the boys would eventually draw their own conclusions. Although quite hot, the women look aggressive, expensive, and maybe even a little dangerous.

My big Texan pal, Trent Evans, sits alone working a whiskey double on the rocks. He motions me over to the bar stool next to his. "One for my friend," he tells the bartender, a tanned and athletically built young woman. Miami must have the greatest proportion of fit and tan women in the nation.

My drink is a double oaked Woodford Reserve, so I certainly won't decline. Sitting next to Trent is perfect. We'll have some good conversation, and after a drink or two will call it an evening.

After toasting to "Winning ballgames" we turn away from the bar to survey the room. "Those boys are looking for trouble," Trent says, pointing to Mitchell, Stanyek, and Griffin. Their engagement with the bodacious sirens grows.

"Yup, they'll learn."

"Like we all did," Trent says. "Hey, are you still dating that same lady?"

Why does everyone seem to be concerned with my love life? "Not sure, we've run into some snags with our relationship." Married and content, Trent's a good source of advice.

"How do you do it, Trent? How do you manage your career and still deal with marriage?"

"I don't know, TC. For me, they are kind of separate. When I'm at work, I'm at work. When I'm home, then I concentrate on the marriage end of things."

"That works okay?"

"It works fine if you have the right woman. It wouldn't be any different if I was a car salesman or something else. Go to work and then come home when I'm done."

Although being an elite baseball player can be a challenge and different from other vocations, I suppose there are also similarities when it comes to one's personal life.

"And you and your wife are able to deal with all of the travel and demands?"

Trent nods. "Yup, just need to build up trust and once you both know you are paddling in the same direction, it's pretty easy."

I sip my drink and digest that for a moment. Jennifer is my ideal, and deep down I know she is right for me. We seem to be aligned in our personal lives, but now it feels like we may not be able to navigate through unease and distrust.

Something catches the big Texan's eye on the television screen above the bar. The sound's inaudible, but the closed caption across the screen cause an immediate reaction. The headline has something to do with the new, female Italian prime minister policy ideas comparing to our own former president's nationalism. Familiar with Trent's political slant I make sense of his exultant grunt.

"Important stuff, the world is teetering on the brink," Trent says pointing to the screen. "Liberty, freedom, tradition, once lost will never return."

"Teetering on the brink, Trent? Why think any of it matters?"

Trent sips his drink. "TC, throughout history we've had political leaders rise to power in a way that once seems inconceivable. Once unthinkable, communism is vastly accepted, and we now live in a divided world. It matters because I know what side you are on in that battle."

A young lady sidles up to the bar and sits on the stool next to me, eavesdropping. Trent ignores the interloper and continues.

"Think about baseball. I'm a little older than you, but when I broke in we had baseball chapel every Sunday. It didn't matter your religion. Teams would supply a reverend or deacon to lead an informal chapel to give thanks to God. Due to our crazy schedule, players can't attend church, but there's rarely chapel any longer. And if we do have chapel the attendance is paltry."

"What does that have to do with something going on halfway around the world?"

"It's all related, you see. Incrementally, traditions and mores are being stripped. If we don't fight back, the world will become unrecognizable."

Chief often rants about something called the *great reset* and curses elitists trying to change the world. When some clown from the World Economic Forum talks about stripping people of their belongings I join with others to raise a collective middle finger, but should I really give two shits? They fly private jets all around the world to meet at summits where they hobnob and eat fancy meals, all the while plotting how the populace is ruining the climate and should all be substituting insects for beef. It all sounds like James Bond stuff to me.

"Even if you're right, what does it matter to guys like us? My father used to say that politics and crime are one in the same, so why be involved in that world?"

The woman at the bar tilts her head to catch Trent's answer.

"Hell, in many ways your father was right. But the guy who robs a bank steals from the company and the shareholders. The politician that lies robs from our children. Their actions impact generations!"

Our eavesdropper nods in agreement. I give her a look to show I don't appreciate the intrusion, but she just smiles as Trent continues.

"You might think you are insulated, but it matters. Go back to the baseball example. You are outspoken when it comes to rules, and you've seen how tradition is being tossed aside. Did you ever think we'd have a pitch clock or that a small group of rabble could force a team to change a nickname?"

I shake my head no. Comparing baseball administrators to the political bureaucrats is a reoccurring theme. Indifference leads to more encroachment, which is certainly clear when it comes to the game and is relatable to problems in the world. Trent makes sense, though I now have a sudden urge for more whiskey.

"Like I said, Trent, I admire your passion, but what are two baseball players sitting at a bar supposed to do about any of it?"

"Ah, that's the exact point. Whether it's an election in Italy or a ballplayer, people crave leadership. They'll rally around those supporting our immutable traditions and basic moral principles. Say, why do you think people root for you to break the home run record?"

I shrug and answer, "Most are fans seeking closure from the steroid era."

No longer feigning unobtrusiveness, I throw another sideways glance toward the strange woman edging even closer. This time, I notice her features. Thin with jet black hair, her face attractive, though her high cheek bones make her appear frail. Her precisely manicured eyebrows provide a haughty look, and I spot a small half-moon tattoo etched on the corner of her temple. Her fingers are marked by strange, indistinguishable symbols, and a larger tattoo of a mysterious horned figure begins on her hand and extends up her arm. Her black short sleeve blouse hides the top of the tattoo and, I presume, many other hidden pieces of artwork covering her body.

"That's right. They root for traditions and love you because you are a throwback. You are also outspoken against lesser men with no accountability making the rules," Trent says. "Ronald Reagan began as an actor and he changed the world. Donald Trump is a real estate mogul for chrissake. There are many examples in history where one individual changed everything. Don't ever discount the power of one!"

Triumphantly raising a finger and with a haughty nod, Trent rises from his stool, satisfied he made his point.

"You know what's strange, TC?"

"What's that?"

"I don't talk to anyone else about this shit, but for some reason I think I'm supposed to have these conversations with you." Trent peers off in the distance "Now I gotta go see a man about a horse."

The unusual woman at the bar smiles awkwardly, and with Trent gone inches even closer. "Interesting conversation," she says, her face nearing mine. "Your friend has it right, I think. Didn't a bunch of baseball players leave the game to fight in World War II? Maybe we'd all be speaking German right now if they didn't."

"Excuse me? Do I know you?"

The woman appears out of sorts and I take a moment to get a better look at her face. She looks vaguely familiar.

"Nay. Maybe we have some mutual friends. I've been following you. Saw you first in the spring training game in Lakeland and called out to you. Remember?"

Nay? I stare at the peculiar woman and the scene flashed back to me. *"Blast the next pitch. You know you've got 'em!"* Fans yell at me all the time, yet those shouts from the stands had risen above the din and were etched in my brain.

"That's right," she says. "You are quite an impressive player, especially considering all the conflict swirling around you. Some resolve you have."

I'm all for interesting bar talk, but there's something unnerving about this woman. She speaks as if she knows me personally.

"Have you been stalking me lady?"

"Nay, not stalking, I'm simply a fan." She taps her long fingernails on her champagne flute. Smiling wryly she says, "I think your friend feels your conflict too. Strip away self-satisfaction and complacency, the power of one is amazing."

Okay, that's the second time she said *nay*. She's either a whack job, or maybe part of a gag.

"Excuse me? Did one of my teammates put you up to this?"

"This is no joke, TC. I'm concerned about the divergence within your mind. I see you looking around the stands, seeking answers." The woman's Boston accent grows increasingly pronounced.

"I thought you said you were a fan. You sound more like a witch or fortuneteller."

The woman's eyes widen, her expression highlighting her angular face, pierced nose and wide cheekbones.

"I prefer to be called a mystic," she says. "I come from a long line, and now that you mention it, I am actually a descendant of Moll Pitcher, a soothsayer from the 1700s."

Okay, I'll play along. This is becoming bizarrely entertaining. Plus, I've often considered seeing a psychic.

She sees me ogling her many tattoos, particularly the pentagram behind her ear. She moves her head to divert my stare and continues.

"Baseball was conjured from the imagination of an entertainment starved American people. Where I'm from was a hotbed for early baseball. Ever hear of a professional baseball team from Massachusetts called the Salem Witches?"

"No, never heard of them. Sounds like you are from Boston. So, what are you doing here in Florida?"

"Yes, from Boston originally, but made my way down south where people leave me alone. I'm also a relative of Laurie Cabot and the way I look, well, I'd often get judged."

"Who the fuck is Laurie Cabot?" I asked. Looking around the bar I expected to find a group of the woman's friends egging her on, but nobody in the lounge seems to be with her.

"Please, no profanity."

I can't tell if she's truly offended, so I put my hand up to apologize. She nods graciously, understanding that certain words were a natural part of a baseball player's vocabulary.

"I'm surprised you don't recognize the name, TC. Laurie Cabot is linked to baseball."

I search the name through my mind's database and recall reading about a witch who claimed to have lifted the *Curse of the Bambino*. Folklore has it that the curse stemmed from when the Red Sox sold Babe Ruth to the Yankees. In the eighty-four seasons after the Ruth sale, the Sox reached the World Series just four times, losing each one in the seventh and final game. In October 2004, the Sox won the Series for the first time since 1918. Cabot took credit for ending Boston's streak of bad luck and claimed partial responsibility for changing the fortune of the franchise.

Before I utter another word she says, "That's right. That's Laurie Cabot." The unusual woman raises her lips into a contemptuous smile, proud that she read my thoughts.

"Alas," she continues, "baseball is your vessel by which you've been selected. Mine is a different craft, but you see I too have a circular connection to the game."

"Lady, what in the world are you talking about? Selected by whom?"

"Ever think that the popularity, the home runs, the records, might all serve a dual purpose? Perhaps something bigger?" The woman's face softens as she stares with pity. Studying my face she adds, "We all have our purpose, TC. You can dampen your personal turmoil if you figure this out. Urgency is headed your way. Broaden your scope and you'll see the possibilities."

What's urgent, the homerun record?

"You need to search your soul for your answers, that much is clear."

Did she just read my mind?

Strangely uncomfortable, I can't walk away. Often failing to pursue my hallucinations, I confront the one before me.

"What else do you see? What's real and what is in my head? Tell me, what's this about."

"I know there's a woman," she says with a sympathetic glare. "And I know there are visitations that are reminders from the past. If you continue to view it as a curse, that is what it will be. The things in your midst, the dreams, the girl, the records... you have the pieces to put it all together. It's all linked, and your destiny is not yet determined."

Shaking her head, the woman's chest heaves as if releasing my mind from her clenches. She quickly pushes me aside and walks away. The room is crowded, and I shout to get her attention.

"What is this? What's your name?"

She stops amid the swarming crowd and looks over her shoulder. Raising both hands toward the ceiling she exclaims, "Theodore Cobb Hunter, indifference is the enemy of leadership. Leadership is based on conviction. Your choice is to inspire or be ordinary. The latter puts everyone in peril!"

I take a few steps to chase her and the drink I'm holding splashes onto my shirt. I grab a napkin from the bar and by the time I look back she's gone.

Trent returns from the lavatory and orders me another drink. "Hey, I know you are popular, but that was a weird one. Especially here with this crowd."

What? He saw her?

Trent squints as he scans the room. "That was one crazy tattooed bitch you were talking to. Where'd she come from?"

"Please, no profanity."

"What?"

"Nothing. She's from Boston. I think."

"Boston, huh? Like the Kenny Chesney song," Trent quips.

I shrug, looking perplexed, still trying to process the encounter and the fact that he saw the woman, too.

Quickly, I finish my drink and despite Trent's protest I tell him I'm done for the night. Trent looks concerned, but I assure him I'm fine and head toward the lobby, my head on a swivel in anticipation of a further encounter.

Thankfully, I make it to my hotel room without incident and sit on the bed viewing an internet search for Moll Pitcher, fortuneteller from Massachusetts. She's described as a legendary soothsayer and is pictured. That's her; tall, very thin, with piercing black eyes and a distinct nose. She's drawn much attention for correctly making outlandish predictions, like shipwrecks and where to find valuable lost items. She's also dabbled in the romantic, often making lovers happy with her prophecies.

I'm right about Laurie Cabot, the world-renowned psychic living in Salem, Massachusetts. Along with helping law enforcement solve mysterious cases, she's known to have alleviated a few sports curses. And son of a bitch, there was once a professional baseball team called the Salem Witches.

If the woman at the bar was not another visitation, how could she know so much about me? If not another conjured image, then maybe I'm not psychologically disturbed after all, or does this realization make things even worse? I'm inclined to think it's the latter. I'd laugh it off if it wasn't all so maddening.

"Indifference is the enemy of leadership," a phrase exposing an identifiable character flaw, but she could not have picked up on that merely from eavesdropping on my conversation with Trent Evans. My self-focus sometimes leads to inaction on many fronts. However, when strangers in a bar expose character defects it seems less than coincidental.

Frustrated, I close my eyes to rest for the night, wondering how the odd, tattooed woman could know about Jennifer and my general emotional state. Resigned to further self-analysis, perhaps working on my imperfections is the key to unlocking my troubles.

CHAPTER 18

WHEN ETHAN ANNOUNCED that he was finished with his cancer treatment and the doctors gave him a clean bill of health, Jen and I put the gears in motion. A limousine will pick up Ethan and his mother, Jane, and drive them to the stadium in Tampa. We'll give him his own personalized game jersey to wear and provide full access to the field during batting practice. Ethan will get a stash of baseballs to use for autographs, and my teammates agree to treat the kid like a rock star for the day. Even though we're the visiting team, arrangements are made for Ethan to throw out the game's first pitch. Then he and his mother will have front-row seats.

I receive a text from Jennifer reminding me of Ethan's itinerary. When I ask her if I'll get a chance to see her at the game she responds that she'd be there. She's either playing it cool, or she doesn't have the burning desire to see me like I want to see her.

The team doesn't have an issue with me staying in my condo for the three-game set in Tampa. It's a formality, but I must seek approval to shuttle separately to the condo after the last game in Miami. Confused and anxious about recent events, I welcome the friendly confines of my own place, and sleeping in my own bed might provide some comfort.

Sitting on my couch with my favorite tropical landscape below, I forego texting and call Jennifer. She picks up right away and expresses interest in seeing me at the stadium. She's in the middle of something at work, and although our conversation is short, I feel reassured that I'll have time with her later in the day. Hopefully, we'll be able to have a substantive discussion to plot a course for our relationship.

I consider driving to our team's spring training site to get in a workout. The trip over the causeway might offer some time for contemplation, but I decide it might be better to do my thinking on my own couch.

The swirling in my head makes me feel lethargic. No matter how I try to make the pieces fit, nothing makes sense. All my life I just wanted to be a baseball player, and now I feel taunted by a sense of urgency to be so much more.

I click on the television and toggle through the channels. Nothing catches my eye until I stop on the classic movie channel. The narrator is previewing the next movie, *No Man of Her Own*. I've never seen the movie, but the narrator snares my interest as he talks about the two stars falling in love after the film in what he describes as "an incredibly romantic Hollywood union."

I learned that Clark Gable was left heartbroken when Carole Lombard tragically died in a plane crash. I previously had no knowledge of the story, and I sat stunned when the screen showed a picture of the former couple. I immediately recognized Carole Lombard as the woman in the Miami elevator, and Gable as her escort who stood beside the Georgia Peach.

The narrator describes the legendary couple's relationship as "the love affair that shocked and delighted the world." He calls Gable an immortal actor who continued acting after the tragedy, though he was never the same.

There was that word again. Why would the narrator describe Gable as *immortal*? After some quick research I found that Carole Lombard died in 1942 and the grief-stricken Gable joined the US Army shortly thereafter. He flew combat missions in Europe for the Army Air Force and contributed in other ways to the country's efforts.

So, dozens of films and an iconic actor known throughout the world made him a legend. He loved a woman deeply and fought for his country, and the things he did beyond his profession made him an immortal, just like Chief described. There's much more going on here than coincidence or irony.

⚾ ⚾ ⚾

The look on Ethan's face is priceless. He watches batting practice and I hear him react each time a player smacks a ball into the seats. My teammates are great, and one by one they speak with the boy, sign autographs and pose for pictures with him.

Jane is having a great time as well, the fear in her face now replaced by joy and optimism. I stare at Jane and Ethan, elated that the young boy can enjoy his days without trepidation.

After I finish my round of hitting, I remain behind the portable backstop and kneel beside Ethan. He throws his arms around my neck so tightly that I think he'll never let go. I look up and smile at Jane and see tears of joy. Standing beside Jane is Jennifer basking in the moment.

We lock eyes and she smiles softly. Jen too is teary eyed, and I can't look away. When Ethan finally relinquishes his grip, I walk over to Jennifer.

"We need to help more kids like Ethan," I say.

"We sure do," Jen responds.

"Can we talk after the game?"

"I'd like that, but I have some things to button up. If not today, then tomorrow?"

"Whatever works, Jen. I'll be patient."

Her expression is reassuring and makes me feel like things might be okay. I turn back to Ethan and ask him to tap my bat for luck. He obliges, and I head toward the dugout to resume my pregame warm up. Turning around, I catch Jen's eye; she's staring right back. We both have things to say and I'm determined to make amends.

After the game I stopped in front of the field box where Ethan and Jane sit. I hand Ethan one last gift, the bat that he touched for luck that I used to pound the farthest home run of the year. He describes the occasion as, "the best day in my whole life," and I promised that we'll do it again real soon. Maybe next time we'll fly them up to Philadelphia for a game, Ethan deserves to have things to look forward to.

They leave to catch the limousine and I watch Jane and Ethan walk up the aisle toward the stadium exit. I scan the seats hoping to see Jennifer, but I can't find her among the departing crowd.

I take a scenic route on my drive home from the stadium, making my way to the upscale Beach Drive waterfront of St. Petersburg. Driving my BMW convertible with the top down, I take my time, moseying on roads running near the water. The streets are relatively quiet at this late hour, and I detour to head to the Pass-a-Grille, a favorite stretch of white sand beaches.

I passed a popular dining spot, the Paradise Grille, tempted to stop for a drink, opting instead to continue along Gulf Boulevard for an extended drive. Being alone and driving my roadster through the Florida coastal air provides a welcomed peace. The familiar brininess of the Gulf sets me in a trance. I drive for a good half hour before heading for the thoroughfares leading home.

Finally, back at the condo, I throw on some comfortable clothes and plop on my couch. I click on the television to watch the baseball channel and catch the show just in time to watch our team's highlights. I know the home run I hit was a missile, but damn if it didn't almost scrape the dome roof before landing deep in the upper deck. The epic blast was dedicated to Ethan, and I glow at the thought of providing him such a thrill.

During a commercial break I clicked on the news and see an interview with an Army Ranger named Peter Graves. The interviewer is absorbed in the soldier's words, and I turn up the volume.

"A man does not die whose memory remains alive in the hearts of those he leaves behind."

Graves reaches for a chain around his neck and pulls out military dog tags of his fallen mate. "Jonathan Larson was an Army Ranger and a good friend of mine," he says. "This day, a little over a year ago, I lost my friend and great warrior in a fire fight while serving our country."

Pointing to the tan beret on his head, the soldier continues. "I honor Jon by wearing his military ID and Ranger beret because I don't want our country to ever forget this man who would have been thirty years old today."

He takes a moment to compose himself and the host skillfully inserts himself into the conversation saying, "I know this is tough for you, but I know you want to speak about how Jon died, so take your time."

The implied drama draws me right into the conversation and I wonder if Chief and Trent Evans are watching. Fighting through the emotions, Graves straightens in his seat.

"Like all Army Rangers, Jon knew what he was getting into. We were involved in assaults against some really bad people who would kill us all if they were given the chance, and Jon fought the hardest. Like so many of our warriors, he happily fought for our country so that others would remain happy and free." Graves breathes deeply. "If he lost his life fighting for the people of the United States that would be one thing. But the firefight that killed this great soldier was tainted. There was something not right about how it went down."

"Go on," the TV personality says.

Graves peers directly into the camera. "Several of our men were directed to a safe house where important information about extremists was supposedly stored. But they walked into an ambush and were killed. It was a revenge attack from an exercise a month prior where we hit a location and took out an extremist leader."

"And you think that the ambush was a setup? Like they knew it was coming and the lives of our soldiers were somehow sacrificed?"

"That's exactly what happened," Graves says. "Those men were used as pawns in some sick, political scheme, and were sacrificed for some distorted end."

"How so? What evidence do you have of that?"

"Sensing something was off, the troop immediately called for backup. Those pleas were denied and Jon along with Army Rangers Joseph Garber, Lance Frankel, Michael Warber, and Mitchell Stanowski were executed."

"Denied by who? How do you know backup was requested?" the host asks.

"I know backup was requested because Jon called me just moments before the attack. He told me everything and I was on the other end of the line just prior."

"Our calls to the Pentagon have gone without response. You are very brave to tell your story," the commentator says.

Graves will no doubt face repercussions for telling his tale, but he has been impacted so greatly he doesn't care.

"I don't ever want people to forget Jon and my other fallen brothers who dedicated their lives to preserving freedom and saving us all. The betrayal within the ranks is too great to ignore. The politicians can do whatever they like to me, but I will never let people forget Jon, Joe, Lance, Mike and Mitch. You see, if we forget them, if we forget their names, they die a second death, and I'm not going to let that happen."

The screen dims and the network goes to a commercial. Immediately, I receive a text from Chief.

You watching the news? Did you catch that?

Fucked up world right now and I don't know where it all comes from.

Goddammit! It's coming from within now.

Peter Grave's accusations are hard to comprehend. Why would our own military leaders knowingly sacrifice five of their own? Why would they withhold reinforcements?

My attention leaves the television when I hear someone fiddling with my entrance door. I bounce off the couch and see the door begin to open. I check the clock to make sure I hadn't nodded off and amid another episode. The clock shows 11:52 pm. I reach for a weapon to combat the intruder.

When Jennifer steps into the lighted vestibule my shoulders drop in relief. She notices my surprise and playfully says, "I hope you don't mind. You gave me a key."

◈ ◈ ◈

Reconciling with Jennifer cleanses my soul. Our relationship might need some work, but it's worth it. Jen fills a void and brings me peace. We are clearly better together than apart, and we agree to put all pettiness aside.

My only regret is that I still can't get myself to tell her about my mental struggles as I see no benefit of burdening her with my issues.

"Uh, Jen, I think a witch from Boston had a hand in getting us back together. Clark Gable thinks it's great we are together too. Oh, and I met your dead parents the other night, they seem great." Such absurdities could scare her off, I fear.

Our reunion provides a shot of adrenalin, and at least this one piece to my life's puzzle feels right. I will never suggest our relationship is predestined, though I do now feel completely different. In light of helping Ethan and looking forward to other things we can do together, our love affair feels like a positive force and that can counter some of the evil in the world.

CHAPTER 19

IT IS OFTEN said that you cannot win a pennant in April, but you can lose one. We certainly did not lose one in April or any of the early baseball months. Instead, we've played great team baseball and sit on top of our division by nine games at the All-Star break. The play is satisfying, but there's a long way to go as the pennant race begins to heat up in earnest. We all know to keep working hard.

For the sixth year in a row, I'm proud to make the All-Star team. Even though the game had lost its luster, I comport myself as an ambassador to the game and put on a good face. It's an honor to be an All-Star, but I'm anxious to start the second half of the season.

Upon returning to our Philadelphia locker room, I notice the restless buzz of my teammates. Troy Miller stands by his locker taking a couple of mock swings with a few different bats to figure out which will be his gamer for the day. Johnny Baugh tapes up his black Marucci using a zig-zag pattern on the handle, concentrating with the precision of a surgeon to make sure the tape is just right.

Members of the pitching staff are doing their routine of medical band exercises and heat therapy, while a few players receive treatment from the trainers to get them ready for play. Others study video or work their gloves in preparation for the game. It's all very typical of a professional clubhouse on game day, but I find myself glancing back and forth from corner to corner in appreciation of mundane tasks being done with determined resolve.

I gripped my bat, a thirty-four-inch P72 model, and study the grain looking for cracks. I try not to get fond of an inanimate piece of wood, though this particular bat has provided dozens of hits over the past several weeks. Throughout my career, I've used several different bat models, experimenting with C243s, C271s, R161s, but the tapered handle and perfectly formed barrel of the P72 provides the right balance for my swing, and this one feels just right.

My phone buzzes with a text from Ethan. *Game day!* I text back, *Yes sir!!!!* and I'm sure that made him smile.

Another text from Jen let me know she's on her way to the stadium. Ever since the carjacking we put more safety practices in place, and I like knowing when she was heading over. I'll check the stands in a half hour or so to make sure she got in safely.

A final text is from an unrecognizable number, and I assume it's from a reporter at the *New York Post*. Over the midseason break I did an interview with Chuck Fairbanks, my favorite sports reporter, and the link on the text is to his article.

Over the years I've had occasion to sit with Chuck, and he always quotes me correctly and in the right context. In fact, I find the *Post* to be a rare New York-based news outlet in that it doesn't have an agenda. Determined to push left-leaning politics, even the sports sections of many newspapers maintain the slant. However, even during the Cunningham incident when others tried to sensationalize the race angle, Chuck defended me and went after the irresponsibility of the others in the media. He always gives me a fair shake and never treats me like a prop.

During the interview we talked extensively about the state of the game and the battle between analytics and old-school baseball. The article explains that data metrics and computer models are a critical tool, but then provides my mode of thinking, which he chronicles perfectly. Chuck writes in a way that provides both sides of the matter, and I find the article to be accurate and impactful.

He's not purely a baseball writer, yet he grasps how my hitting approach had been contagious throughout our team and how we are baffling the competition. Fairbanks addresses the psychological advantage of aggressive play that three and a half months into the season has our squad not only on top of the division, but with the best record in the league.

The new pitch clock has been a boon for us as it distracts pitchers who are making snafus with increasing regularity. We're pouncing on that weakness, attacking relentlessly to further rattle hurlers. These are things that a computer cannot quantify and what many in the league are unable to grasp. Chuck's article dissects the consequences of the league's new rules perfectly. I'm always impressed by how much he understands the nuances.

Chuck addresses my statistical prowess, describing my numbers as historically obscene. No other players in modern history has had as high a batting average at the midseason break, .433, and the fact that I'm also hitting dingers at a record pace is a statistical anomaly. Chuck notes that I'm driving opposing pitchers crazy by never allowing them to dictate the game.

Inevitably, organizations that strictly manage their baseball philosophy by the numbers will be forced to adapt, Chuck writes. To that point I said, "Screw 'em. Let them stay mired in their new world approach," a quote Chuck leaves out of the story.

The article includes perfunctory questions about my pending free agency, but Chuck doesn't dwell on the topic. If Chuck Fairbanks was the commissioner of baseball instead of a reporter, the game would be in a much better place.

Chuck's article concludes that pressure will mount on me as the season progresses if I continue my batting average and home run pace. He hopes I'm up for the challenge. Strangely, the last sentence of the article is foreboding. *"Hunter needs to understand the country craves a glorious chase, and the very existence of the game and the health of a nation are at stake."*

I swipe my finger across the face of the phone to get to the message screen and notice the text originated from a number I don't recognize. I hit the redial button and an automatic message engages right away stating the number is no longer in service.

◌ ◌ ◌

The attention from the press mounts as I hit home run number forty-two on July 31. The coverage has been frantic ever since a two-week hot stretch where I hit another ten home runs and maintained a batting average over .425.

The team rolls to a comfortable fifteen game lead in the division, and we're showing no signs of letting up. Our pitching staff remains strong, and more importantly healthy and not overused. Manager Billy Law remains a maestro, orchestrating winning streaks by focusing on strong pitching and defense, continuing the promotion of Law Ball where we keep opposing teams off balance and confused by not doing what would otherwise be statistically obvious. The city now houses the best team in baseball and its streets buzz with talk of a championship.

My personal life stays on the upswing as Jen and I spend much more time together. She's become an extremely positive influence in my life.

Inspired by young Ethan, she helps me become more aware of how a community presence can be a huge force for good. Not only does she advocate for a bigger involvement with the Leukemia and Lymphoma Foundation, we seek opportunities to raise money for an array of causes.

Jen works tirelessly on this mission. She's busy organizing a huge golf and fishing outing in the off season with the goal of raising millions through my contacts in sports. We intend to match whatever donations we raise, and for the first time I'm reaching outside of my comfort zone, and it feels great.

Ever since we reconciled, I've been episode free. Time will tell if I have permanently expunged the forceful demons along with the unbearable insomnia, but my mind feels settled. Committing to my path with Jennifer is unquestionably a significant improvement to my psyche.

I do still find myself scanning for people who I might consider out of place, but I have not had any recent encounters. On a couple of occasions, I could swear I saw some players from long ago in the stands. However, there's been no interaction and no calling out from the bleachers. A few oddly timed flashes and the sound of magnesium filament igniting is the extent of my delusions.

Staring at the statistics graphic on the baseball channel I shake my head. With a rare day off I have the luxury of lounging around in the morning. I want to see game highlights and stories from around the league, but the show's segment is all about me.

Apparently, I'm on pace to hit 72.73 home runs, just shy of single season record of 73 hit in 2001 by Barry Bonds. Just behind Bonds is Mark McGwire with 70 and Sammy Sosa with 66. Bonds and McGwire admitted to steroid usage during critical junctures in their careers. That's why so many baseball purists are cheering me on. They want an untainted single-season home run record, period.

The record had been held through the early decades of baseball by Babe Ruth, with 60. Yankee great Roger Maris eclipsed Ruth's triumph by one, and his 61 homers in 1961 topped the list until 1998, the year McGuire and Sosa battled it out for the crown. That chapter in baseball is widely known as the steroid era.

With so many other things going on in the league, it agitates me to be the constant focus of attention, though I do understand the enthusiasm of fans and sports writers given the significance of the single season record. I'm trying not to buckle under the weight.

I once read that Roger Maris felt so much pressure during the 1961 season that his hair started falling out. The subsequent record chasers had just as much strain upon them when they vied for the top mark, and I recall feeling sincerely sorry for them despite the fanfare and loud whispers of steroid use.

With the new fishbowl called social media, I have my work cut out for me if I'm to avoid succumbing to the hysteria. Not only am I being put under strain, my teammates and manager are being thrown into the mix. Team ownership and the league wants to capitalize on the record chase, and Billy Law is getting the brunt of it anytime I don't swing for the fences. I feel for Billy because he knows I am not going to compromise my principles and change my methods, and he gets hammered by critics any time I decide to bunt for a base hit or intentionally slap a ball the other way for a single.

If I'm going to break the record it must be within the framework of my hitting philosophy. To me, it's most important to win, and I have no intention to deviate. Playing the game right in honor of the players of yore is equally important. I wonder how people will feel if I come up just short of the record, not because of my hitting beliefs, but because of the suspension I earned earlier in the season for standing up for the country.

The irony is that with each home run my value on the free agent marketplace increases, and with each article or television segment my popularity grows. Occasionally I receive a text from Tom with an increased contract extension offer. The owners increased their bid to just under $400 million, but since we had all of the leverage there's no need to jump at anything. If I continue on the current pace and we win a championship, Tom said I'd easily be worth $500 million on the open market.

○ ○ ○

My phone buzzes when Chief texts, *Tell me you are watching this. How the hell do you hit 72.73 home runs?*

These people are all nuts, I text back. His timing is uncanny, though I suspect Chief knew that on an off day I'd be planted in front of the screen watching the early morning baseball review.

You know this is going to get stupid, right? Chief continues.

I'm not worried about it.

Good. As long as you realize the record is important.

I get it, Chief.

Although I'm coming around to the historical significance of my personal exploits, I'm still determined to downplay it. Especially with the pundits, I'll provide nothing but cliché responses so not to stir the pot. Keep it simple.

I have to take Jen to the airport later as she is heading back to Florida later in the day. I'm heading out for a ten-day road trip to Minnesota, Colorado and Arizona, so it'll likely be a couple of weeks before I'll see her again. I'm not looking forward to being away from her for that long, but we'll get through.

Jen is still in bed, and I plan to join her shortly.

My phone buzzes and this time it's a text from Tom. *Not to worry, but letting you know that the carjacking story is now public. It was inevitable and not a big deal. Call me later when you can.*

Tom knows I'm with Jennifer and doesn't want to disturb me on my off day. I'm on the couch with a pensive look when Jen walks in the room. I tell her about the carjacking news, and she just shrugs and smiles. She's wearing one of my T-shirts and looks amazing, even after just arising from her slumber. She runs both her hands through her hair and lets her long brown curls fall naturally on her shoulders before draping herself over the couch.

She rubs my shoulders to ease my tension and then wraps her arms around me in comfort. "Not to worry," she says. "I've been thinking about that, and I've got a plan, but nothing that needs to distract us right now."

Dropping Jen off at the airport this time around makes me quite sad. Her recent stay spanned eight consecutive days and I already long for the routine of waking up with Jen in my arms after a satisfying day, and a full night's sleep. Our days together were straightforward and uncomplicated, and our future together had begun to feel like a given.

My improved disposition helps me manage the media frenzy, and my play couldn't be any better. Locked in as a hitter, the game slows, and no matter how hard the opposing pitcher throws, the baseball looks like a grapefruit coming in. The pitch clock continues to encourage pitcher mistakes and every hanging curveball or fat fastball out over the plate is headed for the stands or to the outfield gap.

Hot streaks in baseball come and go, and like many players I get superstitious. So, I don't want anything to change, including Jen and me. The best thing a player can do when during a streak is to maintain a routine, which is now disrupted with Jen leaving. To compound things, the carjacking story erupted, and the media hounds won't leave me be. Given the sensitive nature of the juvenile case, and also due to my celebrity, it had been effectively kept under wraps throughout the entire investigation.

Tom is reassuring and as usual he isolates me from any of the dirty laundry being aired by critics. My job is to stay quiet on the topic and just play ball. If asked, I am simply to say that I was involved in an unfortunate incident that is being handled through the legal system. For any further comment they should speak to law enforcement or my attorney.

I almost blew a gasket when I saw a particular commentator editorialize that instead of breaking the kid's wrist, I should have simply given up the car. After all, I'm already rich and headed for what might possibly be a record-breaking contract, and these poor kids are downtrodden and desperate. Of course, he minimizes the fact that the main instigator brandished a gun in my face. That I could have been killed seems not to matter.

Instead of addressing individual articles and slants, Tom prepares a generic public statement, which he distributes to media outlets and through social media. He effectively paints the picture of the assault and encourages full prosecution for the attackers.

The statement from my attorney presented to the courts expressed that the crime meets the standard of being so egregious that the main perpetrator should be tried as an adult. Tom wants to meet with the district attorney, and they set an appointment a couple of weeks out. Thankfully, I don't have to be in attendance. As always, Tom will handle everything.

Upon landing in Minnesota, I'm determined to spend much of my stay on the baseball field or in my hotel room. Being on the road provides a small degree of cover. Not in the mood to deal with answering questions about the carjacking and talking about baseball records, my goal for the entire trip is to avoid the limelight.

Even though we'll be playing in relatively small markets, Tom still expects a media frenzy.

In need of a friendly voice, I call Jen from my hotel room. She too arrived safely from her travel day and is also melancholy from being separated. I warn her that my strategy to stay cooped up in my hotel room might mean I call her more often. She's more than fine with that.

We're on the phone for nearly an hour talking about an array of things. Jen has some thoughts about the carjacking and the troubled boys. We also strategize at length about alleviating the pressures of the media and what might be ahead. When things get even crazier, she may find herself in the middle of the media blitz. She laughs off the notion, saying she could handle anything thrown at her. With her temperament I'm sure that she can manage.

We circle back to talking about the game and Jen's viewpoint proves interesting. She's realistic about baseball statistics and records and prods me to view it from the fan's side. Fans need distraction from the mundane, and the press is simply an extension of the people she lectures.

"The country craves a hero," she says, echoing the thoughts of others around me. "Don't run away from it."

We even talk about rule changes and the state of the game. "If there's something you don't like, fix it!" she says. "You can be more influential than you think!"

Thinking outside of my purview is often difficult and I appreciate Jen's perspective. My defense mechanism is to insulate and put up a wall between myself and outside issues. Jen helps me explore beyond my bubble, and she once again provides food for thought and something to ponder as I lay my head on the pillow for a restful night.

The clock on the hotel nightstand blinks 3:48 am. Back into the haziness of an unexpected occurrence, the last thing I remember is speaking with Jen and falling asleep. Optimism shattered, I now rule out personal contentment as a precursor of emotional peace.

Walking over an infinite span of emptiness, the sand at my feet is white and as fine as powder. No matter where I turn, the barren expanse appears endless, yet I run in search of something amid the blankness. Eventually, I notice an anomaly far off in the sandy distance, and I sprint to the figure now standing before me. Almost within reach, I'm swept away by the sand, and I awake disoriented and out of breath.

Tossed back into the abyss, extreme urgency weighs heavily. Flippantly, I coin the imagery "The Allegory of the Sand" in deference to Plato, and as a defense mechanism. Like the people in Plato's cave, I struggle to understand what's real and what's distorted. What has changed? Angered by persisting madness, the feeling of disappointment is nothing compared to the new degree of panic I feel through my core.

Prepare for a game. Play the game. Hide away. Sleep. Wake up at 3:48 am. Repeat. The latest adaptation of my woes is a pattern like never before. There are no encounters, no flashing bulbs, yet there's a shift to a daily episode, restlessness and mind-numbing angst.

I force myself to entertain a usual routine, kidding myself that maintaining an elite standard of play should be my focus. Hiding in my room as if I'm a dying man, I hop in my hotel bed at an early hour to sleep, knowing I'm going to wake up again at an ungodly hour.

After three consecutive morning occurrences in Minnesota, I pray for a reprieve, only to get three more days of my nightmare.

The dream perpetually reoccurs, though in Colorado I find myself confronting more intense imagery.

One night, the sands take me to Jonathan Larson, the soldier who faced betrayal at the hands of his own government. Standing at attention the serpent on the Gadsden flag he was holding thrashed with life, the words of the banner *Don't Tread on Me* glow as if presenting a clue. His face is lined with agonizing concern, and although utters not a word, he implores that I aid his plight. His troubles seem but a microcosm of a world bereft of loyalty and nourished humanity.

The next night I come face to face with my three namesakes, each stand with regal confidence, staring with disapproval. I disappoint them in some way, but they say nothing. Their glares convey panicked urgency, their terse smirks a plea for response amid their silence. What do they want from me? Reading into their posture is irresponsible, yet their manner suggests inadequateness.

The sixth consecutive day of episode-spurred insomnia is even more bizarre. Running endlessly over a stretch of white sand, I chase a plume of smoke wafting in the distant air. Sprinting until my lungs cave, I find the source, a familiar round-faced man with a salt and pepper beard. He puffs on his cigar and raises a golden microphone to his mouth. Smiling and full of confidence and patriotic spirit he exclaims, "The flag stands as a beacon of peace and hope for those willing to protect her. She'll always be there as long as our ideals are never lost!"

Sitting in my bed I considered the words, instinctively knowing they were another piece to an unsolvable puzzle. In the morning darkness, an even worse thought occurs. *Maybe there is no solution, and the constant mania is unconditionally random.* Six nights in a row of madness; my only recourse is to pray for God's intervention.

CHAPTER 20

THE WHITE SAND at my feet is incredibly soft, even softer than the Gulf Coast sand from back home. The surface is so yielding that my feet sink to my ankles with each plodding step. As if defying physics, I continue to move forward despite sinking deeper into the fine dust.

I survey the terrain in all directions like I have done each of the last eight mornings and find myself still trapped in an odd wasteland. A small dot off in the distance forces my direction, and I pace toward the far-off speck; whether a mirage or another figment of my imagination it's as good a direction as any.

I try sprinting toward the dot and stop after some time to catch my breath. I wipe the sweat from my brow and squint in the object's direction. The incongruity is getting closer, so like each dream sequence I begin to swell with anticipation.

I struggle to turn my jog into a sprint as the small speck starts to form into a discernable outline. Initially, I think it's a rock formation or perhaps a piece of driftwood. But the silhouette takes the form of a woman.

My sides split with the pain of overexertion, but I continue to run toward the figure. I stop to again catch my breath and holler toward the figure. Whoever it is remains motionless and I switch to a walk so not to scare the individual.

It's a woman with long, dark hair, her body positioned awkwardly, and she peers outward as if looking over a cliff. Completely still, I think I might be marching toward a dead body. Wobbling from the long hike that seems to go for miles, I'm determined to reach the woman who for a brief second looks like Jennifer. Edging closer I can tell it's not Jen. Moving closer still, I see the woman breathing while leaning up against a rail, her hands cupped and pressed up against a glass barrier. My breathing short from exhaustion I ask, "Are you okay? Where are we?" She keeps her hands pressed up to the glass, and as I approach, I see there was no rail. The barrier she leans against is translucent, like a glass wall.

"Ma'am, can you hear me?" I'm now a couple feet away but afraid to reach out. Turning toward me, I see movement and a human face, although I do not recognize her. The woman is small and her outfit from a different time and place. She dons a brown, long-sleeve dress that reaches her feet. Her facial features are hard and her nose slightly pointed, yet there's an attractiveness. I think she might be the woman from the pub, the mystic, but without the tattoos I presumed it to be her ancestor.

Silently, I stared at the gypsy, not backing away even though my instincts tell me to maintain a reasonable distance. The peculiar woman turns her head toward me, looks back at the glass and then repeats the motion several times. Finally, her neck stiffens as she lifts her body away from the barrier. The apparition straightens as if trying to take up a proper speaking pose.

"There's much to do," she says, facing the glass.

"Who are you? What is there to do?" I'm losing patience.

The woman grimaces. "It's all collapsing, and soon nothing will be the same."

I repeat. "Who are you? What is collapsing?"

"It's teetering on the edge. Which way will it fall?" She motions toward the glass, but I'm reluctant to move closer. I want no part of her apocalyptic world. "It's all up to you Mr. Theodore Cobb Hunter."

"What's teetering, the game? What's up to me?"

"Tsk, tsk, tsk. She's worth saving, you know."

Tsk, tsk, tsk? Who says that? Who am I talking to? "I'm confused, I already saved Jennifer. What are you expecting me to do?" I shout. I quit, it's time to find someone else to deal with this enigma.

The woman moves closer to the glass, her eyes darting back and forth. As if reading my thoughts, she continues. "You've been guided and maybe they've selected poorly. You can quit, but nothing will ever be the same."

"What won't be the same? Stop talking in riddles!"

"You continuously fail to understand your place and the impact you can make. Figure it out."

I say nothing, once again haunted by words that were from my father. This hallucination is different; the lady's tone feels ominous and unyielding. The vision infers finality.

"History tells us that one man can change everything. Search your soul."

I begin to protest, and the woman lifts her hand to silence me. "Remain idle and things will go along the same path. FIGURE IT OUT!" she shouts.

Her eyes grow dark and her face becomes unrecognizable. I immediately flash back to the airplane episodes when the men's faces were blinded by prosopagnosia. Her face morphs into that same empty, puppet-like appearance.

Tensing, I reach toward the woman's shoulder. I need to see if she is real, but before I can make contact her image puffs into vapor. Stepping toward the haze the mist hits me like walking into a sea spray on the seashore, the warm steam drifts into my face.

I move toward the ledge and lean forward. My feet rest in the sand and stare ahead. I see endless blue before me. The azure vista is crystal clear, providing a calming peace, like staring into a place of virtue and morality.

The panorama below is wholly different. I see unexplainable scenes. Historic and nostalgic, the scenes are both exhilarating and full of dread. It's as if the landscape is being viewed for the very last time.

I see an old baseball field with players from the early 1900s. A player lashes a hit to left centerfield, races around first base and flies into second base with spikes angled high. He brushes himself off and then steals third on the very next pitch. The runner then darts home, but the play is whisked away into a wind-swept vapor before concluding.

Next, I see a big lefty hitter pointing toward the stands and striking a fastball deep into the bleachers. The hitter breaks into his home run trot with short, staccato steps then vanishes before he even reaches first base. It's as if the vastly changing game of today threatens to eliminate the historic exploits of the past. Can history be forgotten so easily?

The landscape shifts again, and this time the players are from a more modern era. I watch as a commotion in the outfield ensues when a spectator runs out into the field to burn an American flag. The outfielder nearest the protester snatches the flag away before the fan commits the vile act. The scene blows up just as the spectator is wrestled down by security.

Next, I see a woman racing toward a burly, butcher boy coifed player standing at home plate. His batter's helmet is replaced by a crown with the etching *Hit King* across the front. The woman's bosom bounces with each step toward the batter, and I recognize the folk figure as Morganna, "The Kissing Bandit," seeking to plant one of her famous kisses. She too disappears before reaching her target.

Suddenly, the imagery moves swiftly and away from the game, morphing into chaos. Burning buildings gave way to a mob of people chasing a man carrying a shotgun. That image gave way to a firebomb going off in a church and then a shooting in a school while adults and police officers stood helplessly watching.

I press against the glass feeling a mix of anger, anguish and hopelessness. The manic feeling mirrors my episodes but amplified tenfold.

Next, I see several young boys carefully stalking a car, one holding a gun. That image yields to a reel of my punch hitting Jamie Cunningham's jaw. Next, I see a police officer with his knee on the throat of an unarmed man and then a jacked up pickup truck flying the Gadsden "Don't Tread on Me" flag. It's being chased by several dark, federal Crown Vic autos. Pensively, I watch as dark vans approach to raid a luxurious tropical estate when suddenly the panorama erupts in flames. Each scene represents our country being ripped apart, and my anger and sadness grow knowing each event is preventable.

As the flames of hell lick upward, I think I see the devil reveling in the chaos. The fire is so intense that I quickly push away from the glass so as not to get burned. Looking back one last time, my feet begin to slide backwards as the sand pulls me away from the fiery lair.

I am now flat on my back in the powdery sand. I have no traction in the strong undercurrent even as I flail my arms and legs hoping to wedge my limbs onto anything solid.

I struggle to see what might be ahead. Suddenly, I hear sand smashing up against glass. The swirling eddy moves clockwise and came upon me without notice. A whirlpool is sucking down sand and through a hole at least twice my body length and width. With my eyes closed, I go into freefall. I hear voices shouting "Salvame! Figure it out! She's worth saving!"

Flailing, I bounce in the air, landing on my back. The sound of the box spring should have woken my roommate, but Johnny Baugh snores loudly in his bed a dozen feet to my left. Doused in sweat, I look around the dark hotel room to let my eyes focus.

Catching my breath, I awoke more lucid than usual from this surreal bout. The sensation is odd, especially when considering the clear messaging and symbolism of the dream. Lying in bed, I measure the fortuneteller from centuries ago. The world is collapsing and on the brink of becoming unrecognizable, and I'm being pushed to do something about it. Me? Preserving morality and principles is my cross to bear?

When did my purpose in life change? My purpose on this earth is to entertain others in the great game, not to counter progressivism. Whether it's the game of baseball or social engineering, what is expected of me? I'm inadequate, just an outfielder for chrissakes, not someone to make rules, answer religious questions, or combat dogma.

I stand, my T-shirt soaked with sweat, so I stumble around the darkness to find another. I rip the cell phone from the charger resting on the nearby desk and use its light to navigate a path to the door. Before leaving the room, I catch my reflection in a full-length mirror near the bathroom entrance. My body wilts and my shoulders sag. Moving closer to the mirror I notice my eyes are bloodshot as if I haven't slept in weeks. In the midst of one of the greatest baseball seasons any man has ever had, I feel defeated and pathetic.

The safety lock on the door is engaged. Carefully, I turn the latch so not to make noise. I stick my head into the corridor, and as expected nobody is up at the early hour. I hit the up button and the elevator doors immediately open. For no good reason I expect to see someone standing in the elevator car or maybe even a blinding camera flash. The elevator rushes upward to the thirty-third floor. The hallway is empty, and I seek out stairs up the remaining flight to the roof. No alarm sounds when I exit outside into the morning darkness.

The late summer Arizona heat hits me. The day's temperature forecast is one hundred and five degrees, and the early morning is only slightly cooler, although a much drier heat than the humid East Coast.

I'm alone on the roof and see a glimmer of sunshine in the distance. The stars and moon provide a glow. I study the orbs searching for some sort of sign from above. A couple of cleansing breaths clear my head, certain that the peace I feel indicates a solid decision coming up here. I expect my heart to be racing but instead feel calm and tranquil.

Robotically, I march to the east corner of the hotel roof. Looking out over the metropolis below makes me feel even more isolated, and I can only make out formless shapes of desolate buildings. This seclusion symbolizes my life in that even though there are plenty of people around, my malady keeps me emotionally isolated and alone with my thoughts.

Even though thirty stories high, there's no wind to threaten my position. Normally, I'm not a big fan of heights, but this time I sit on the parapet without fear. If I had my druthers, I'd toss myself into the ocean, but the nothingness of the desert will have to do. Why such self-destructive thoughts? How in the world did I get to this juncture?

I'm a famous athlete and perhaps the best player in my sport, arguably one of the best ever. Yet, I feel empty and tormented.

The lack of sleep, the vividness of the images, the premonitions, the clairvoyance, the odd encounters strip me of pride and dignity. Unsolvable and endless, my trauma is something a team of psychiatrists couldn't exorcise.

"Christ help me," I say out loud. My words fall empty into the desert air as I look again into the stars. "Here I am," I verbalize, "the great TC Hunter, unable to cope with my own head." The absurdity of it all makes me laugh. The fame, the money, and the girl are worthless without my faculties.

"The girl," I scoff. Jennifer deserves better than this life of uncertainty and psychosis. She should not suffer along with me.

Even if we marry and she stays with me each night, the latest occurrence confirms my hauntings will persist until I accomplish some incredible feat. I don't know that I'll ever be the savior that I am being prompted to be, and I certainly can't drag her into this bizarre world. Sitting in the darkness with my legs dangling, I begin a text:

Jennifer, you are the love of my life. The moments I have spent with you enriched my life more than you can ever know. You showed me a love that I never thought I could have. I cherish the time we spent together, and I know I am closer to you than anyone who has ever been in my life.

It would not be fair to go into details, but I have spent a long period of time tortured by my own thoughts. I often cannot sleep and the anguish that I feel has brought me to the point that I can no longer live. It would not be fair to you to go on like this and I need to feel peace. Do not be sad as I am no longer in pain. I love you.

I reread the text and pause before I hit send. I have never been overly religious, though I have a firm belief in a magnanimous God. I asked God to forgive my sins and hope that given the circumstances, I might find absolution. Reciting the Lord's Prayer provides me with peace, and upon opening my eyes I move my thumb to hit the send button. Before I take one last breath the phone vibrates and rings.

"Get down from the goddamm ledge, TC."

Looking around I wonder who has seen me on the roof, certain that I'm alone. "How do you know where I—"

"I just know, kid. The images, the voices, all of it. It ain't just in your head. You can't fix things if you're dead so get down now, TC," the voice on the phone demands.

"What do you mean?"

"I'll explain, but just get off the ledge you crazy bastard!"

I pull my feet over and hop down to the roof's floor. Shaking, my feet fell firmly on terra cotta. Confused more than ever, I listen intently to the voice saving me from myself.

The last game of our road trip is a blur. I think I had an okay game, but my mind is clearly elsewhere as I have renewed clarity and purpose.

Despite a modest stat line, we win 5-3, and when the team boards the plane back to Philadelphia, I'm completely drained. The day had been mentally exhausting, and I wonder if I might be able to sleep for the first time on the plane. I'm filled with optimism about a lot of things, and normal sleep is pretty high up on the list.

It was a successful West Coast road trip for the team, which demonstrates an air of confidence and professionalism. Confidence goes a long way in the game of baseball, and the guys are enjoying their accomplishments.

An uncommon move, I sit by a window. I typically let a teammate take the window to make it easier to prop up a pillow. I'm sitting next to Bobby Jenks, a utility player who's been with the team a couple of years. He gives me a confused glance and with a shrug hands me a pillow. He flashes a wink and wishes me good luck.

Billy Law is the last to turn off his overhead light. He was reviewing something on his laptop, probably a scouting report for the next series. The scouting report can wait for now; we all needed to take the foot off of the pedal even if only for a few hours.

I wedge the pillow into the corner of the seat and the window and I lean back as much as I can. With my eyes closed I think briefly about sitting atop the hotel ledge. Amazingly, only my rescuer will ever know what I was considering. Not even Jennifer can know. Thank goodness I didn't send her that text. Instead, I replaced the morose text with a quick *I love you and I miss you.*

Jennifer had texted later that morning and I convinced her to hop on a plane and head to Philly. She quickly agreed. The timing is perfect as I have a few things to take care of in the morning and then can spend the rest of my off day with her.

I keep my eyes closed and take long, deliberate breaths. My final thought before falling asleep is that I could not wait to take on the rest of the season with new resolve.

CHAPTER 21

EVEN THOUGH WE returned to town in the wee hours I feel refreshed when I meet Tom at the municipal building. My status and schedule are why the district attorney accommodated me with a morning meeting.

We exchange pleasantries then gather in a large meeting room. The deputy attorney hits me up for an autograph, and I kindly oblige. He says it's for his kid, but that's what they always say.

The boys are escorted in by several police officers and a public defender. They're shocked to see my face and try to remain stoic. All wear blue short-sleeved, button-down shirts with dark blue pants, the uniform of inmates at the juvenile facility.

The public defender directs the boys to folding chairs and they sit in order of age, with the ringleader in the first seat and his young brother in the last. Even the oldest looks like a child. He wears a curious expression and looks tattered. His left arm is still in a heavy cast that wrapped around his hand and rose up to just below his elbow. The hard outside part of his cast caked with dirt.

Seemingly, the other boys look toward the sixteen-year-old for guidance and mimic his actions. Reading more into their expressions, I saw six scared boys now trapped within a punitive system that's ill prepared to offer any sort of productive future. To be confident in moving forward with my plan I need to see sincere repentance that is not based on desperation. I wonder if I would be able to distinguish the difference.

Jennifer helped me formulate the strategy, and it didn't take much to sell the idea to Tom. Instead of considering only what had happened, we considered what happens next.

"Hello boys, do you know who I am?" I ask. The boys look at each other as if deciding who will answer. "Just blurt it out. I want to have a conversation with you, that's all."

"You are the guy with the Range Rover," one of them says.

"And you are TC Hunter. We didn't know it was you," says another.

"Would that have made a difference?" I ask.

The oldest, Mickey, clears his throat. "We weren't looking to hurt anyone. And we wouldn't have messed with you if we knew."

"Are you fans?" I ask. "I mean, do you guys follow the game?"

Mickey's young brother, Jason, chimes in. "Used to. Sometimes I watch the ballgame looking through the window of the bar near our house."

"Where do you boys live?" I ask.

"Hunting Park," one of the boys blurts. I figure he's thirteen or fourteen years old.

"North Philly? What were you doing so far from home?"

"When it's nice out we roam all over. Sometimes we stay away for days, you know, just trying to survive," Mickey says flatly.

"That block was dark, so we were hanging out there," says Ronnie, the second oldest. I recognize his thick chest and wide shoulders that make him appear squat.

"You the guy I hit with the car?"

"Yes sir. That was me."

"You okay?"

"Yeah, the car just grazed me. I went into a roll and landed on a patch of grass past the curb." The boy reminds me of a kid I played with in the minors. Strong and athletic, I'll bet Ronnie could excel in sports if given the opportunity.

"Where did you get the gun?"

"Used to be Mickey's old man's gun," Ronnie says. Ignoring a menacing look from Mickey, he shrugs to signify he has nothing to lose.

"Is your father still around, Mickey?" I ask.

"Nah, hasn't been back around for about a year. Just me, Jason and our mom."

"So, it's just your mom to take care of you?"

"Yeah, she does her best, but it's hard, you know."

"She gets depressed sometimes, likes to drink our dinner," Jason adds. I appreciate how the boys were speaking openly.

"Well, how about you boys?" I ask the other three. "What's your home life like?" The trio look at each other and the youngest, Mark, speaks.

"Same stuff, you know. We all live off the streets. Do what we have to do. Right?" he says as the others nod.

These kids are in no way evil, just a pathetic product of their upbringing and in need of guidance. It's not an excuse for attempted robbery, though I could easily see how things could get to a point of such desperation. Beyond that, I questioned how any of them would have a chance to move beyond this incident. Bureaucrats talk about rehabilitation, but what does that really mean for these boys?

Looking squarely in the eyes of each child I feel empathy. Maybe Jennifer's making me soft, but the same boys need help—not punishment. It was the right thing to do, and my experience on the rooftop in Arizona spurns me on.

"Do either of you know who Hammerin' Hank was?"

"Hammerin' Hank? That's Hank Aaron, right?" Mickey's response is immediate, and the others echo in unison, "Yeah, Hank Aaron."

"Well boys," I say, "In honor of the late Hammerin' Hank, this is what we are going to do."

I lay the groundwork for a plan that I had developed with Jennifer. The boys need to pay their debt to society, and I will work that out with the powers that be. Upon their stint of rehabilitation, I'm going to make sure they have an opportunity to recover and have a good life.

I look at the district attorney and the public defender, both showing agreeable, but curious expressions. Both seem to appreciate the outside-the-box thinking.

"Does this work for you?" I ask the kids. "I promise that if you do what is asked, I am going to help each of you. I want you leaving here feeling like you can turn things around. I promise if you do your end, I'll do mine."

The kids look puzzled as I rise from my seat to shake each boy's hand to seal our compact.

After the boys leave I detail what I intended to do once they were done with their time in the juvenile facility. The punishment needs to be significant, but it should be brief if they demonstrate exemplary behavior.

Tom is instructed to not publicize the plan. He wholeheartedly agrees with it and declares that he will check on the kids from time to time to see if they're living up to their part of the bargain. The only pat on the back I want is from the spirit of Hank Aaron who demonstrated how one man can make a difference.

I go about my routine and work out before heading to the airport. Jennifer's flight arrives in the late afternoon, which is perfect after a busy morning. Energized, I can't wait to see her. More than ever, I realize how she's an integral part of my life moving forward.

Trying to remain incognito, I change into jeans, a Van Halen T-shirt and a beat up No Shoes Nation ball cap that I bought at a concert. Arriving at the terminal, I pull the hat low to cover my face and avoid crowds. I notice a couple of fans pointing at me and I give them a quick wave, but for the most part my beat-up look seems an effective disguise.

As always, Jen looks terrific, wearing a long coral halter dress that shows just enough of her toned and Florida tanned legs. She immediately spots me hanging back in the corner and runs into my warm embrace. There's so much I need to say and plenty of time to say it, so I opt to simply enjoy the moment.

We walk hand in hand through the airport as we've done before, but this time feels different. Once in doubt, our love and commitment are cemented. We feel as one, absorbed in each other's company. Excited at the prospect of spending each minute together, Jen is thrilled to have the rest of the day to ourselves.

Before heading to the condo we stop at the Italian Market in South Philadelphia. The market is on 9th Street, but the smell of the Italian bread and pastries spreads for blocks around the perimeter. Along with bakeries and pastry shops, the marketplace has fruit stands, Italian butchers, pasta shops, and other unique stores.

The aromas nearly have Jen jumping out of the car. Given her Italian heritage, I know she'll appreciate the stop, and we fill up numerous bags with ripe fruit, warm bread, olive oil, tomato pie, and fresh pasta. We also take home Italian pastries and cannoli, which will necessitate some extra cardio exercising in the days ahead.

I have a bit of an ulterior motive with the stop as I want Jennifer to see the charm of the area. Concern with crime in the vicinity due to the carjacking, I want her to see the other side of the city. There are still hard working, law-abiding people living here, and this area of town is like a time capsule from a simpler era.

We stroll along the streets, stopping occasionally to talk with fans. Jen embraces the interaction with the community, and any reluctance with the area wanes. I can tell that she appreciates the joy that a winning team provides a city, especially given her devotion to philanthropy. Nothing can stop a community with people determined to triumph, and although baseball is just a sport, its uplifting spirit is significant. Jen understands ways that we can help, and our union can become a tremendous force.

After the market we head to the condo to spend time alone. Maybe it's my imagination, but even our intimacy reaches another level. I feel more absorbed by our love, and any prevailing fear or vulnerability dissipates. Haunting thoughts have given way to refreshing ideas, allowing me to be completely captivated by this woman.

Even our pillow talk is different. I want her to know things about me that I've never shared with anyone, and I finally feel free to display that openness. We relax in bed and talk about an array of things, both of us willfully bringing up topics we have not previously mentioned. We talk about our pasts, our families, our childhoods, finding many parallels with each other's upbringing. We both talk about our parents as we share the same feelings of loss and anguish over having them depart our lives too early.

She tells stories of her upbringing, which run adjacent to mine. As a young boy, I grew up as the athletic kid in school, yet I never fit in. My popularity as an athlete made me reserved and untrusting. I saw jealousy in others I never knew whom to trust, which made me seem aloof and pretentious. Often, I'd retreat to the bubble that I created for myself, and I used baseball as my outlet and place of comfort.

Jen had similar experiences. She too was an athlete growing up, playing basketball and soccer. Her athleticism was often overshadowed by her beauty, causing her to erect walls to manage her insecurities. She too found herself isolated and struggling to find her place.

She spoke extensively about her parents, and I could tell the conversation was cleansing. Jen does not have siblings and was very close to her mother and father. Her parents provided her with the life lessons that continue to shape her. When they died, she threw herself into her work. By helping others, she gains self-assurance and purpose.

I relate to it all. Our burdens of expectations, feelings of isolation, and quests to find belonging are remarkably similar. It's completely out of character for her to approach a strange man sitting at a bar as she did that fateful evening at the bar in Ybor City, and we're now leading, and sharing, purposeful lives.

"Maybe you're finally in a good place mentally," she says.

If only she knew the half of it.

We spend the rest of the week making love, growing our relationship, and plotting our course. Reaffirming my new mindset, I also begin hitting the absolute shit out of the baseball.

CHAPTER 22

A LIGHT IN the far corner of the training room provides a subtle glow. Several of the team trainers jostle about in preparation for the day, and I watch with admiration as they take inventory and schedule afternoon treatment for the squad.

Sitting in the shadows by my locker, my attention moves to the number nine uniform top hanging a few feet away. Emulating my namesake, I proudly wear the number to honor Ted Williams, a man I've been connected to since childhood. Meditating in my familiar habitat, many questions swirl. In between the lines, my association with Teddy Ballgame and his influence upon me is clear. Still, I never knew how baseball is just the conduit to so much more.

"Hey, ain't your lady friend in town? Why'd you want to meet so early?" Chief asks. Agreeable to an early meeting, his voice ringing through the empty stadium locker room snaps me from my rumination.

"Jennifer's at the apartment, but she's got work to do. Just wanted to run into you before the day gets started," I say.

Chief rubs his trimmed beard and grunts in anticipation.

"Why me Chief?"

The old man scoffs loudly. Pacing the floor in front of my locker he seeks the right words.

"Ain't your eyes wide open yet? Look around TC, it ain't just you. The whole country needs a good kick in the ass and maybe you're the guy to do it!" He pauses. "What does it matter anyway? I mean, here you are so why ask why?"

Everything matters. Truth and reason matter most.

"I dunno, Chief. I've always viewed myself as some guy who plays baseball. Then I got pretty good at it and was thrown into stardom. The media scrutiny and the baseball stuff never bothered me, but then crazy things start happening in my life, so I need an answer to that simple question. Out of everyone why me?"

Still pacing, Chief laughs. "You think you are just some dude who plays baseball? You ain't just some guy, TC. For a long time, you've been special."

"Why special? Is it because I work hard and have become good at something? Does that make someone special?"

"Work without talent doesn't make a hill of beans," Chief sneers.

"So it's because I have talent? A lot of people have talent."

Chief stands directly in front of me, still nervously scratching his beard as if a father nervously giving his son the sex talk.

"It's the whole picture, TC. It's your talent, it's your drive, but it's also your past and the circumstances you've overcome. It's your character and your being. It's your faith, your loyal patriotism, your work ethic, your appreciation of family. All those things that are absent in today's younger generation that need fixing by example. It makes you the right man in the right place at the right time, period."

"Then who decides when you are the right man in the right place? How does a player go from legend to immortal?" I ask.

"By not only being the best, but by leaving a permanent mark," he snaps. "It's not just athletes, you know. It's those immortals chosen to be a dedicated force for good. The very few who by their stature can distribute principles and preserve traditions!"

Chief is right. Immortals are those who impact society in such a way that they can never be forgotten. They are our link to the traditions of the past and to a simpler, more wholesome life. I don't know if I'll ever reach that standing, but he's prompting me to try.

"Outside of Aaron, who do you look towards Chief?"

As if anticipating the question, he answers quickly. "Lou Gehrig, John Wayne, Jackie, Aaron, and Ronald Reagan. Patton, too."

With a loud click, the lights of the locker room switch on. Just arriving, Billy Law also anxious for another day of baseball enters without a word and passes through. Chief waits until he's gone. And smiles wryly.

"You know what's coming, don't you?"

I nod. "I think so."

"The closer you get to the home run record, the more nuts it's going to be. If you keep hitting over four hundred it's going to get even crazier." Chief face became more animated "Don't let any of it get in your dome! Go do this and take your rightful place!"

Rising from my seat I extend my hand to thank my friend who pulls me into an embrace for an extended bro hug. No further words are needed.

Finally letting go, he bolts toward the tunnel leading to his office. Checking his phone and muttering profanities about government overreach he turns down the hall. I appreciate every fiber of his being.

A full baseball season is a hundred and sixty-two games over eight months. The seasons starts with the optimism that the men in the locker room might come together and challenge for a championship. If performance dips team confidence wanes into a death spiral. If players do not perform to their expected abilities or key injuries disable key players, a season can quickly turn into a painful grind. My second year in the league was like that. We were out of the pennant race by July. We had lost some key players to injury, and some of the veteran players soured the team with their nagging and negativity. Some of those players had signed to life-changing contracts and stopped working hard, taking little pride in their craft and blaming others for the team's woes. Big money makes some players rest on their laurels, a tragic irony.

After that woeful second season the club fired the manager and hired Billy Law. Billy made an immediate impact, taking charge right away and becoming a positive force for the organization. He pressed management to trade away lazy or negative players, cutting all who plagued the squad. Miraculously, everything changed once the malignancies were gone. Billy knew that a team needs hungry players and not big money athletes who got fat off the hog.

Once Law cleaned house and established a no-nonsense mindset, the subsequent seasons became enjoyable as we vied for a championship each year. However, this year is different. Managing the weight of high expectations is an art, and thankfully Billy knows how.

It's September, and we're winning games at an unprecedented level despite the media circus circulating around the clubhouse. My batting average holds firm at .422 and I've slugged fifty-six home runs.

It's still conceivable that I might challenge the single-season home run record of seventy-three long balls. If I were able to accomplish the feat while also hitting over .400, well that would go down as the best batting season in history.

Ridiculously, several sports channels created a pace tracker to project my home run total. With each at bat, the new number flashes across television screens and social media sites, tallying my long balls and predicting the anticipated sum. At the same time, my batting average shows directly under the home run prediction.

This hyper focus on me and the records has been a distraction for the team, one that Billy masterfully navigates.

"There's nothing to be sorry about. We are going to embrace the attention, TC. There's no need to shy away and hide. Let's have some fun with the ride!"

Billy agrees that I'm not to alter my approach in search of the home run record. It's more important to get on base and score wins for the team. Screw the owners and the media.

I hear a ruckus in the far corner of the room. Several of the reporters that were scheduled to meet with Billy Law for their weekly meeting invade the locker room. They're trying to sneak by to get to me, but some of my teammates block them, knowing my aversion. I thank my teammates and then step into the throng. It's an opportunity to put theory into practice and to set the tone for the days ahead.

I remain calm and manage the scene. I spread the reporters out so I can clearly note who is asking questions and require they speak one at a time. Happy with the unfettered access, they all agree.

The reporters have a job to do, however, I also have an agenda. First on my list is to review the exploits of my teammates who, without their exemplary play, I would not be having the historic season. I emphasize the importance of team chemistry and noted how Billy Law has been the mastermind. I also note that winning games comes before all, and the real story is how well we were playing as a unit, a concerted effort just like old-time baseball.

When asked about the records before me, I'd rattle off clichés like, "I try not to think about home runs, but yeah, it would be historic to break the mark." I also credit the fans by saying, "Breaking the record would be for the crowd. They've been supportive throughout my career, and I want to do it for them more than anything else."

Asked about any movement on a contract extension I repeat that we're not negotiating during the season, and they should ask my agent about such things. I even pull a quote from the movie *Bull Durham* to let them know my only focus is on the game. "I just want to give it my best shot and the Good Lord willing, things will work out."

No matter how the reporters try to trip me up, I keep my mood upbeat and focus mostly on the fans, my teammates, and the game. I chose my words carefully while making sure I hit my points, providing little controversy. My only contentious remarks are about the station-to-station approach that many other teams follow.

"The more the game moves from its founding, the more important it is to reinvigorate it with traditional doctrine," I say.

I'm asked what that means, exactly. My answer is simple.

"I like to bunt on occasion."

CHAPTER 23

ANY TIME I drop a bunt or intentionally slap a pitch the other way to gain an easy base hit, the writers suggest I've got a screw loose. In one game I drop three bunt base hits in a row. The media howl at the atrocity, even though I score on all three occasions in a single run win.

When I need affirmation of my strategy I simply look into the stands. Even though my life is absent of insomnia and odd occurrences, recently, if I look hard, I can find one of the guardians of the game who seems pleased with my play. Sometimes it's as simple as following a camera flash to locate one of the ghosts of the game.

The press becomes more unrelenting each day as the numbers become more attainable. Reporters show up at the stadium earlier and earlier no matter if we are on the road or at home. As we head into playoff season, it all starts to feel overwhelming.

When home, I use Chief's office as a bomb shelter. He encourages me to hide out at any time if the media blitzes the locker room. I think Chief likes being my guard dog and he has no problem playing the heavy. If a reporter attempts to follow me back to his office he plays the part of the crazy old clubhouse manager, lacing a string of profanities that echo through the hall.

"Get the hell out of here you two-bit beat writer," he shouts. "The next time I see you in here I'm going to shove that microphone right up your ass." Such encounters always leave him smiling.

Hiding in Chief's office also gives me more time to spend with the old man. Our relationship has morphed over the years and ever since Arizona, our conversations angle toward the spiritual. He still provides baseball instruction from time to time, but most of our conversations veer toward life and the soul.

I discover many new things about my old friend. Although I knew of his firm religious base, I'm surprised to find he is so devout. He likes Jennifer partly for her own religious footing. Wanting me to have that same foundation, I assure him I'm not the pagan he might think.

"Belief in an almighty keeps you grounded," he often says. "When you firmly believe life is more than just yourself you can then have a fulfilling path. Don't forget that."

Often, he points to Jennifer's charitable efforts, sometimes making mention of some of his own. When his wife passed on many years ago, he became more altruistic. He knows Jen pushes me to be better in that regard and he's unrelenting in his messaging.

"You and that young lady are a great force. You've got the platform to mold things the way you want them, the way things ought to be. Make a difference, kid, never sit back," he says. "Who knows, maybe the two of you can straighten out this country so I might die in peace!"

I hate it when he suggests his time in this world is limited, but he scolds me when I say so. "For chrissakes, I'm eighty-five years old. Feel great and ain't dying yet, but get real kid, my skis are pointing down the slope."

⚾ ⚾ ⚾

We clinched the division on September 13, the same day I hit home run number sixty-two, tying modern day slugger Aaron Judge and eclipsing what many consider the truly impactful home run record of sixty-one by Roger Maris. I set the mark at home in Philly, making the occasion even more special.

The probability of reaching the standing mark of seventy-three is waning, yet the fans still shower praise and adulation. With sixteen games to go, the mathematics put me on pace to ding between sixty-eight and sixty-nine home runs. All my bunts, singles, and walks are seen as missed opportunities by critics, yet getting on base bolsters my batting average, which is an obscene .423. Accumulating team wins, which remains my foremost priority, we clinched the division and also garnered home-field advantage throughout the playoffs.

Before our next game I stick my head into Billy Law's office door. "Billy, it's time." He knows exactly what I mean and didn't say a word. Instead, he smiles and winks.

I'm not going to start swinging for the fences on each pitch. The simple adjustment of not slapping the ball or bunting against the shift on some at bats should alone equate to more long balls attempts. I might show bunt once in a while to keep the opposition honest, and besides, there are still a couple of hitting marks that I want to reach.

The next two games produce no home runs, and the collective sigh from the press is palpable. The fans too are disappointed.

The collective pause from the home run chase allows the team to catch its breath, though when I hit two home runs the next game and then another two to start the following series the buzz cranks up again. A home run in each of the next two games to close out the series set me at an astounding sixty-eight home runs with ten games to go.

With each home run the roar of the crowd grows, and I make sure during my home run trots to scan the faces in the crowd as a note of appreciation. Sometimes I think I see one of baseball's immortals smiling down on me from the stands. Whether it be Ruth, Cobb, Yogi, Robinson, Catfish, the Splinter, the Clipper, or Hank, I tip my cap and receive affirming recognition that can be described as nothing outside of magical.

With ten games to go I need five home runs to tie the record. We travel to Pittsburgh for a four-game set and then back home for six games to close out the season.

The anticipation grows exponentially with each at bat. After two home runs in four road games in Pittsburgh my home run tally reaches seventy. It's an unthinkable number and hard to grasp; it's downright mythical.

When I hit numbers seventy-one and seventy-two to open the home series against Milwaukee the entire country burst into frenzied celebration. Tying the record in my first at bat of the final three game series of the year against Chicago blew the roof off the stadium, though it was the next plate appearance that unexpectedly set the world on fire.

Chicago pitcher, Kurt Jones, toed the mound for the opposition. One of Chicago's high-level prospects, Jones is a tall, hard-throwing lefty who throws with a fiery edge. As commonly done by teams who have been eliminated from contention, he's a late season call up from the minors, so I have no history against him.

Young and wild, the kid is also cocky, and his goal is to make sure I don't take him deep; the kid understandably doesn't want to become the answer to a baseball trivia question.

I want to break the record quickly, but off of the brash kid the safer route is to shorten my swing and try to punch a ball through the infield. I do exactly that and slap a pitch for a single. I could feel the air come out of the stadium crowd, but that changed with a simple gesture.

I had not run into Jamie Cunningham since the fateful incident on opening day. Cunningham had been injured for several weeks, so when we played them in Chicago in June he was not in the lineup. We played them again in early August and somehow I never ended up on first base in those games.

With so much going on, an encounter with Cunningham is the last thing on my mind. As I stand at first base, Cunningham extends his hand. "Congratulations on an incredible year, TC," he says.

The buzz of the crowd turns into a full roar when I grasp my adversary's hand. Shaking the stadium with wild applause, the fans realize the impromptu moment is something special. Turning to the big first baseman I say, "I just realized, I never apologized for hitting you, Jamie. I'm sorry."

"Nothing to apologize about, we're good."

Impulsively, I put my arm around Cunningham. The simple

gesture of burying the hatchet provides an example for people across the nation. Two baseball players, one black and one white, with diametrically different positions being able to put their differences aside sparked a change. The innocuous handshake and embrace are replayed night after night on news channels and through social media, making a palpable difference in the tenor of a polarized nation.

I look over my shoulder toward the stands. Above our dugout, walking up the aisle is a tall, athletically built man wearing a 1960s plaid print suit. He speeds up the aisle, but before disappearing into the crowd we lock eyes. I nearly well up right at first base when I realize Cuinningham and I have just made Hank Aaron proud.

⚾ ⚾ ⚾

Fanfare for the following game is over the top. We have what seems to be hundreds of reporters milling about in games leading up to the home run mark, close to three-times the normal number. Even gossip columnists and pop stars attend. Baseball-loving countries like Japan, Mexico, and Italy have also sent reporters, and with so much excitement surrounding the event I have butterflies for the first time since my rookie year.

Chief guards the locker room like a hawk, shooing away reporters all day. The press was promised access to the locker room a couple of hours before game time, but that doesn't stop some from trying to sneak in early. Nobody messes with Chief. At eight-five years old he was still full of piss and vinegar, he looks crazy enough to pummel any rogue sportswriter hunting me down.

I want to strike quickly and put the home run record behind me, but Chief reminds me to not get overanxious. "Find a way to relax," he says. "Take a few deep breaths and absorb the crowd. Enjoy the moment like you've done from the beginning. That's the key." Chief is of course right. I must find a way to slow it all down.

I like the matchup with the opposing starter, a veteran righty who's not going to pitch around me. Steve Cartnick has a good sinking fastball and a sharp curve, and he'll try to attack the strike zone. Studying his patterns, I see that he likes to establish his fastball inside to left-handed hitters. I'll look for one inside, and if he doesn't get the pitch in close enough I'll launch it into the seats.

My anxiousness abates as I move through the tunnel to the dugout. It's the same path I've walked hundreds of times, and despite the anticipation I feel at ease. As I pace toward the dugout, the clicking of my metal spikes against the concrete floor give way to the sound of an already roaring crowd. The excitement rushing through the stands fills me with energy. My only thought is that I wish the game would start immediately instead of still being over an hour and a half away.

A horde of reporters wait impatiently at the front step of the dugout. I know I must give them a few minutes of time, but I time it so that our team batting practice gave me an excuse to keep things short. The reporters were given strict instructions not to enter the dugout, so I take my time. I pour a cup of Gatorade from the large orange dispenser at the far end of the dugout and take a few sips. I put out my index finger to indicate I need a minute and find amusement in watching the reporters get antsy. I climb the steps of the recessed dugout and once at field level I announce, "I'm happy to give you a few minutes before batting practice. Let's just keep it organized, so no stampedes."

The reporters form an arc of bodies, seemingly leaning on top of one another a dozen deep, scrunching together in a jumbled mass of humanity. It seems like hundreds of microphones and recorders extend in my direction, and I envision some reporter who misses the entire interview because of not hitting the right button.

Amid the organized chaos I'm impressed at how orderly the questions rain down. As if there's an understood pecking order of who was to ask questions, they come one at a time, and everyone in the throng conducts themselves with the utmost professionalism.

I keep my answers short in order to give more reporters a chance to ask me something. Each question is similar and predictable. Am I nervous? How do I feel? Is today the day I make history? Do I have a strategy? Did Billy Law give me the green light to swing away?

After twenty minutes I excuse myself to take my round of batting practice. I gave the reporters a good amount of time and they appear satisfied. I tell them to meet me in the same spot at the end of the game if I do happen to hit the record-breaking home run.

Batting practice helps me get refocused. I joke around with my teammates and treat the game and preparation as just another day. Even so, I hear the cameras click with each batting practice swing. Off in the distance, I hear the distinct whoosh of a few old-time magnesium filament flashes, too.

Some of the bolder reporters pull a few teammates away from the batting practice backstop to get more interviews, and the buzz of the crowd builds toward a roar. I try to keep an even keel approaching the game as usual business. Despite my legs feeling weak from nerves, I hear Chief's voice in my head and tell myself, as he has, that I was born for this moment.

Our starting pitcher works quickly and disposed of Chicago in the top of the first. The crowd doesn't even wait for us to get off the field defensively before roaring with anticipation. They grow louder when I step into the on-deck circle to warm up before my first at bat.

Billy Law gives me a quick smile and says, "Let's do this, kid." Billy had toyed with the idea of batting me lead off for this game to get the first at bat under my belt right away, but I implored him to keep things the same.

I give him a thumbs up and go about my routine, which includes swinging a heavy lead pole before taking dry swings with my game bat. I had set my young friend Ethan up with front-row seats and I extend my bat toward him and ask, "Are you ready to go?"

"Hell yeah," he says at the chagrin of his mom sitting beside him on his left. Laughing, Jennifer, sitting to his right, notices the exchange and gives me a calming glance. Ethan slaps my extended bat for good luck, and I flash him a sideways smile. His presence certainly brings perspective to the moment.

Our leadoff hitter grounds out to shortstop, and when I take my strides toward the plate the fans stand and erupt into a deafening roar. I take a few deep breaths and tell myself to take the first pitch.

As anticipated, I take an inside fastball. The flashes of what seemed like tens of thousands of cameras leave me momentarily stunned. I must find a way to block it out.

The umpire calls the pitch a ball. It was clearly inside, and I know Cartnick is simply applying some gamesmanship to gain an advantage on the next pitch. That tells me he's going to throw another inside fastball, and now ahead in the count I look for a pitch to drive.

I step out of the batter's box to take another few breaths and scan the masses. My eyes move about each section of the stadium, and I see a small army of men strewn throughout the crowd wearing out-of-date suits.

I shake my head and force the images into the background and regain footing in the box. Digging in I clear my head and visualize the next pitch. A rush of confidence courses through my veins and I hear my father's voice say, *"Figure it out,"* as the pitch hurdles toward the plate.

I turn hard on the inside pitch and watch the ball explode off the bat toward the right field wall, flying deep into the Philadelphia night. The decibel level of the roaring crowd is almost frightening and louder than a jet plane engine as I start my home run trot. I don't feel my legs as I round each bag.

When I reach home plate I'm mobbed by the team. One by one I embrace each teammate and coach, making sure my baseball brothers know that my glory was a collective effort.

Billy Law gets an extra-long hug. Without Billy having the courage to buck the trends and manage without distraction, I would never have come close to the great feat. Along with sheer joy, I see relief in Billy's eyes. He stuck his neck out for me and the team throughout the season.

The last person I hug is Chief. Normally, he's not on the field, but he made his way into the dugout before my at bat. He says he knew I was going to do it on my first swing of the day. That old man has something more than uncanny intuition. We were meant to share the moment together. But I have one more thing to do.

After the long embrace I say, "Hey, Chief, I decided to take your advice."

He gives me a quizzical look as I walk him over to the front row of seats next to the dugout. Motioning to Ethan, he pulls the black box out of his pocket and tosses it to me. Right there on the field, amid the bedlam, and in front of my dearest friend and redeemer, I drop to one knee and ask Jennifer to marry me.

⚾ ⚾ ⚾

The scrum for the home run baseball looked more like a riot with people diving on top of each other all looking to snare the piece of history. The auction value of the record-breaking baseball is estimated to be well over three million dollars, and the lucky fan who came out of the pile with the ball will likely cash in. Stadium security immediately ran to the section where the ball landed to preserve order and safely escort the lucky fan to safety.

The home run video is scrutinized over and over again to find the blessed fan. The film shows the baseball hitting off a man's bare hand and then falling between the bleachers. Dozens of fans threw themselves on the ground and struggled to find the ball, each eventually climbing to their feet with hands raised suggesting the ball had disappeared. And for the rest of the game, which we win 6-2, speculation runs rampant.

Sports announcers theorize that someone must have shoved the ball into their pants out of fear the valuable relic would be swiped. A couple of charlatans claimed after the game to have the historic ball, but they were proven to be frauds when they produced a generic baseball not used during the game. The commissioner of the league had special markings put on the baseballs for the game in order to draw a distinction between the true ball and any other.

Detectives were called upon to analyze the video to identify the fan in possession of the ball and they went so far as to track down and interview several fans who were in the vicinity. Each of the interviewees claimed they saw the ball on the ground and reached a split second too late. A half a dozen fans claimed they distinctly remember the hand that grabbed the baseball belonged to a young man wearing a dark brown suit. But no one on video matched who they saw.

With the pressure off and the team securely in the playoffs, Billy Law wants me to sit out the final regular season game. In fact, he wants to rest all the regular players and vehemently declares his decision is final. He'd have some serious explaining to do if he allowed me to play and I got hurt, but I appeal to his love of baseball history to make him understand why he is going to have to physically drag me off the field.

With 247 hits in 590 at bats, my batting average is .4186 which rounds to .419. My goal is to hit .419 to match Ty Cobb's best batting average that he obtained in 1911. Cobb had 248 hits in 592 at bats, so mathematically he had me beat.

It's like a repeat of Ted Williams going into the final day of the season statistically hitting .400 but demanding to play in the last day's double header instead of sitting it out to protect his record. The parallel to history was just too juicy and I pressed Billy Law to reconsider. We agreed to a compromise.

He allowed me to start the final game, and in my first at bat I lined out to the right fielder. For my second at bat, I hit a sharp double down the line. Time was called and as agreed, Billy Law sent out a pinch runner. My season was officially over and with 248 hits in 592 at bats, I precisely matched Cobb's season from 1911. Pretty damn cool.

We flew through the baseball playoffs en route to the first championship the city experienced in over a dozen years. With the final out, I dropped to my knees and thanked Heaven for the moment. God had provided the talent cultivated for many years and culminating in this one instant.

As we sprayed champagne all over one another, I focused on the sheer joy in the faces of each of my teammates. We had grown together and became one of the best teams in baseball history and most importantly, we did it in a way that represented old-school, hard-nosed baseball.

"Law Ball" received vindication. The team owed everything to Billy Law's leadership and the look on our manager's face as he hoisted the championship trophy was priceless. I could not imagine playing for any other manager, and when my agent, Tom, pulled me aside and whispered in my ear, I knew I'd never have to.

Grabbing Billy from the throng, I thank him personally for everything he provided me. His face glows when I tell him Tom's news, and he interrupts the party for a special announcement. Holding his hands up in the air and calming the room he yells out, "Listen up everyone, Ts has something he wants to say."

The room goes silent out of respect for our revered manager, and I step forward. "Gentleman, I need each of you to know how incredible it's been to be your teammate." I look around the room and each player is focused on my words. "No matter what lies ahead for each of us, we will always have this moment and we will always have this championship," I say. I make eye contact with each of my baseball brothers and continue. "And I just have to tell you... I AIN'T GOING ANYWHERE!"

The room cheers at the news and will later learn that as a condition of my contract, Billy Law is to receive a contract extension to match the span of my time with the team. Not only had Tom negotiated a record half-billion-dollar deal, but he also used leverage to make sure I had my manager in place, effectively ensuring that the game would be played right.

With the demons of the steroid era gone and a championship proving the merits of the game's history, baseball itself is no longer in jeopardy. With my path now clear there's yet another thing left to do.

CHAPTER 24

SACRED HEART CATHOLIC Church in the heart of Tampa is magnificent. Although not officially recognized as a principal church since it does not house a bishop, the structure resembles an ornate European cathedral.

Built in 1905, the church is adorned with numerous stained-glass windows portraying Biblical scenes. The windows are original to the structure and offer an ancient touch to stand out among the many modern highlights. The mere historic aspect of the church is inspiring, and the intricate artwork, windows, statues, and moldings emphasize tradition.

The pews of the church are packed, and the over flow stand in the side aisles. More people fill the choir balcony, and I figure some of my teammates must have snuck upstairs. They'll probably get kicked out, but I have other things to worry about at the moment.

Jennifer doesn't have a big family. Like me, Jen was an only child, and our invitation list is relatively short. I suppose I should not be surprised to find the event has turned into a spectacle with a bunch of wedding crashers making their way into the church. I probably should have hired a security team, but it was too late to be overly concerned.

I have played in front of more than fifty thousand people at times, and I can firmly say that I rarely get nervous. Nevertheless, here I am at the front of a church, my hands clammy and sweat dripping from my brow.

Looking into the crowd I recognize many of the faces and see plenty of current and past teammates along with players who I've befriended through my career. We invited everyone within the organization including team executives, trainers, current and former coaches, and most are in attendance. It's a full house, and I feel honored.

Ethan and his mom sit in a pew close to the front. He's dressed in a sharp, dark-blue suit, fidgety from the tie, but thrilled to be part of the occasion. It's funny how life works. This little boy has no idea how much he means to me and how our growing friendship has made me realize many things about myself.

My dearest friend, Chief, stands beside me as my best man. He's almost unrecognizable with his beard manicured and sporting a well-fitted tuxedo. Chief often jokes that people should not judge him on face value, and he cleans up well. "Only for you, kid," he says when I compliment his transformation.

The music sounds and everyone rises. The pipe organ and cellist played Cannon in D as Jennifer appears in the vestibule. Maybe it's the sun reflecting behind her, but I swear she's surrounded by a glowing aura. They say brides often beam, and Jen always sticks out in a room, but today she looks even more radiant.

Our eyes lock when she's halfway down the aisle and my nervousness dissipates. I'm not much for ceremonies, and I do have a good degree of social anxiety, but looking at my bride gives me strength. I was meant to marry Jennifer.

Chief gives me an approving nudge and I look down at the old man. His expression is that of pure joy, his smile reassuring. "She's beautiful, TC. She could get me out of mourning," he unceremoniously jokes.

Breathing deeply, I'm completely focused on Jennifer and barely notice my manager and good friend, Billy Law, who is to give the bride away. Svelte in his immaculate, black tuxedo, the classic look is as dignified a fit as his baseball uniform.

Jen became friends with Billy's wife, Erin, after sitting beside each other at several of our games. She became like a stepmom and Billy a stepfather. Billy looks swollen with pride as he walks slowly down the aisle.

I am not devoutly religious, although I have a firm belief in God.

Like Jennifer, I was raised to have faith but had stepped away from the church for a variety of reasons. Jen maintained her religious base throughout her life, and it's reassuring that she has that foundation.

In preparation for the Sacrament of Marriage, we were required to go through several consultation sessions with a priest. I went into the Pre-Cana meetings feeling as if I'm a heathen for having left the church. Jen and I are now spiritually aligned, wanting the same out of marriage and beyond.

Billy and I embrace, then he gives Jen away, smiling from ear to ear. Father Jake, as we call him, has a forceful voice, displaying an energy and enthusiasm that keeps all attentive. He's pious but with a jocular charisma that evokes smiles and laughter.

He speaks of how he can see us grow as a pair before his eyes and is confident that we will have a marriage filled with everlasting love. He tells the crowd that he's impressed with our devotion to helping the less fortunate and adds that a marriage with purpose is destined for success.

He even throws in a few baseball lines, suggesting I hit a grand slam when I met Jennifer. Father Jake also compares life to baseball, suggesting that both can be filled with plenty of strikeouts and pop ups, but when you are with the right woman, it's easier to deal with the outs because you know the hits are coming. "It looks like there are plenty of baseball old timers in the crowd to attest to that," he says, "although I think I recognize a few out there who like TC, make baseball seem a little easier than it should be."

Facing forward, Jen and I cannot tell who he's addressing, but he points in several directions to acknowledge players in the crowd and balcony. Weaving the game into the ceremony is masterfully done as he speaks to the purity of the game in conjunction with the sanctity and the blessings of marriage.

"Without further ado, please help me welcome this wonderful couple into holy matrimony. Do you TC Hunter..."

I concentrate on the priest's words, while images of my parents flash before me. I imagine my mother and father in Heaven, thrilled that I'm settling down. I'm sure they've toiled in the afterlife thinking this day would never come, but here it is, and I can feel their love and approval.

Did our parents have a hand in cultivating our relationship? Perhaps they touched us from the afterlife, but they certainly influenced us through our similar upbringing.

When pronounced man and wife, the throng erupts in deafening applause, including strident hooting and hollering from the balcony. The shouts only drown out when the massive pipe organ blares Jennifer's traditional choice for the recessional, Beethoven's Ode to Joy.

The cheers as we walk down the aisle as husband and wife resemble those of a stadium crowd. With each step they grow louder and more raucous as the many overzealous baseball players let loose.

Chief tugs on my tuxedo jacket. Turning, I notice a strange grin. Lifting his eyes and bobbing his head toward the balcony, my best man is giddy. The images up above, although utterly implausible, provide clarity to the mysteries that have haunted me for well over a year.

On that fateful day when I was talked down from the ledge of the Arizona hotel roof, I knew mystical forces were at play. I also knew that Chief was somehow part of the scheme, but now I had my proof.

Jennifer is oblivious to the strange gentlemen in the balcony, so I tap her on the shoulder and point upward. "Isn't the façade of the balcony just beautiful!"

Staring upward with my mouth agape, I see the apparitions of Cy Young, Rogers Hornsby, Jimmie Foxx and Stan Musial huddled to the far left of the terrace. Nearby, Big Train Walter Johnson and Christy Mathewson are conversing, Ty Cobb stands near Civil War general and baseball designer, Abner Doubleday.

I recognize Honus Wagner from his infamously valuable baseball card, and next to him stands Frank Robinson and Tom Seaver leaning from the balcony rail. Henry Aaron. Mickey Mantle and Joe DiMaggio are in the center of the balcony, and Catfish Hunter along with Roberto Clemente dawdle behind.

Many others who were not baseball players also roam the space. To the far right of the stage, Rush Limbaugh smokes a cigar while chatting with Andrew Breitbart. Charlton Heston stands nearby, rifle in hand replicating his "From my cold, dead hands" pose in support of the second amendment. Nearby, John Wayne leans against a post and behind him, Clark Gable and Carole Lombard, looking like lovebirds. Could that actually be Lincoln and Washington standing near JFK and Martin Luther King, Jr.? Even though he's standing to the far end, I know I recognize Ronald Reagan speaking to Winston Churchill and Margaret Thatcher.

The balcony is packed with these mystical immortals, and I can't see them all. Ruth, Gehrig and Berra are nearest and sit with their legs dangling from the balcony ledge. Ruth points toward me and says something that Berra finds funny, while Gehrig nods in quiet approval.

Each legend appears youthfully vibrant, moving with confident animation as if captured in the prime of their careers. Prodded by Jennifer to continue walking toward the exit, I could have stood in the same spot in the church to watch the interaction for hours.

With each step moving under the balcony ledge, the images leave my sightline. Nonetheless, I hear several shouts above the din, "Way to go, kid!" "*Nos salvaste.*" "Welcome to the club." "Save us all, slugger!"

Craning my neck toward what everyone else sees as an empty balcony, my fixation on the space must have appeared odd. Jennifer seems not to notice as she basks in the admiration of the living.

The episodes and encounters over the previous year pointed me in a direction to save the game while also saving myself. Breaking the record, patriotically popping Cunningham in the face, marrying Jennifer, helping Ethan, forgiving those kids... it all converges. Mostly I wonder about Chief, just a few steps behind and staring into the balcony smiling. I wonder if Chief chose me, or if the immortals made the selection and charged Chief with making it come to fruition.

Chief puts his hand on me as if to reassure me that what we're seeing is real. I look over my shoulder and he gives me a wink. Prodding me to continue moving forward he pulls a baseball from his jacket and hands it to me. "Here you go," he says. "Snared from the cranks."

The ball is pristine outside of one scuff mark from my record-breaking home run. I stare in awe at the inscription above Cobb's autograph that reads, *She's worth saving, kid!*

The sun sits low in the late afternoon sky and will soon yield to an ideal late fall night, perfect weather to complete a fantastic day.

Father Jake has already taken off his cassock and stands outside greeting people wearing standard short sleeve vestments and collar. He's enjoying chatting with a few of my teammates. Father Jake is a baseball fan and makes the trip across the causeway to the Clearwater Beach resort for the reception so he can continue to mingle with the players.

Jen is chatting with guests who come over to wish congratulations and compliment her on her beauty. Sensing a presence to my right I turned away from Jennifer and find myself face to face with a tall, young gentleman. He was about my height and has short brown hair. His smile highlights his boyish face, and I immediately recognize the legendary figure.

"Congratulations, TC. You are one lucky man," he says.

Jennifer remains deep in conversation with some guests, but it's like someone hit the mute button. I could not hear what she's saying, nor the words of those she's speaking to. I hear only the dapper man beside me.

"Thank you," I mutter. "I sure am lucky."

The man lets out a booming laugh. "Lucky in ways you probably don't even realize yet!" he says. Looking down he kicks at the ground with childlike self-consciousness before continuing. "Say, I hope you don't mind that some of the boys crashed your wedding."

Unable to respond, I manage an anxious grin. I see Chief standing a few steps behind the man, giggling like a school kid at our conversation. Captured by the man's piercing eyes, I stand frozen.

"The boys just wanted to let you know how thankful we are for all you've done. We put you through the wringer, and you were a hard nut to crack. Just glad you've figured some things out and are now on the right track," the man says.

"It's been an interesting time," I squeak, managing to gain at least a small amount of composure.

"Yeah, we definitely made it interesting for you," the man bellows. Changing the subject he says, "Helluva season you had."

"Means everything coming from you," I respond, slightly less nervous now.

"Different time and different game, but damn, I'd like to get a crack at the baseball the way it is now. Live balls, beautiful stadiums, better bats, hell if I wouldn't give all those records a run."

I muster an encouraging smile. One of the great things about baseball is the debate about how players of a different era would match up in the current game. A great irony is that Ted Williams was the first player forced to deal with a major defensive shift. It was deemed more of a psychological ploy than a tactical one, but since he was so hot at the plate the opposition preferred that he bunt instead of launching another home run ball into the seats. I have a feeling Ted would do just fine if inserted into today's game.

"I hope you forgive us for some of the stuff we put you through."

"Forgive?"

"Well, yeah. I know what we asked of you ain't easy, the dreams, the visitations and the rest of it are enough to drive anyone crazy. Pushed you to the limit there in Arizona, had to you know. Needed you to feel some urgency. Things are dire out there and the easy route is to remain unaware."

"Unaware?"

"Well sure, kid. You know the old saying that 'ignorance is bliss?'

It's much easier to push truth and reason aside and follow along. But history and truth trumps propaganda, and it was our job to make you fully aware of the consequences of the current path. It's what we do and how we preserve the guiding principles of the past."

"It still feels like I've got much to figure out."

"Well, sure you do," he says. Pointing toward Jennifer he continues. "This is all part of it, you know. Letting this young lady into your life, you need her, she's a big piece. Virgil here knows it, he helped with that. We did whatever needed to get you to this point, but it's up to you to take action."

Chief gives me a heedful glance, knowing he constantly harped that Jennifer fortified my soul. He smiles and nods with approval at the recognition, and it's at this moment that I understand Chief's involvement.

"That young lady completes your life. You did great to save the game of baseball, but she's gonna help you save the rest," my namesake declares. "That lady won't let you get complacent, there's more that needs to be done and she knows it!"

"Save the rest?"

"Well yeah, kid. *Salvame*, as our friend on the plane said. You saved us ball players by saving the game. Saved yourself too, but there's much more to do. She's worth saving, you know."

The former Triple Crown winner and Korean War pilot flashes a wry smile while staring intently. "The game predates movies and film, you know. The foundation of our country is a fascinating miracle of human history, and baseball has been married to her almost from the onset. You were selected to preserve that link, and also to bring balance back to the game and stability to the country. I know how that's a tough thing to get thrown upon you, kid."

I nod encouragingly, wanting to hear more. Some say that when you enter the gates of Heaven all of life's mysteries are revealed; this feels like my troubles are now lifted and I'm receiving answers to the things that have haunted me.

"The country's gone astray, she's divided. Happens every so often," he continues. "The pendulum needs to swing back, and she needs a hero. The country needs a champion of freedom, and baseball's just the conduit."

Still unable to grasp the full extent of the man's words, I do at least now realize how the game and the country run parallel.

The left-handed prodigy continues. "Hell, just like baseball needs some fixing, so does the country, and now you are in position to do both." His eyes grow glassy with patriotic pride. "Anyhow, we knew you were the one to take on the responsibility. Virgil confirmed it, told us you could handle it."

Chief is biting his lip, less out of concern and more from relief. Trying to figure out what's real and what's in my head has been the most maddening.

Glancing back at my father's childhood idol, I notice his immaculate suit jacket and perfectly creased pants. His clothes hid his flawless athletic build, clearly strong and muscular, but not bulky. If I had a bat, I'd ask him to take a few swings right there in front of the church. I want to cherish every moment of the encounter.

"Say, you know how your dad named you after me? That must have been a little tough, you know, having to always get compared to me."

"I wouldn't have it any other way," I say. "It's an honor to even have my name mentioned in the same sentence as yours."

"The honor is mine, kid," he says softly. "Let me say it again, though, I'm still the best hitter that ever lived! Hell, if I didn't miss all those years from being in the military, just think of the records I'd have had."

"I know," I chuckle, shaking in disbelief. "Can I ask you a question?"

"You can ask anything, kid. But there are rules that connect your world with mine, so I can't always answer." He smiles cautiously.

"Can I start with why it always had to be 3:48 am?"

"Oh, that?" he laughs. "I can answer that one. Up in the balcony, did you see those three damn Yankees sitting together on the ledge?"

I pictured the balcony and sitting together on the rail during the wedding were Yankee legends, Ruth, Gehrig and Berra. The digits 3, 4 and 8 were their uniform numbers.

"Babe, Lou, and Yogi have an odd sense of humor. Ruth is the instigator out of the three, but you know how baseball players can be. Those gents like their gags and their mischief. Had to be early to shake you, but they added the extra detail for their own amusement."

Funny, life would have been a lot easier if Yogi and his number eight lead the instigation. Baseball players do have an odd sense of humor, likely due to the strain of the game. Being a little goofy provides an outlet, and I do appreciate the gag.

"Why me?" I next ask.

"Chief already answered that one." Shifting his weight onto his hip, he tilts his head and pensively continues. "I can ask the same thing, no? Like you, all I wanted to be was a ballplayer, but there were other even more important concerns in life. Why me way back when?"

Because you are the best hitter ever and a war hero! I nearly blurted my thoughts, but the smarter choice was to just listen.

"You were selected for the same reason as me and the others. It takes a man with a presence, someone with fortitude and character who ain't afraid to go against the grain and buck the trends. Nobody's going to listen to a wobbly fellow without principles, you see."

He looked off to the side at Jen still chatting obliviously.

"With your character, baseball prowess, and your drive to be the best, naturally you were the choice. Your journey has provided you with wisdom and courage, two things that are badly needed these days. Now, you can use your status to lead on and off the field and get things moving back in the right direction."

The same thing Chief told me. I get it now. But I still don't know precisely what I am to do. Perhaps that will become clearer with time.

"One last thing," the prodigious lefty says. "There are some who desire to replace the past with the present. The closer they come to that fundamental change, the more tradition needs to be preserved. Baseball and history need preservation, despite the shallow attempts of some who ignore the significance of both. Those who throw away morality and ageless ideals have little regard for consequences. Under the auspices of progress, they try to eradicate history both in the game and the country. But it's our history that guides us, and there's great responsibility in preserving legacies and safeguarding our future. Like freedom and liberty, baseball requires convention to live on!"

His demands for a simpler, more just time are as applicable today as during his prime. I now understand why he and the others from the past push me to the brink.

The greatest hitter in the game's history turns in Jen's direction. A blunt spasm of disappointment reaches my soul as I realize our conversation is at an end. Looking toward Jennifer who was headed our way, I feel an encouraging pat to my shoulder. I swivel back and the image was gone.

"Why did that guy just salute you?" Jen asks. "He looks familiar."

CHAPTER 25

BASEBALL IS A revered institution that moves beyond the stadiums and the pageantry of sport. The diamond, the bases, home plate, the laces of the ball, the balance of a bat, the smell of a leather glove, all remind us of a game we played as kids in parks with beat up backstops and uneven fields. It's that deliberation of familiar comfort that ties into past eras and traditions like no other endeavor.

Some consider the pace of the game too casual, but it's that cadence that allows for discussions and strategy that often move beyond the untailored viewer. The incomparable beauty of the game is fortified with numbers, statistics, and generational comparisons like no other sport. Records provide a baseline to understand what we see right before our eyes, all the while we understand the game is one of failure, where even the best hitters fall short most of the time. The best players can have poor games, while the average player can have a great game, seemingly with no rhyme or reason. But consistency is the measuring stick that marks the game from day to day, player to player, generation to generation.

In my final year, the entire country was in great anticipation as I vied to break the career home run record. I began the season with 742 home runs. With each blow, the fans went wild as a stadium billboard made for the occasion tallied the numbers. Boom, there goes home run 750. Bang, 755 ties Henry Aaron's mark. When I got to 760, the expectancy and excitement was off the charts.

Ticket sales went crazy as everyone wanted to be in the building when I hit the magical mark of 763, breaking Barry Bond's mark.

I hit the final home run, number thirty-five for the year, and number 777 lifetime, on my last career at bat. Pittsburgh pitcher Phil Cuevas threw a fat fastball, and I planted it deep into the right field stands. Throughout my career I hit Cuevas pretty well, and his pitches sometimes look like batting practice to me. However, this pitch was an intentional meatball, something I'd typically frown upon. But the veteran pitcher threw the gopher ball out of respect. On the bright side, Cuevas would now gain notoriety for being the pitcher who let up my final career home run.

The final blast drew further comparisons to Ted Williams who also hit a homer in his final career at bat. Even so, I'm still uncomfortable being compared to Williams.

My wife and three children attended the game along with my dear friends Chief Daley, Tom Bader and Ethan Colbert. Chief was frail and it was a tremendous effort just to get him to his seat. Ethan gladly volunteered to help, and took good care of my old friend and confidante.

I celebrated the home run with my wife and three children. Georgia, Carole and TC, Jr. rushed the field with mom and greeted me at home plate. Jen flew into my arms and the kids were jumping all over and for a moment I lost myself in their bond, completely oblivious to the fifty thousand elated stadium fans. Satisfied with the family moment, I went on to celebrate the achievement with the raucous home crowd who supported me throughout my career as well as the entire nation glued to their television screens.

Chief was unable to storm the field like my family, although I bet he wanted to. He stayed behind at his box seat, and we instead planned to meet up in the locker room. Tom, still my agent, made sure Ethan had credentials to get to the clubhouse; however, I think wheeling Chief in was the only authorization needed. I'm pretty sure that even without the credentials, Chief would have made sure they got in.

The league commissioner came out to the field to congratulate me. Initially apprehensive, he seemed hesitant I might use the moment to settle some scores. I eased his pain quickly, putting my arm around the man. It was time to promote the great game, not to cause a spectacle and I was happy to celebrate with him and bring exhalation to the national pastime.

Serendipitously, I ran into Mickey Bruther on the way to the locker room. Mickey had worked at the stadium for about a dozen years and took over for Chief when he retired. There were several stories in the media when Mickey took the position as club house manager. He went from attempting a carjacking of the team's most prolific player to complete rehabilitation. It was truly a Cinderella story of how he straightened his life out and ended up replacing a legend, but there was even more to it than that.

Jennifer did an amazing job seeing our plan through for Mickey as well as his band of would be thieves. All the boys had paid their price to society and were sincere in their desire to turn their lives around. We labeled the endeavor the *What Would Hank Do Project*, and Mickey, his brother and four other young men became our first mission.

Upon atoning for their actions, Jen and I made sure these boys had a chance to succeed in life. They had their initial expenses taken care of while we worked diligently to secure employment. Team ownership was gracious enough to hire Mickey, his brother and two of the other kids. Two more were hired by the local professional football team. They understood the importance of what we were trying to do, which was not just get a few kids jobs, but to make a cultural change that would spread throughout a community.

The young men became examples in their neighborhood with Mickey and three others receiving college degrees and the other two working towards theirs. Henry Aaron knew the difference he could make in kids' lives and his example gave us the impetus to do the same. It was tremendously rewarding to see the young men soar and immensely gratifying when they would tell us how others from their neighborhood looked to follow suit. Jen and I have lost count of how many we've helped along, although I think we've made Hank proud. My dearest friend, Chief, too.

Chief was sobbing in the locker room the day I set the homerun record, so I decided to talk to him in a manner that he would appreciate. "Get it together you pansy," I joked. "I love you old man," I said.

"I love you too, son." Chief's eyes were penetrating, saying things that need not be verbalized. "Now I can die in peace!" were the last words he said to me that night. Chief passed away two days later and somehow, I was not sad. He lived a full, wonderful life and he was waiting for me to hit the big home run. I knew he was in his glory and would not want me to mourn.

In his coffin I placed the record-breaking home run ball I received at my wedding, along with the Hank Aaron glove he had bestowed on me many years ago. Chief was put to rest wearing his wedding ring from his marriage to his only love and he was buried with full military honors. Someday I intend to see this great man again and maybe have a catch with his ball and glove in the afterlife.

The inscription on his tombstone reads, *Virgil "Chief" Daley, Devoted Husband and Friend. Ambassador to the Greatest Game in the World!*

◊ ◊ ◊

The baseball record books now enshrine my name, but I will always maintain that the championships won in Philly are what makes me most proud. We won the first championship as an answer to the computer analytics that had dominated the game. We continued to make a mockery of the new rules by destroying the competition the following four years as well. In all we won eight championships.

We were so dominant that the league had to back track and eliminate the pitch clock, the bigger bases, the shift ban, and the limit on pitcher pickoff attempts. They even got rid of the electronic strike zone to swing some advantage back to the pitcher. Human home plate umpires are susceptible to a degree of error, but they add texture and strategy to what is intended to be a complex, intricate game. Through sheer force, we brought the game back to its roots.

Scoreboards still display launch angles, exit velocity, and pitcher velocity, however, the charm of the game has reemerged with traditional play as the focal point. The game is again more competitive, exciting and dramatic.

Named Theodore Cobb Hunter, I might have been destined to impact the great national game, yet I had no concept of how swiftly the arc of baseball needed change. The legends of the game faced a threat to their own immortality, and with baseball history at stake I was used as the conduit to sway the sport back to its rightful path.

The origin of baseball includes many strong-willed, God-fearing men who emerged larger than life and who helped frame our country's history. They played a kid's game with youthful enthusiasm and became sewn into the nation's lexicon. Some even became war heroes, but they all were giants and patriots on the field and off. They lived in a very different time where most of the population viewed themselves as proud Americans.

Still, I wonder why me and why baseball as the conduit back to sanity? My only conclusion is that ball players are best groomed to persevere. Baseball is a game of failures and even the best hitters succeed three out of every ten at bats. In my best years I went four for ten. The point is that baseball requires the ability to cope with failure to prevail. It's a game requiring character, strength, and determination, matching the attributes needed to battle the power hungry, self-gratifying forces that threaten to push the nation toward the unrecognizable. I hope my brief presence on this earth has helped nudge us back in the right direction.

⚾ ⚾ ⚾

Retirement has proven more interesting and purposeful than my baseball life. Sitting in the home office of our family's waterfront estate in Tampa, I peer out the window at the tropical vista and watch as a pod of dolphin splash about in the distance. It was one of those sunny Florida days where you can see for miles out into the Gulf, and the crystal-clear water below looks more green than blue.

My smile grows wider as I look down toward the dock below. Jennifer and the kids have already boarded our yacht in anticipation of our trip to the Keys and then to the Caribbean.

With Jen's help I finally found our super-yacht, a tri-deck cruiser with staggered levels of living space, four bedrooms, a living area, three bathrooms and a galley kitchen. Complete with a sky lounge, an amenity that allows me to do my nature watching in luxury, she is a little more extravagant than I pictured when selecting a vessel. Jen knows how to spend money and convinced me to splurge on the purchase. After considering several names for the luxury vessel, we settled on naming our home on the sea, *My Pal Chief.*

Alone in my office I leaf through the old picture album that I inherited when Chief passed. I look at the old images from time to time, not with any sadness, but with humility. The great men depicted in the scrapbook shaped my life and I was now using what I've learned to mold my own three children. The men stood for honesty, honor, hard work and decency. Patriotic to the core, they in many ways represented the American dream. Vitally important is that our children get to carve their own path because of the principles and sacrifice of those before them.

No matter what they do, it is our intention that each grow up in a God fearing, country loving, family oriented, benevolent environment where they always realize there are important things outside themselves. Jen conscientiously sets the example through our many charitable endeavors, often including our kids in all we do.

Together we run the JTC Foundation to help with an array of causes. The kids call him Uncle Ethan, and his winning battle over leukemia spurred us to be involved in charities fighting childhood cancers. In tribute to Catfish Hunter and Lou Gehrig, we've dedicated tons of resources to fighting ALS. On the patriotic side, we contribute to the Wounded Warrior Project and the Tunnel to Towers Foundation in appreciation of the warriors who fight to preserve our freedom. The men and women who fight for liberty and protect the citizenry will always garner our attention.

To honor Henry Aaron, we expanded on our original What Would Hank Do Project. Providing college scholarships to underprivileged kids who demonstrate the character and desire to achieve; we've been able to make quite an impact in Philadelphia and other inner cities.

Once a foe, Jamie Cunningham joined the effort. We turned a confrontation between two misaligned ballplayers into a positive societal force and created something I'm quite proud of. Jennifer encouraged me to reach out to Jamie and we've been able to do great work by providing hundreds of scholarships throughout the years. Jamie and I forged a strong bond, realizing we have much more in common and want the same things for society.

We've had our hand in building hospital wings, parks, Little League fields, schools. You name it and Jen gets us involved. One thing that getting involved in an eclectic assortment of projects has shown me is despite our differences, the majority of people want the same things. No matter the political affiliation, religion, race or where someone is from, when the noise and propaganda are swept away, good people can unite to achieve great things.

Sitting in my office chair, I know my latest project will trump the others. In my life, I've been granted fame and fortune, but more importantly I was given a nudge to use my status to enact change. Whether due to the power-hungry gripping the government, the devil corrupting our ideals, or maybe just too many people honoring perverted priorities, the country has lost her way. Divided and with freedom waning, our great nation is becoming unrecognizable and in desperate need of a uniting voice.

An American revival is just beginning, and when the phone rang I quickly answer, anxiously awaiting news from my good friend, Trent Evans. Trent retired several years before me and moved his focus to politics, dedicating his life to preserving liberty. I hope today will connote the culmination of years of work for the people of our great nation.

Trent didn't even say hello. "Yeehaw, we did it dog!" he hollers, the big Texan's prideful jubilation infectious.

"You are kidding! It's actually done?"

"Arizona makes it thirty-eight states! All the other states will have no choice but to join the movement now."

"I don't know what to say, Trent. This is incredible."

"Couldn't have done it without you, TC. The government is going back to the people!"

Through an amazing grassroots effort we worked to gather enough participants in a Convention of States. Under Article V of the US Constitution, Congress is provided the authority to propose amendments. When Congress itself becomes self-serving and ineffective, through the infinite wisdom of our Founders, states are also provided that power. It takes thirty-four states to call the convention and thirty-eight to ratify proposals. Through approval from state legislatures, we now have the mechanism by which we could restrain the power of the federal government.

Patriots, both modern and past, believed a proposed solution as big as the problem is the only way to strip the consolidated power of Washington bureaucrats. The elitists will never voluntarily relinquish an ounce of their power, so the people must lawfully take it from the executive, legislative and judicial branches of government.

Capturing the attention of a nation by breaking baseball's most cherished records provided the necessary status; divine intervention did the rest. Fully grasping my chosen path, I parlayed baseball heroism to influence state officials to jump on board. My calling guided me to write letters, record public service announcements and even travel around the country to meet personally with state legislatures.

Some were immediately receptive while others would have the gall to ask if I was promoting the next Civil War. In turn, I'd explain my pursuit was merely a resolution put in place by the genius of our American designers to prevent conflict. The federal government was overreaching, and the people must put a stop to it. A divided nation now had a chance to heal by using the tools granted by our forefathers.

"I'm lost for words, Trent."

"Hot damn, TC. I wish I could be a fly on the wall to see how the entrenched bureaucrats begin to realize they are now excluded from controlling our lives. The people will now have the final say."

Swelling with satisfaction, I hang up the phone and fly back in my chair. The immortals set the groundwork and provided the impetus to fight. In retrospect, I'm pretty sure it was their intention all along.

The sound of fireworks interrupts my thoughts and I peer out the window, only to realize it's not fireworks at all. Jennifer and the kids are on the aft deck of *My Pal Chief*, still waiting for me to make our departure, and they don't notice the sound or the celebration on the bow.

I had not had an episode nor had seen any visitors from the afterlife since my wedding day, but the men look to be right out of 1776. They wear tri-corn hats and dress like minutemen, jumping about and shooting celebratory musket fire into the air. They're only visible to me, and I'm certain they'll be gone by the time I make my way down to the yacht.

On my desk, the album of nostalgia is opened to the last page. Formerly blank, the sheet now shows a collage. In the center, a glorious picture of the American flag is surrounded by an array of photos of me. Some are action shots from the field, others candid pictures from everyday life.

There are still mysteries of this unearthly world, but I finally have figured it out. Now welcome into a club of immortals, I fulfilled my destiny and completed the circle. At times I thought the providence might never be settled, but the burden is now lifted.

The roar of a stadium crowd, the smell of the ballfield and the sensations of the game will continue as my sanctuary and inspiration. Although being out on the sea is great, I will always look forward to visiting baseball cathedrals and enjoying the Greatest American Game.

ACKNOWLEDGMENTS

BEHIND THE BACKSTOP atop the hill, we watched a ton of high school baseball. Not only did we talk about the game and the players, we talked family, history, statistics, politics, patriotism, relationships, batting styles and virtually everything in between.

Thank you, Jerry Winchester, Sr. for your friendship and support. The back-and-forth banter provided underlying themes to *Immortal* and our time spent watching the games filled a void that cannot be properly put into words. I am forever grateful for our friendship.

I would also like to acknowledge the brotherhood that is the game of baseball. I took plenty of literary licenses in *Immortal* and the work is of course fiction. Although poetic liberties abound and the characters are conjured, the underlying themes and dialogue are a fusion of experiences and stories from both professional and amateur baseball. I am hopeful that some of the features of my novel bring a smile to those I've played or coached with or against over the years.

Printed in the USA
CPSIA information can be obtained
at www.ICGtesting.com
LVHW050738050923
757187LV00001B/2